AN ARMY OF ONE

THE EXTRAORDINARY SERIES

PAM EATON

COOPER AVE PRESS

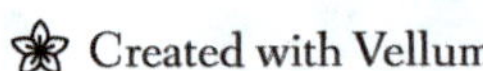 Created with Vellum

CONTENTS

ONE

"Don't be careless." Tiberius's harsh whisper cuts through the balmy night air of Barcelona.

I drag my eyes away from the illuminated red warehouse door we've been watching for the last ten minutes, waiting for Lucy to rejoin our group that's hiding in the darkness. He's close enough that I can *just* make out the stern purse of his mouth.

I avert my eyes. "I'm never—"

"Yes. You are," he says, inching nearer to where I'm crouched. I can feel him close to my shoulder. "You keep acting like you've got nothing to lose." His voice lowers, trying to keep this conversation between us, which is virtually impossible since our small group is all pressed against another warehouse.

I focus back on the dark alley we're waiting in on the outskirts of one of Spain's biggest cities. The scent of saltwater mixes with a nearby dumpster, and it smells as disgusting as it sounds. But I do my best to ignore it, knowing full well I'll need to shower the minute we get back to Brazil.

This isn't the first time we've hidden in the dark, waiting to infiltrate a secret lab, but I don't know why we're talking about this *now*.

"I know this is the worst possible place to have this conversation." He's got that right. He couldn't have waited until we were back in Fordlandia? "But after the last mission…" His voice drops even lower, somehow thickening his prominent Russian accent.

I honestly don't think the last mission went that badly. I mean, it was only a bullet graze on my left arm. Barely a scratch, and hardly any blood. I did have to toss that shirt, but big deal. And when I lit the building on fire, we made sure that no one was stuck inside. All in all, I considered it a success. And I hope they know that when their labs burn, it's because of me.

Tiberius gently places his hand on my arm. And the sudden, violent urge I have to rip it away startles me, but I fight it. Aside from Walter patching me up, no one has touched me recently. Almost like they knew they could lose a finger if they did. "I *just* found you." His words are bordering on angry, but they're filled with an urgency to get me to listen to him. "You're the last part of my brother I have. I *do not* want to lose you too. Neither do Lucy, Walter, Bronia, Tony, or anyone else at Fordlandia. We're family. Whether you like it or not."

My stomach bottoms outs at the word *family*. My family is gone. Burnt to ashes in the one place I felt safe, and the only home I've ever known. Everything I loved—*everyone* I loved—was ripped from me in the cruelest way. When I close my eyes at night, I see the vacant look on my grandparents' faces, I see the gun pointed at Gregory's head, and I swear tendrils of smoke are trapped in my nose. All I have left now is vengeance. But if I tell him that, they'll never let me come on these missions again.

Tiberius grips my shirt sleeve a little tighter. "I need you to be careful," he says, begging me this at this point.

I know his words are meant to make me feel comforted about how he cares about me. But all I feel is guilt. Heavy, draining guilt. And some days I'm not sure how I walk with the weight of it. Because I burned that lab in Myanmar. I made dangerous decisions knowing my grandparents weren't safe. And if I had worked harder at honing my powers, I could have prevented Gregory's death. I could have transported us all out of Myanmar to the safety of headquarters.

The past couple months, all I've done is worked on using my enhancing power to boost my transporting. Now I can take a group anywhere in the world. And I can also hit the center of a bull's eye with my Glock.

The sound of soft footfalls coming from the opposite direction brings me back to the matter at hand and puts me on alert. Dante and Adriana shift closer to us. Ever since we saved those two from that hell hole in São Paulo, they've stuck close to me. Haven't decided if that's out of loyalty or the knowledge that I can get us out of here in a hurry. Either way, they seem to have my back.

Lucy's face is the first thing to come into view and everyone visibly relaxes. She crouch-runs over us.

"How many are inside?" Tiberius asks Lucy as she squats down next to our little group.

"Get close and let me show you," she says, motioning us to huddle in.

We all lean towards her as she pushes a button on her watch and a small projection appears before our eyes. She manipulates the image with her finger, allowing us to see past these cinder block walls. Who needs x-ray vision when we have Lucy? "Looks like two guards, a doctor, and three Blessed in cages," she tells us, her voice choking up a bit when she says *Blessed*, but she quickly clears her throat.

When Tiberius first told me that he called those hiding in Fordlandia the Blessed Many, I fought a cringe. And I still do. There are so many times when this power I've inherited doesn't feel like a blessing at all.

"It'll be easy for Becca to transport in unnoticed." Lucy touches something on the screen and the building's blueprints overlap the images on the hologram. "The guards are in this front room," she says, and we watch one of them sitting at a desk, while the other leans against a wall.

She touches her watch and the scene shifts to the doctor, who's standing at a computer. "I've got the security cameras on a loop right now, and all cell phone signals are jammed." And this is why we bring Lucy with us.

Ever since she was captured as a teenager and they merged the DNA of someone with powers with her own, she's been a master with technology. These missions wouldn't go as smoothly if it weren't for her.

"Becca, do you have the syringes?" Tiberius asks.

I pat my pockets; all four are still in there. I only need three: one to knock out each guard, and one for the doctor. I nod and reach into my pocket, pulling out two syringes. "Good to go," I tell him.

Thank goodness Walter and Bronia came to Fordlandia. Seeing them there was one of the biggest surprises, but I know it's the safest place for them. Especially since Bronia has her mom, Ania's, strength. A ten-year-old walking around with the strength of a hundred men is terrifying, but Walter being a doctor has really helped. We wouldn't have these syringes if it weren't for him. And these people are a lot easier to deal with when they're unconscious.

"This supply closet's door is ajar." Lucy points to a closet near the doctor on the screen. "This is your best bet to get in there unnoticed."

I study the room for a moment longer and look closely at the closet Lucy wants me to transport into. There's a better idea she hasn't thought of.

"See you guys in a few minutes," I say and transport into the room right behind the doctor.

In a blink, I stab the syringe into his neck, pushing down on the plunger as quickly as I can, which totally disregards Lucy's suggestion of sneaking in. I swear I can hear Tiberius curse through the thick cinder block walls for my going rogue.

That doctor's hand reaches up for his neck. He staggers to the side, eyes wide and afraid. "Wha—" He doesn't even finish the word before he starts staggering to the side. I reach out to catch him in my arms as he loses consciousness. Last thing I need is him crashing to the floor and alerting the guards. But seriously, whatever Walter has in this stuff is super powerful.

The rustle of fabric against metal has me spinning and raising the other syringe like a knife. But a pair of widened bright blue eyes, peering out at me behind metal bars, stays my hand. A little girl with white-blonde hair cut super short inches her way to the back of her cage. They put her in there like she's an animal. If there was any guilt about injecting that doctor, seeing this little girl in a freaking cage has completely erased it.

I put a finger to my lips. "Shh."

Her eyes drift to the doctor sprawled on the floor and then back to me. She nods.

I walk softly across the tile floor, scanning the room. Tanks for embryos line the wall to my left, causing me to pause. My hands clench, but I force myself to focus and keep going. If I stop now, we'll be discovered. And I still have two more people to take out. The door ahead stands slightly ajar. I sidle up next to it and look through the gap in the opening. Two armed guards stand against the metal-clad wall, chatting. Damn it. I rub at my forehead, trying to think. The first time I stumbled upon one of these labs I was in Myanmar, and we didn't subdue anyone that time. I still set the place on fire, but I just assumed everyone got out. Ever since then we've had to subdue everyone, because I won't take lives like they so easily will.

I study the guards some more. These are big guys. One of them has arms the size of my head, and the other looks like he could crush me easily. I could transport in between them, but as soon as I appeared, I'd have to stab them both with a syringe at the same time. What if I miss? What if I'm not fast enough? What are even the odds that I could pull that off? Probably super low.

I could try drawing one of them in here. I look back at the little girl, her blue eyes watching me carefully. Or I could have her call out? But they're expecting the doctor to be in here. And what if they both come in? *Think, Becca.*

I bite on my bottom lip, having no clue what to do. I look through the gap again. And soon the decision is made for me as one of the guards takes a cigarette pack out and heads for the door, while the other sits down at the desk.

I hold my breath and watch as he walks out, leaving the other guard sitting at the lone desk in the room. He's a big guy, a lot larger than the doctor. But don't they say big guys go down hard?

Here goes nothing.

I transport to the spot right behind him and plunge the syringe into his neck. His left hand reaches across his body and grabs my arm in a punishing grip. "*Qué demonios!*" he roars.

I punch at his arm with my free hand, but his impossible grip tightens even more, wrenching me forward and throwing me across the desk. My hip slams into the top of the wood and I flip over, slamming to the ground below. I scramble to my feet, the empty syringe still in my hand, poised like a knife to stab. Why isn't he down? The doctor passed out super fast.

The guard stumbles to his feet and screams out something in Spanish. He sways to the side, his other hand still covering his neck. The door behind me bursts open, banging against the wall. Time freezes as the other guard watches his friend collapse to the floor. He swings his gaze toward me, and then time suddenly picks back up and he rushes me. I reach down to grab one of the syringes out of my pocket, but as soon as I pull it out, he tackles me to the floor. My head bounces off the tile. And my vision starts to blur. His arm rears back and I quickly transport out from under him and a few feet to the left. His fist cracks the tile as he punches the floor. How strong is this guy?

I take a running jump and leap onto his back, but as soon as I stab the needle into his shoulder, he's flinging his body, and me, backwards. The needle skids across the room as my body flies back. I transport to the syringe, but the needle is broken and most of the drug is still in it. I've only got one more.

I grab the other one out of my pocket as he grabs for the firearm on his hip. No time. No. Time. He raises the gun, finger pulling the trigger.

I transport behind him again and plunge the syringe in as the gun goes off, hitting the wall where my head just was. I hang on as he tries to reach any part of my body clinging to his back. He yells and slams us back against the wall. My head hits again and I fall off, hitting the ground.

The door explodes off its hinges, and the rest of the team storms into the room as the guard falls to his knees and then slumps to the floor.

I collapse against the wall behind me. The movement causes Tiberius to turn and look at me. "Apparently," I say, taking in a huge lungful of air, "I need to work on transporting and fighting at the same time," I tell him as I wipe the blood from my lip.

Lucy rushes over to me, first aid kit at the ready. Tiberius and Dante move to clear the rest of the lab, while Adriana stays stationed at the door. "Anything broken?" Lucy asks.

"No, but my body is going to be covered in bruises tomorrow."

"Clear!" Tiberius yells.

She goes to open the kit, but I wave her off. "Go, they've got a little girl and two others in cages."

She runs into the other room. And I bend forward, resting my hands on my knees. The back of my head pulses with pain. Gonna need Walter to check for a concussion.

I take a deep breath. My back protests at the movement, but I slowly climb to my feet. I need to head back into the exam room to finally take a look at the horrors in there. You would think since this is the fifth lab we've found, I would get used to what we find. But it's still like a punch to the gut every time. How many more places are there? How many more kids? When will it stop?

Adriana walks over and sets a can of gasoline next to me, holds out a lighter.

"I'll start pouring the gas if you guys can drag these guys out of here," I say.

She nods once and I slowly climb to my feet. Got another building to burn.

TWO

"Well, *robaczku,* you don't have a concussion, but you've got quite the bump back here," Walter says in his thick Polish accent. He prods at the back of my head and I wince, even though he's trying to be soft.

"How did this one happen?" he asks while he places something cool on my scalp.

I reach up and hold the cold pack to my head. "Haven't learned how to fight and transport at the same time. It's hard going up against two guys whose thighs are the size of my waist."

He turns and starts putting things away. "You can't rely on just your powers. There may come a time when you can't use them. Why do you think Ania was so trained in fighting techniques when she had such immense strength?"

How does he say her name without pain in his voice? How can he talk about her with such ease?

We're lucky he escaped here with Bronia after I visited them. I still hate that the first time I met him was because Ania died, but I'm grateful he's in my life. It may be because he reminds me so much of

Grandpa, and that thought makes a huge lump form in my throat. I shake my head. I can't let my thoughts go there. The pain is still too raw.

"Good to go?" I ask him as I hop off the exam table.

He reaches out and lightly touches my arm. "Becca—"

"I've got to find Tony," I say without looking at him. I head out the door, but not before I hear his deep sigh. I know he wants me to talk about what's happened the past few months, but I'm fine.

I head out of Walter's home-slash-clinic, and out onto the dirt lane.

Dante pushes off against the side of the house. "Do you know where Tony is?" I ask him.

He points to the old rusted-out water tower. "*Lá em cima.* He's been there since we got back."

I follow his finger and can just make out Tony's profile. "Thank you," I tell him. "I'll catch up with you later."

I step away from him and transport to the spot high up on the walkway of the water tower, right next to Tony. He only makes the slightest flinch, signaling that I surprised him with my sudden appearance.

"You get them?" Tony asks, his eyes looking out into the distance. I know he can see for miles, because that's his power. I wonder what he sees. I stopped asking a while ago. It seems like such a long time ago that we were lying on a rooftop and he was talking about the astronauts on the space station. He would point things out to me that I'd never see with my own eyes. Any time I asked what he saw, he would tell me.

"Don't we always?" I ask.

He makes a humming noise. "Set another fire?" he asks.

I don't bother answering. He knows the answer. I slide down and plop my butt next to his.

We both look out into the trees, staring at the setting sun. My mind keeps wandering to the little girl we found in the cage tonight.

Her eyes followed me everywhere I went in that lab. What was really odd though, was that she made no sound, showed no emotion when Lucy picked her up so we could leave. The other two kept thanking me in Spanish, but that little girl stayed quiet, watchful.

Tony clears his voice, dragging me back into the present. "It's been four months, Becca," Tony says to me—like I don't already know that. And it hasn't been four months; it's been four months, thirteen days, and five hours. "You haven't mourned." He's trying to be comforting, but there's no point.

"You're being reckless," he states.

Did these guys have a meeting earlier in the week? Because this is the second time in only a few hours I'm being lectured about this.

"I'm waiting for the day you don't come back from one of these missions." His voice drops, letting me hear the pain he's in.

I turn away from him and look out over Fordlandia from our perch on the old water tower. It's definitely not the safest place to be sitting—there're more rust spots than paint—but I hardly give a damn about my safety anymore. That's not what I'm living for now.

"It's only a matter of time." He's begging me, just like Walter has and Tiberius have, to care more about myself. But it's like that part of me died with Gregory and my grandparents. And I don't think I want to revive it. The only time I feel anything is when I'm on that edge between death and success on our missions.

He lightly touches my arm, and I rip it away, bringing it close to my chest. "Don't," I warn him.

"This isn't living!" The words burst out of him with the most feeling I've heard from him in a while. I'm not the only one who hasn't moved on. I haven't even gotten him to leave the compound since I transported him here months ago.

"You're one to talk," I tell him in a calm, controlled voice. There's no point in yelling back at him.

"It's not—"

"It *is* the same thing," I say, cutting him off, finally looking at him in the eye for the first time. He's too thin, and in desperate need of a hair-cut. "I've asked you to come with me repeatedly. You know exactly what these guys are capable of. You've seen the people I've brought back here. I've been patient, but I need to know what went down in Myanmar."

His shoulders cave inward, and he looks down at the ground far below our dangling feet. "Talking about it won't do any good," he says, and I know not to push him more, otherwise he's going to lock himself in his bedroom for the next three days.

"Well, aren't we a pair," I say, and he huffs out a harsh laugh.

We're a mess. And we both know it. Both of us self-destructing in our own ways. He's hiding, and I'm putting myself in the path of bullets.

Voices carry up from below. I look down at my watch. "You coming to training today?" I don't know why I bother asking, because it's been *no* every time.

"What's on today's agenda?" he asks, like he actually cares, when I know he doesn't.

"Firearms," I say, my voice getting a little more animated from the anticipated rush of pulling the trigger and hitting the target. It's basically its own high.

"Is that the only thing that gets that scowl off your face these days?" He may not like it as much as I do, but if he would only try, with those eyes...he'd be amazing.

"Why don't you come watch? You don't have to shoot; you can just help me work on my aim." It's an olive branch I know he won't take, and I'm proved right as he shakes his head.

"How did we start talking about me?" he asks, genuinely sounding confused.

I shrug my shoulders. "Gotta stop hanging around and doing nothing all day. Your brain's going to mush."

He opens his mouth, but before he can say anything, I salute him and transport to the ground below. "Hey, I wasn't done talking with you!"

"Come join me at range then!" I yell back, flashing him what is probably a strained smile.

He turns his head away, eyes scanning the treetops. "Maybe later." His reply isn't shouted, but I can still hear it and the lie he's telling both of us. He won't come, just like I probably won't ever finish this conversation with him.

I HEAD down the dirt-lined streets, waving at all the people calling my name, trying to keep my emotions in check. Because that talk with Tony has me a bit rattled. I'd gone at least a couple hours without thinking about my grandparents or Gregory. But with that one conversation, my reprieve of the constant heartache was obliterated. Mourning isn't going to bring them back. Nothing will.

I make a turn down the main avenue of houses. Even though I've been here for four months, this place is still surreal. It looks like a war-torn Californian suburb, but we're smack dab in the middle of a Brazilian jungle. I don't know what the Ford Company was thinking putting small-town America here, but it's been a refuge for those of the Blessed Many.

"*Ciao*, Becca," a deep Italian voice calls to me from the front porch of the house I'm walking by.

"Hey, Luca," I say, stopping at his fence. "How's it going?"

He steps out from the cover of his porch, and I steel myself not to flinch. Luca is one of the prime reasons for this place. The teal scales on his exposed skin gleam in the sunlight as he makes his way closer to me. He scans the street, probably looking for the kids who run around here. They're still not used to him and usually run screaming when he's spotted.

"Same old, same old," he says in his thick Italian accent. He keeps his body angled, like at any moment he's going to run back to the cover of his porch.

We found him a month ago, trapped in a cage in the bowels of some abandoned warehouse in Rome. I'm pretty sure they'd left him there to die because he wasn't a success, and the lab was completely cleared out. We had been a day too late. Tiberius had found them, and by the time we'd organized to go, they had deserted the place, leaving Luca there alone. It's not very often I see a grown man cry, but when we opened that cage he stumbled out and fell to his knees, tears raining down his face.

We haven't found who's taking DNA from the one hundred yet and trying to create more of us, but I've burned down every lab I can find, and save the people I can. I know Luca's life has changed forever, but I'm hoping he'll find a life here.

"I'm headed to the range if you want to tag along," I offer him.

His tongue peeks out to lick his lips, and ugh, that's disturbing. I didn't know it was forked. Luca has got it rough, but he needs this place. He'd never survive out in the real world. We're pretty sure they tried to morph the genes of someone who can shift into any creature with his, but it's like he's locked in this half-human, half-scaly-reptile state. And every time I talk to him about working with me so we can get him to try and shift, he freaks. Can't really blame the guy. It took me twenty minutes to convince him to leave the filthy lab and come with us.

His eyes keep scanning the area, searching.

"The more they see you, the faster they'll get used to you," I tell him.

The more I talk to Luca, the more I learn he's the kindest guy I've ever met. Oddly enough, talking with him helps temper the rage that consumes me on a daily basis.

"*Si*, I'll come." He squares his shoulders a bit and walks past his gate, joining me on the dirt road.

We head to the clearing, thankfully not encountering anyone on the way. Either that means we actually didn't walk by anyone, or they looked out their windows and stayed inside. It'll change in time; Luca just happens to be the first to have his power on full display.

"Have you ever shot a gun?" I ask him, trying to ease some of the tension that's coming off him in waves.

"Never," he says as we approach the small range I helped build two months ago. Guess I'll have to teach him some safety tips first.

"Okay. Right off the bat, never point a gun at anyone. Don't care if it's loaded or not, don't do it." My voice is very firm, because I need him to realize how serious I am. Walter may be an amazing doctor, but he's not God.

Luca nods his head, his face matching my serious one.

"This is a 9mm Glock," I say, drawing the side arm from the holster hidden under my shirt. "We'll start with only five rounds in the magazine."

I show him how to hold it, how to stand, how to line up the two sights on the gun with the target. It's an odd thing seeing his scale-covered arms hold the gun. I wonder if the shifter in him makes his grip better.

After his first time pulling the trigger, he places the gun down with the slide pulled back and the magazine out like I showed him. He looks down at his shaking hands and then up to me.

"Adrenaline rush, huh?" I ask him.

He nods slowly, hands still subtly shaking.

"In some ways it's the scariest thing. You realize the destruction and power you're holding," I tell him, eyes on the handgun. "But at the same time, it makes you hyper focused on what's around you—it makes you feel alive. It's a balance of feeling powerful but respecting what you're holding and what it can do."

He lifts the gun up, not as shaky, and empties the clip. He's an awful shot, but not everyone can be a natural.

"*Grazie*, Becca." He only says two words, but in those words, I hear everything he isn't saying. Maybe he's regaining the control he lost, maybe he's feeling acceptance—but he's not running scared, and that's the most important thing.

"Hey, Becca, Lucy could really use your help," Tiberius says as he comes walking up behind us. "Hey, Luca," he says, raising a hand.

I take the gun out of Luca's hand, take out the magazine, and after putting them both down, turn towards my uncle.

"What's going on?" I ask.

"It's the little girl we found in Barcelona. She's at our house right now."

"I'll head right over," I tell him. I pick my gun back up and put it back in my holster.

THREE

"She hasn't said anything. Not one word," Lucy tells me, her voice lowered so it won't carry.

"Really?" I ask, looking at the door that separates us from the little girl.

Lucy crosses her arms, eyes focused on the door. "She hadn't been in that lab long. There aren't that many needle marks on either of her arms," she tells me in a hushed voice.

"She let you check her?" I ask, surprised.

"She understands what I'm saying, she just won't respond. She kept showing me the locket around her neck. I'm assuming the pictures in it are of her parents; she looks just like her mom."

"Was she kidnapped?" I ask.

"I have no idea," she says, shaking her head.

"What did the others say?" I ask, referring to the two other people we found in the lab in Barcelona.

Lucy runs her hands through her hair, eyes still fixed on that door like she can see through it. "They can't remember when she got there. These guys were so heavily drugged, I'm not surprised. They're the roughest we've ever rescued before. Thankfully Adriana helped get them settled."

I want to ask if they were worse off than her, but I bite my tongue. Lucy's the real reason behind the start of these missions. If Tiberius hadn't found her when he was walking down the street in Miami—no, I don't want to go there. She's a part of us now, and I'm so grateful she's here. I missed out on having an aunt for years, and I don't know if aunts and nieces typically spend their Saturday afternoons at the shooting range, but I love it.

"What do we do now?" I ask.

She finally turns away from the door and looks at me with pleading eyes. "Would you go talk to her?"

Wait, what? "Me? What am I supposed to say?" This is not my area at all.

"You rescued her, maybe that connection will make her talk."

I stare at the door now too. I doubt she'll talk to me. This is probably a huge waste of time.

"Please, Becca," Lucy says, putting a hand on my shoulder.

"I'll give it a shot, but no promises."

She nods, a small smile gracing her face.

I take a deep breath and let it out slowly. I knock lightly on the door. It creaks slightly as I open it gently. The little girl with the piercing blue eyes stares back at me from her spot on the bed. In one hand I can see the chain from the necklace she's clutching. In the other she has a stuffed giraffe.

I sit on the edge of the bed, as far away as I can get. I don't want to freak her out. We stare at each other. She's not cowering; her eyes are more curious than anything else. "My name's Becca," I tell her.

She stares at me. I reach out and softly touch the giraffe. "I had one of these growing up. His name was Jeffery. I slept with him every night."

A sharp pain hits my heart. He burned up in the fire, along with everything I owned, loved. I lost so much that day. And I'll never get any of it back. I take a shuddering breath and push the memories out.

"Do you have a name for your giraffe?" I ask her, my voice a lot more hoarse than before.

She shakes her head.

"Do you have a name?" I ask, hopeful she'll answer.

She tentatively reaches out her hand and grabs mine. She opens my fingers and I hold my breath as she places her locket in the palm of my hand. "Is this yours?" I ask her quietly. I don't know why I lower my voice, but this feels like something sacred to her.

She nods.

I open it and bring it closer to my face. Inside is a picture of a young woman who has matching spiral curls like the little girl. On the other side is a man in an army uniform. "Are these your parents?"

She stares at me, not answering the question either way.

"Are they your family?"

She reaches out and slowly pulls the locket back to her. She looks at the pictures, her eyes full of a haunting sadness no little kid should ever feel. She closes it, and then softly kisses the locket. She places it around her neck and hugs her giraffe closer to her.

We sit on her bed in silence. I don't know what to do.

I'm looking around for something when I hear my stomach growl. "Are you hungry?" I finally ask her.

She nods, so I rise from the bed and step back out of the room. Lucy's standing on the other side, her arms folded tight across her chest. Her head snaps up at the sound of the door.

"Anything?" she whispers once the door is closed.

"No more than you got. She nodded her head when I asked her if she was hungry."

"What are we going to do?" Lucy asks, but I think she's talking more to herself than to me. "I'll go make her a sandwich." She walks out of the room.

I sit down at the dining room table. There has to be some way we can help her, figure out who she belongs to.

And then it hits like lightning. And the name that pops into my head makes me break out in a cold sweat.

Xavier.

I need to find Tiberius.

"HIS POWER IS to be able to touch something and to see what's happened with that object for the last three days. I got him to see to four days once, but that was before I worked on my enhancing power," I tell Tiberius.

He rubs a hand across his jaw. "Are the risks worth it?" he asks me, his voice measured.

I haven't seen Xavier since my life imploded. I have no idea where he is, but with Tiberius's power it won't be a problem finding him. But I can't go back to Project Lightning. I won't go back. And what if Mr. Smith wants him to make me come back?

I see those bright blue eyes in my mind again, and the decision is made. "We need to help her, and I don't know any other way to. She's not talking—I don't even know if she can. Plus, maybe if we take Xavier to that warehouse, he can find out who's behind all of this."

"You know him better than I do. I'll leave it up to you," he tells me.

I need to help this little girl. I need to know who's kidnapping these people. But being here in Fordlandia, in the middle of the Amazon jungle, under the secrecy of Lucy's inventions, has allowed me to drop off the face of the planet. "Time is not on our side," I tell him. The longer we wait, the less information we'll get.

"What if they find us here?" I ask, voicing my biggest fear. I can't put all these people in danger.

"They won't, and even if they did, I would know they're coming," he assures me.

I bite my lip, trying to think of any other option, but nothing is coming. "I can't think of any other way," I tell him.

"Well, let's see where in the world he is," Tiberius says as he reaches out his hand.

I grab it and close my eyes, picturing Xavier. His long raven hair. The well-worn jeans he always wears. And the soft smile he readily shows. Images bombard my mind, like stills in a movie. I haven't let myself think too much about him, or anyone at Project Lightning. My mind wants to drift, but I strain to keep the image of Xavier at the forefront.

"We're going to need Lucy," he says in a shaky voice, breaking the image of Xavier in my mind.

I look at him, totally confused.

"He's in Brazil," Tiberius says.

FOUR

Tiberius and I sit on the couch behind Lucy's workstation. She's typing furiously and clicking things on three different monitors. I don't bother to ask any questions; I learned pretty quickly to just let her do her thing. Interrupting her is like poking a beehive. Just don't do it. Plus, she's on a mission to help this little girl. Nothing is going to interrupt her.

"Aha! Got him," Lucy crows triumphantly.

She pushes back her chair and turns to us with a smug look. We walk over to the screen, and sure enough, there's Xavier standing at Beira Do Rio, the original restaurant where I met Lucy for the first time in Itaituba. He's a lot rougher than the last time I saw him, like he's been traveling for weeks. His beautiful raven hair is unbrushed and tangled, and he's in desperate need of a shave.

"When was that taken?" I ask, anxiety filling my stomach.

Lucy leans forward and types in something. "Looks like about two hours ago. Those cameras I put up around town are excellent quality."

"I'm going to give Paulo a call and see if he talked with him," Tiberius says, and walks out of the room.

I stare at the picture of Xavier. "He's here for me," I say, not taking my eyes off the screen.

"He is," Lucy says, her tone careful.

I rub a hand across my eyes. How would he know where to look? No one knew about Tiberius. I was so careful. But was Grandpa?

"I wonder if he found something at my home," I tell her.

"But how?" she asks. I know she's thinking that there wasn't anything there to salvage. Anything in that house is gone. But we haven't talked about that. I can't.

I fill her in on Xavier's power. She lets out a low whistle. "He must have found out by using his powers at your home," she agrees.

I start pacing back and forth behind Lucy, her eyes tracking my every move. I know I'm agitated, and I can see that she's concerned, but I can't deal with that now. It's not a new look for her. I see it all the time, especially when she thinks I'm not looking.

"But why wait four months to come and find me?" It just doesn't add up.

She leans back in her chair. "Maybe he doesn't want anyone to know he's looking for you."

I stop at her words. Maybe he doesn't. But there's only one way to find out. "I need to talk to him. I need to know what he knows, and we need his help. We don't have much time."

"You won't go alone," Tiberius says as he walks back into the room. "Paulo talked to Xavier today. Found it odd because not many Americans visit this area. He just asked some generic questions. Nothing to raise concern."

I run a hand through my hair. "He was probably trying to *see* if I had been there recently. It's been a while since I've been to town though," I tell them.

"That's good. And Paulo gave him real generic answers back."

"Well, let's go pay him a visit then," I say and hold my hand out to Tiberius.

He looks at my hand. "I want your word that if he's there for nefarious reasons, we're leaving right away," Tiberius says.

"I won't put this place in danger," I vow to him. I won't do anything to ever jeopardize the people here.

He nods and places his hand in mine. "He's staying at Hotel Açaí, that's not far from Paulo's place. I don't know if he's alone, just that there isn't anyone with powers around. He's there now."

I close my eyes and with Tiberius's help we transport to the alley behind the hotel. Tiberius staggers out of my hold and props himself up against the building. It takes only a moment for him to get his bearings, and that's such an improvement.

After I realized that my second power was to enhance, I practiced and practiced being able to transport people. At first, they would only let me try it with one of the village chickens, Henrietta. She got to travel the globe, but she's still alive. Since then I've been able to transport all of us on missions. I can only take three others with me at a time, but it's been worth it...and no one has died, so that's a plus.

A subtle shudder goes through him.

"You good?" I ask him. The first time I tried enhancing his power he passed out, but since then I've learned how to control it. It's taken a lot of trial and error, but it's gotten better. Tiberius is still the only one who knows about me being able to enhance.

He shakes out his hands and lifts off against the wall, standing to his impressive height. "That was a lot better than last time. Hardly any draining," he says, and I let out a little sigh of relief. That first times I transported others after Tony, they all needed to sit down for a good ten minutes.

"All right, let's go upstairs and pay him a visit," I say.

We head up the back staircase to the second floor and down the hall to Xavier's room. Tiberius stops in front of the door; he lifts his hand and looks at me questioningly. I look up and down the hall one last time. Seeing nothing out of the ordinary, I nod. I lay my hand on his back, just in case we need to get out of here quickly.

As Tiberius's hand knocks softly, my stomach flips and my mind races. What's Xavier going to say? How's he going to explain what happened to Gregory? Why wasn't he there, or was he? And where's Raven?

Xavier's door slowly opens, and his face appears in the crack. His mouth pulls in a hard line when he sees Tiberius, but as soon as his eyes swing to me and connect with mine, he rips the door open all the way.

In a blink, his arms are wrapped around me and he's crushing my body to his. Everything in me seizes. I haven't let anyone touch me, outside of my hand to transport, since I lost everyone I love, and it's like my body doesn't know what to do. "I never thought I'd find you," he says into the top of my head.

I struggle in his arms, making his arms drop. My hands start to shake, and I cross my arms tightly across my chest. "Let's step into the room for this conversation," Tiberius says as he steps in front of me.

"Who the hell are you?" Xavier asks, getting into Tiberius's personal space.

I step out from behind Tiberius, back into Xavier's view. "Meet my uncle Tiberius."

FIVE

Xavier's eyes linger on me for a minute before he comes to a decision, and he slowly backs into his room. We follow him inside and Tiberius shuts the door. Xavier sits on the end of his bed, his eyes going back and forth between us.

The silence in the room stretches, causing the tension to ratchet up several notches. I scan Xavier, looking for clues as to why he's here, but all I see is a tired man with wrinkled clothes, bags under his eyes, and his long beautiful hair a mess.

"Since when do you have an uncle?" he asks, sitting on the edge of his bed.

"We're not talking about that right now, because I'm pretty sure you're here hunting *me* down." I pull out the chair in front of the desk and take a seat. "Why are you here? *How* are you here? Did they send you to retrieve me?" I ask, my voice deadly quiet.

He takes a deep breath and leans forward, clasping his hands between his knees. "I'll get to your questions in a minute, but first, I'm so sorry about your grandparents." His eyes pierce me, and his words alone drive a spike right into my heart, letting agony wiggle its way past the numbness I've encased myself in. If I weren't sitting, I'd probably collapse to the floor.

"When we left Myanmar, we'd only been in the air for a few minutes when things took a drastic turn. Those men dressed in black...two were behind me and Raven. I didn't even feel the initial stick of the needle, I just heard Raven cry out."

I close my eyes at the images his words are creating. That one guy, the only one that spoke had sounded so familiar, but I still don't know who it was.

"They injected us with a tranquilizer, and as my vision started to go, I felt the plane landing. Gregory leaned into me and whispered into my ear to get to you, to protect you."

A sound starts to fill the room, a low keening. And it takes me a moment to realize it's coming from me. Tiberius puts a hand on my shoulder, but I shake it off and take several deep breaths.

"The kids?" I ask, my voice rough.

Xavier stares at me, but I turn my head and look at the window. I don't want to see his pity. "Back with their parents," he tells me gently.

My whole body deflates at that. But why would they leave the kids? Why leave Raven and Xavier? Things aren't adding up. I get to my feet and head for the lone window. I scrub a hand over my face.

"Did Mr. Smith send you after me?" I ask, because that's the only reason he'd be here.

"Yes, sort of, but not for the reason you think. He's worried. We all are. When we showed up at your grandparents'—"

The silence in the roof is deafening, and I know they can see my whole body stiffen, but I still don't turn around.

"I found your phone there. I don't think you realized it, but you whispered 'Brazil.'" I hear him take a quick breath. "Why didn't you come back to headquarters?" Xavier asks, genuinely sounding confused.

"There's nothing left for me there," I tell him, no emotion in my voice. Just dead, like how I've felt for a while now.

"Step back," Tiberius orders.

I turn my head, surprised at Tiberius's tone, and even more so at seeing Xavier up from the bed. Tiberius stands between us, acting as a physical barrier.

"We needed you. We needed your help in finding Gregory." Xavier's voice is harsh, cutting.

I turn fully to face him. "What?" I ask, completely shocked at his tone. He's never talked to me like this. Or to anyone, from what I've seen.

"I thought you loved him! How could you not come back and help find him? Was it a lie? Are you just hiding with him?" He points at Tiberius. "Why do you think I'm here?"

I shake my head, anger washing over me. How dare he? "Don't you dare." The words snap out of me like a whip. "I saw the pictures. I had to look at those damn things while my grandparents' house burned to the ground with them in—" My voice cracks, anger quickly giving way to the ever-present sadness that resides within my heart.

"Enough." I've never heard Tiberius so lethal before.

"What are you talking about? What pictures?" Xavier asks, his eyes darting between Tiberius and myself.

"Gregory's gone." I know my voice is cold, dull. But I can't let it be any other way. As it is, I'm breaking inside. And I promised myself that I wouldn't break again. But I can feel the agony ripping my heart to shreds.

Xavier takes a step back, bumping into the bed behind him. "What? No."

His hands shoot up and grip his hair. He starts pacing back and forth in front of the bed. Tiberius steps closer to him and tells Xavier what I can't—that the pictures were of Gregory being killed.

"No. He can't be gone." Xavier says the words, but they're not directed at me or Tiberius.

How did he not know? It's been months. Did they not send Mr. Smith messages like they did me? When they kidnapped Tony, they didn't wait this long to send a ransom. But, maybe?

"Tiberius?" I look up at him. And this stupid little niggle of hope tries to sprout, but I shove it down.

"You never asked. And I've never met him," he says, basically reading my thoughts.

Xavier stops his pacing. "What are you guys talking about?"

"Do you trust him?" Tiberius asks me.

"Trust me?" Xavier asks, but I ignore the question.

I look over at Xavier. His face is set like stone. *Do* I trust him? A memory flashes in my mind. When we were rescuing Tony in Myanmar, he didn't want to leave me there. They had to force him to leave. And I *know* he'd do anything in his power for Gregory.

"There's so much you don't know," I tell Xavier, but most of that information will have to wait. I take a deep breath and trust my gut. "Tiberius can find anyone in the world with powers. If Gregory is alive, he'll find him."

Xavier curses, but I don't pay him any attention. I never bothered to ask Tiberius to look. Those pictures they sent me—there's no way they were fake. I take a step towards Tiberius and put a hand on his arm. I steel myself, and then let the onslaught of images flood my mind. Gregory's smirk the first time I rode in an elevator with him. He knew I was ogling him. I picture our time in the basement at the cabin, working to perfect my power. I watch as he charged back down that hallway to kiss me for the first time. And finally I think of the smile he gave me before he boarded that plane, and how he told me he loved me.

Tiberius's body sways a little as he closes his eyes. I'm probably pumping too much of my enhancing power into him, but I can't help it. My emotions are way too involved at this point. He taps my hand twice, our signal for me to let go, and I step back.

My breath comes in short bursts. Did he find him? Were the pictures fake?

After several moments of his eyes still being closed, I can't wait anymore. I'm on the verge of a heart attack over here. "Well?" I ask.

He opens his eyes and with that look he doesn't even have to open his mouth; I already know. "I'm sorry." He says the words so gently, but it feels like a gunshot to the chest.

Xavier drops to his knees, a tortured moaning sound coming out of him.

I take a deep breath. Desperately seeking that numbness I've been living in the past four months. But it's so hard when things feel so fresh. It's so hard when I hear Xavier's agonizing grief.

Breathe, Becca. Just. Breathe.

A heavy, oppressive silence hangs in the room for several minutes. But I can't take it anymore. I can't dwell on it. It hurts. It hurts so much.

I drag in a lungful of air, and then blow it out slowly. "We didn't come here to tell you this. We came here because we need your help," I tell Xavier, desperate to get past this. To focus on something I *can* control.

He looks up at me, his face drawn. "What is it?"

I clasp my hands together, trying to stop them from shaking. "Remember all the things I found at the lab in Myanmar?"

A shudder runs through him. "Yeah."

"That lab we found when we rescued the kids in Myanmar. That's not the only lab out there. It was just a drop in the bucket."

His face becomes haunted, because he knows about the experiments that were occurring there. About the embryos, and the things they did to those kids we saved. "How?" he asks.

"We don't know who's behind it. That's the big problem. After every lab we raid, there's another out there that we don't know about. We keep getting tips and some are nothing, but last night we rescued a little girl who won't talk, and we can't help her. I think you can," I say.

He sits up taller. "I'll help," he says without hesitation.

"Thank you," I say, letting the relief pour into my voice. "But I need to know: does Mr. Smith know you're in Brazil?" I ask. Because if he does, this won't work.

"No. After not being able to find you after the first two months, he told me they were calling off the search for the time being. I've been trying to track down Gregory, but I knew I needed to find you. Because I was hoping if I found you, we'd find him," he says.

"Are you carrying your issued phone?" I ask. Tiberius shifts next to me, like he knows the answer to this question can cause a whole host of problems.

Xavier looks between the two of us. "No. I left it so I could keep looking for you." The relief is instant.

"There's something, a place actually, I need to show you," I tell him. I turn to Tiberius. "Want to give Lucy a heads-up?"

He takes out his cell and shoots out a text to her.

"You're going to need to hold my hand," I tell him.

Tiberius walks over to me and grabs one hand and I hold the other out to Xavier. "I thought you couldn't do that," he says, staring at my hand.

"Things change," I tell him matter-of-factly.

He reaches it and grabs it. "I'm trusting you," he says.

"This is going both ways," I respond. Because aside from Tony and myself, they've never had anyone from Project Lightning come to Fordlandia.

I squeeze his hand and transport us out of the room.

IN A BLINK we're standing beside the old rusted-out water tower.

"What is this place?" Xavier asks in awe.

I don't blame him for being floored. This place is like the set of a 1950's dystopian movie, with its rusted outbuildings and random old Fords half-covered in vines. It's pretty surreal.

"Welcome to Fordlandia," Tiberius says.

Three little girls run by us, their giggles filling the air. A huge smile spreads across Xavier's face, and then little Melanie shoots a lightning bolt at the feet of Becky, and his jaw drops.

"Melanie Ann." Tiberius's Russian accent always gets thicker when he scolds someone. Melanie stops and slowly turns around to face us.

He squats down to her eye level. "Are you supposed to shoot people with your lightning?"

"Lightning?" I hear Xavier mumble to himself.

"No, Uncle Ti," Melanie says in her sweet little voice.

"You could have really hurt Becky," he tells her, and Melanie's face collapses. He places his hand gently on her shoulder. "Don't cry, little one, just be more careful," he tells her kindly, but firmly.

She nods and runs off with her friends.

"Did she just...?" Xavier asks.

"Yes," I tell him, while he continues to stare at Melanie in complete shock.

"Welcome to the safe haven for those who shouldn't exist," Tiberius tells him, making Xavier look between us and the little girls running off.

"We told you. You saw those kids in Myanmar," I say to him. "Some of those experiments worked."

He runs a hand roughly through his hair. "I never thought...so this place is called Fordlandia?" Xavier asks, like we're making up the name of the place.

Tiberius's eyes roam the area. "This was once a settlement for a tire factory built by the Ford Motor Company. They tried to take a Midwest American town and plop it into the middle of the Amazon jungle."

"Well, that's different," Xavier says, more to himself than to us.

"Now, it's a safe haven for people like Melanie," Tiberius tells him.

All of us watch the little girls run through the tall grass, probably heading to see Maria. She always has fresh-baked cookies in the afternoon.

"How?" Xavier asks.

"Someone out there is kidnapping children and adults so they can experiment on them and try to make more people with powers."

My stomach rolls in disgust at the memories of where we've found these people and the conditions they were in.

Tiberius tells him a little about Lucy and rescuing her. About the horrors we've seen since we started raiding these labs. And about some of the people we've saved. "Fordlandia is a place where these people can feel safe and have a life. Some of them will never be able to live in the normal world again."

"You're gonna see things that will startle you; try to hide it," I tell him, thinking about Luca.

He raises a brow at that, but nods.

"One more thing," I say in all seriousness. "No one knows Tiberius is my true uncle, and it needs to stay that way for obvious reasons."

"No one? Not even Tony?"

"Walter, Tiberius's wife Lucy, and now you. That's all. Again, I'm trusting you with all of this. Don't blow it."

Xavier holds my stare and nods once.

"Let's take you to meet Lucy, and the little girl we're hoping you'll help," Tiberius's gruff voice says, breaking our tense standoff.

SIX

Lucy leans against the doorframe waiting for us. I'm not surprised; she was probably alerted the second we appeared by some gadget she created. If whoever kidnapped her knew that their experiment worked with her, she would be hunted to the ends of the earth. Nothing was more amazing than the first time I came here and watched the jungle landscape peel back like a curtain, revealing a hidden dock.

Thankfully they don't know about her, and we benefit from her scarily genius knowledge of all things involving technology.

"Lucy, I'd like you to meet Xavier," Tiberius says, walking up to her.

Xavier holds out his hand for Lucy, but she just stares him down. "Don't betray our trust. There's nowhere on this earth you can hide now," she says to him.

"Wouldn't dream of it, ma'am," he says while lowering his hand.

She stares him down for a moment longer, and then turns and walks into the house, Tiberius following close behind.

"She's scary," Xavier whispers.

"She's awesome," I say.

We walk into the house and follow Lucy to the back where the little girl is staying. She opens the door and we see her on the bed, legs curled under her. "Hey, we've got someone we hope can help you," Lucy says as she kneels in front of the girl.

Xavier steps forward and gives her the biggest smile to her. Her whole face lights up, but I swear every kid loves him instantly. "My name's Xavier."

She waves back at him, her giraffe clutched tightly in her other hand. He sits down next to her on the bed. "What you got there?" he asks.

She lifts her giraffe in front of Xavier's face. "Very nice to meet you, Mr. Giraffe," he says, shaking one of its feet.

She gives him a huge smile. He points to her locket.

"Well, isn't that pretty? Can I see it?" he asks.

She lifts it over her head and hands it to him. He takes it gently from her and closes his palm. He closes his eyes. I walk closer and sit next to him. I put my hand lightly on his shoulder and make like I'm trying to get a better look, but I pump a lot of my enhancing power into him.

"Whoa," he says, almost breathless.

"What is it?" Lucy asks as she steps closer.

I shush her with my free hand.

Xavier opens his eyes and looks at the little girl with a gentle smile. "Hi, Eloise," he says softly.

At the sound of her name, tears stream down her face. And I swear I hear my heart crack a tiny bit.

"No one will ever put you in another cage. Do you understand?" He asks her, and she slowly nods. "Good. I won't ever let that happen, and neither will they," he says pointing at the rest of us.

"Can you sit with Lucy while I talk to Becca and Tiberius?" he asks her.

She nods, and Lucy comes over, sweeping her into her arms. Xavier stands and runs his hand down the length of Eloise's hair. She gives him a watery smile.

We follow Xavier out of the room and into the living room. "What did you see?" I ask.

He places his hands on his hips and puffs out a strained breath. "I don't know if she realizes they killed her parents in front of her. But I'm thinking she does. It was a hard thing to watch. Someone was strapped to a bed, but I couldn't focus well. It was a strain to see that far. Only the more powerful events stuck out. And unfortunately, that was what happened to her parents."

I turn around at his words and see Eloise looking me straight in the eye. And my heart just breaks, because she knows what happened. It's there in her haunted eyes. It's probably the reason she won't speak.

"She had been in France with her parents," Xavier says, causing me to turn back at the sound of his voice. "They were holding her in another lab. Lots of tests, some blood draws. They gave her some shots, but I've got no clue what was in those needles. I'm not sure why they moved her to Spain, but it wasn't in a hurry. There was no rush to get her out of France. She traveled in a tractor-trailer with others." His eyes spear mine. "This is human trafficking at its worst." His voice is heavy with disgust and I don't blame him.

Tiberius lets out a low growl, and man, I can relate. I want to find these people and end them. End whatever horrors they're inflicting on people. Stop this mess that's already gone too far.

"Do you know where in France she was?" Tiberius asks, his voice dangerously low.

Xavier shakes his head in frustration. "All I saw was Collégiale Saint-Laurent carved into stone with some Latin words that I don't understand."

"That's a big find," Tiberius tells him. "We'll have Lucy do some research on it later. See if we can figure out where Eloise was."

The room falls silent as the three of us stand in the middle of the room, all lost in thought.

Tiberius lets out a heavy sigh. "We're not going to figure this out right now." He looks over at Xavier. "Can you give Becca and me a second?"

Xavier looks between us and nods. He heads out of the living room and back towards the room with Lucy and Eloise.

I follow Tiberius out the front door. "How do you feel about setting him up in your house?" he asks.

Wasn't expecting that. But am I okay with it? I look back at the house, but I can't see through walls. I've never felt unsafe with him, and I don't now either. "It'll be fine. But it's not just me. Tony probably won't care, but let me go talk to him. Send Xavier over in ten," I tell him.

"Sounds good. But if anything changes, we'll be here."

I wave and walk across the dirt-packed street to the little shack where I've been staying at. I can't call it home. It's not that; I don't know if anything will ever feel like home again. I open the front door into the living room and right away I see Tony lying on the couch.

"How was the gun range?" he asks, not even looking at me, his eyes trained on the book in front of him.

I sit down in the chair next to him and push the recliner back. "Well, we ended up having to cut it short because we tracked down Xavier from Project Lightning. I transported him here."

The book falls to the floor with a heavy thud, and he shoots straight up. "You brought someone from *there* here? Are you completely insane?"

I sit up too. "Hey, Xavier was one of the guys that helped rescue you. Don't forget that."

He grips his hair with both hands. "Mr. Smith is going to come knocking on our door any time now and you—"

I reach out a hand and grab onto his arm. "No. He's not. Xavier went rogue. He's not supposed to be looking for me at all right now."

He shakes his head back and forth. My stomach sinks; he doesn't believe me. "I want you to meet Xavier," I tell him.

He stands up and walks past me, probably to lock himself in his room. "I'm grateful for him helping to get me out of that hell hole, but I want nothing to do with anyone from Project Lightning."

He's almost out of my sight when I let the real bomb drop. "He's staying here with us."

Tony's whole body freezes. He slowly turns and locks eyes with me. "Why would you want one of them here?"

I can hear his anger clearly, but I want to rail at him. If he would help us on these missions, he would get why Xavier is here and how important it is we get his help.

"Because during our last mission we rescued a little girl from a cage. And she either won't talk, or she can't."

He looks away, but not before I see the guilt in his eyes. "We needed Xavier to help us figure out who she is, and where she came from before we rescued her from that laboratory from hell."

He won't look at me, just stares at his feet. I know they ran experiments on him, but he won't tell me *anything*. I can only imagine this is bringing all of those memories to the surface, but he needs to tell us something. He needs to deal with this. And I know that I'm being super hypocritical, but maybe he saw someone or heard something that could help us figure out who's behind all of this. I want to yell all of this at him, but we've been there before and the results were disastrous.

"Just keep him away from my room," he says, and storms off.

I want to throw my hands up in the air. I want to yell at him to fight me more. I want him to explode. But I just sit here in my chair. We make quite the dysfunctional pair. Neither of us wanting to deal and yet wanting the other to succumb. But maybe having Xavier here will help Tony more than he realizes. Because I need Tony to help us. We can't tackle this problem without him.

SEVEN

A knock at the door startles me from my thoughts. I ease from the chair, not really wanting to get the door, but knowing Xavier's probably on the other side of it. There's another knock, but this time it's more hesitant.

"Coming," I say as I reach for the knob.

As I open it, Xavier steps back, his hands shoved in his pockets. We stare at one another, too many heavy things between us. I take a deep breath and stand a little taller. "Come on in," I tell him while I make a sweeping gesture into the house. "I'll show you where you get to sleep."

I step back and allow him to walk inside. He stops just past the entryway and I wonder what he's thinking about what he sees. This place is bare. Aside from the thread-bare couches, old model TV, and Tony's video game set-up, there's nothing here. No pictures, paintings, throw pillows, nothing. It's pretty depressing, but I try to spend as little time here as possible. Being here gets me lost in my own thoughts. And that's not a place I like to be.

"If you're thirsty, the only thing I've got to drink is water and soda," I say while I shut the door.

"I'm fine, thank you," he slowly drawls.

"Have a seat and I'll see if I can get Tony out here," I say.

He raises his brow at the mention of Tony. "We're roommates," I tell him.

He nods and slowly sits on one of the couches, his focus drawn to Tony's video games.

I head down the dark hallway towards the back of the house. He hasn't been in there long, but I need to at least give him the chance to come out and really meet Xavier. I reach Tony's door and knock once before I push it open.

He's lying in his bed, his body facing away from the door. I can't see what he's holding, but it has all his attention. "Can you come out here and meet him?" I ask him.

"Maybe later." His words are muffled against his pillow.

"*Tony*," I say, completely irritated.

"*Becca*," he says, trying to mock my tone.

I walk over to the bed and reach around him, pulling on whatever is making him refuse to look at me. It's a picture of him and his dad. *Oh, man.*

"Hey," he yells, lunging for the picture and ripping it out of my hand. "You've got no right." He spits the words at me, his eyes showing the most fire I've seen since we rescued him.

"I'm sorry," I say. "I didn't know what was in your hand."

His only answer is a growly huff. But I can't back down now.

"Please get out of bed and come talk to us," I say, my voice still even, calm. And I know it sounds like I'm trying to coax a wounded animal, but in some ways I am.

He locks eyes with me, and I fold my arms across my chest. I will wait him out if I have to. After a few moments of our standoff, he sits up. "You're not going to leave me alone until I come out there, are you?" he asks.

"No. I'm not." If this is how I have to push him, then I will.

He blows out a breath, causing the hair dangling in front of his eyes to move. "Fine, give me a sec and I'll meet you out there."

I stare at him a little longer. "I promise I'll be right out," he says, throwing his arms out to the side, completely exasperated with me.

I give him one last warning look and then walk back out into the hallway. I lean against the wall next to his door and hang my head. His dad was his world, and I came in and pushed into that memory. But he needs the push.

It takes him five minutes, but true to his word, Tony comes out to join us on the couch. Xavier stands and extends his hand. "We haven't officially met. I'm Xavier."

Tony shakes his hand and clears his throat a few times. "Thanks for everything you did," he says, and quickly drops his hand to sit down next to me on the couch.

Xavier takes a seat across from us, and an awkward silence fills the room as the two men stare at one another.

"So, uh, Tiberius say anything to you before you headed over?" I ask Xavier.

His eyes leave Tony and focus on me. "He said he'd be coming over here soon so we could plan out a scouting mission. Lucy is trying to find out where that stone with Latin on it is."

"Scouting mission?" Tony asks me.

I adjust myself on the couch so I can face him. "The little girl we found came from another lab in France. She wasn't rushed out of there in a hurry, so we're assuming it's still active. We could use your help on this one," I say, and he tenses at the suggestion.

"I'll think about it." Which means no.

"This might lead to whoever is behind all this. Behind your kidnapping," I tell him, pushing past where I know his comfort zone is.

Tony's hand slices through the air. "I said I'll think about." The words whip out of him, fast and fierce.

"You can't hide out forever." Xavier's words are delivered in a calm but firm manner.

"Who the hell are you to judge and say I'm hiding?" Tony leans forward and stabs a finger in his direction. "You've got no clue what happened to me."

Xavier stands abruptly and I latch a hand onto Tony's arm in case I need to transport us out of here. Xavier takes off his shirt to reveal a tanned chest covered in dark hair. But I soon see the faded scars that start from his hipbone and climb up all the way to the top of his ribs. There are seven of them on each side, and considering how wide they are, they must have hurt like hell when it happened.

"When I was eighteen, I was on one of my first missions for Project Lightning. I was taken hostage in the Middle East for weeks. Every day I got the crap beaten out of me. I was waterboarded constantly. Every interrogation tactic they could think of they did. And when they realized I wasn't going to talk, they kept up their tactics, but at the end of the day. Every. Damn. Day. They took a knife and ripped me open from groin to ribs."

Tony and I sit frozen, both of our eyes tracing the deep gouges in his skin. "If it weren't for Gregory, I would have died in that sand pit jail cell."

He puts his shirt back on and sits back down. "I understand more than anyone what you've been through."

Heavy silence blankets us. I look at Xavier and try to match the story with the guy I've worked with. How did he come back from that? How is he still doing this?

"When does it go away?" Tony asks the question so quietly I'm not sure I hear him.

"Which part?" Xavier asks, his voice gentled.

"The fear," he whispers.

Xavier leans forward, and now it's just him and Tony. Like I'm not even in the room anymore. "Never. It never goes away. You just learn to be stronger."

I watch Tony slowly nod. And they don't notice me, but I nod too. Because I might not have been kidnapped, but that fear...I feel it every day. And I pray like crazy I'll be able to be stronger, because if I can't, then how am I going to find the person responsible for my grandparents' and Gregory's deaths?

EIGHT

After watching Xavier and Tony go down a video game hole, I left to go wander the streets, and now I've been walking aimlessly for an hour.

"*Ciao*, Becca." I turn at the sound of my name, and squint to make out Luca sitting on a nearby bench.

"You do realize it's super creepy to be sitting out here alone in the dark," I say as I make my way closer to him.

He shrugs his massive shoulders. "It's the only time that most people aren't out." He tries to hide the sadness lacing his voice, but it's familiar to my ears.

"The more you show yourself, the less it'll startle people," I say, telling him something I've already said a dozen times.

"It's hard to get past the screams."

Sadly, he's got a point. "The kids will get used to you."

He shakes his head like he doubts it. I take a seat next to him. "Have you tested the range of your powers yet?" I ask, trying to change the subject. But also, maybe if we can help find a way for him to morph back, that would help.

He shifts in his seat. "A few things. My skin feels like a shield.

The scales seem impossible to cut. And my strength has increased very much."

Whoa, he's basically got built-in armor. "I wonder if that makes you bulletproof." He takes in a quick breath. "Don't worry." I put my hands out, trying to calm him. "I don't have any plans on trying to figure that out."

Even in the dark I can see him deflate.

"Have you tried shifting?" I ask tentatively.

"No," he answers softly.

"How about we try something? Give me your hand." I hold mine out and he stares at it for a few moments, making me wonder if he'll trust me.

He places his hand in mine and it's the first time I've really felt how different his skin is. When we rescued him from Rome, everything was chaotic, and I didn't really pay attention to how his hand felt. But now, alone on this bench, I can. And it feels smooth, but like a polished fingernail, and warm to the touch.

"I want you to pretend you're staring in front of a mirror looking at yourself the way you look now. Can you see yourself?"

He squeezes my hand. "*Si.*"

I take a deep breath. Here goes nothing. "Okay, now I want you to keep looking at that image, but I want you to look at your arm and change it to what it looked like before. The scales are gone, and it's replaced by your natural skin tone and hair."

I keep my eyes trained on his face. His eyes squeeze even tighter, and I pump some enhancing power into him.

Slowly, the teal scales on his arm fade, leaving tan skin with dark hair in its place. I suck in a deep breath.

"What?" Luca's eyes snap open.

"Your arm," I say pointing towards it with my free hand.

He looks down, just in time to see his skin change back to scales, except for one little patch around his wrist that stays. "*Madonna santa!*"

Uh...what?

"It worked. Can you believe it?" He asks the question in awe, still looking at his real skin peeking through.

"Can you change it all back to scales?" I ask, pointing at his wrist.

He pulls his hand away, cradling it to his chest. "Why would I want to do that?" he asks like I'm completely crazy.

"Because those scales could save your life someday. I think it would be pretty useful to be able to go between scales and regular skin."

He looks at the patch of skin. And the war on his face almost makes me tell him to stop, but he squares his shoulders and holds his hand up at eye level. We both watch as the skin turns back into teal scales.

"Now what about changing your hand into all skin?" I ask, hoping he won't need me to enhance him.

He focuses on his hand and squints really hard. I wonder if it were daylight if I'd see sweat beading on his brow. Slowly, three of his fingers turn back to the same tan skin. He slumps forward, sucking in huge gulps of air.

"You did it." He smiles slightly at my excitement.

"*Si*, but not the whole hand," he says, still breathless.

"No, but it's more skin that you had yesterday. You just need to practice, and I can help sometimes too."

He takes a deep breath and sits up a little taller. "It's a start," he says with more conviction than he had a minute ago.

I pat him on the shoulder and stand up. "Hey, maybe you can start going on missions with us."

"I'd like that. I want to help," he tells me. And I wonder if the vengeance I hear in his voice can be heard in mine at times.

"We could use you. Especially when it comes to dealing with the guards." I wipe my hands on my legs and move a step away from the bench. "I'm going to call it a night. See you tomorrow, Luca."

"*Grazie*, Becca," he says, his voice solemn.

"Don't worry about it. Remember, you're not alone, and you're in a place where people understand you. Remember that when you're afraid to come out."

He nods and I walk back to my place, every now and again turning to see if he's still sitting there. Like most people at Fordlandia, he has no family, no friends outside of this place. He was an orphan just like Lucy. So even if he gets his powers under control, I doubt he'd ever leave here.

I stroll down the desolate lane until I get to the house I'm living in. The flickering TV lights up the front window. I wonder if they're still playing video games.

I stop at the gate and stare at the house I've lived in the past couple months. This isn't home for me. But just like Luca, I have no place to go back to. No one waiting for me. And even though Tiberius is the last family I have, I still barely know him. I don't know if I'll ever be able to call this place home. But it's better than nothing.

NINE

Asoft knock drags me from a deep, dreamless sleep. Most of me
is grateful for that. The cryptic dreams with my mother were
driving me insane. But there's a small part of me that misses it. I miss
her letting me know what's coming. And if I'm honest with myself,
there's a teeny tiny part that misses her.

The knock comes again, and I sit up in bed, rubbing my eyes.
"Yeah," I say in raspy morning voice.

"Is it safe to come in?" Xavier asks from the other side of the door.

I look down at my t-shirt and shorts. "I'm decent," I tell him.

The door opens and he slowly enters the room, like he's still
afraid I'm sitting here in my underwear or something.

"Morning," he says. He's way too awake.

When I came inside last night, he and Tony were completely
transfixed on a video game. It was after midnight and I went to bed,
but they seemed to just be getting started. Does the man not sleep?

"Morning," I respond.

His eyes drift around my room, and I know what he sees. Nothing. There is nothing personal in this room aside from the picture on

my nightstand. There's no personality in this room. It's a place to sleep and hold my clothes, and that's it.

"Tiberius stopped by, asked if we could come over when you woke up." My legs are swinging over the edge of the bed at the mention of Tiberius.

"Let me get dressed," I say, hopping up.

He nods and steps out of the room, shutting the door behind him.

I dress quickly, wanting to get to Tiberius. I'm hoping Lucy knows where in France Eloise was before we found her in Spain.

I walk out of my room and down the hall to the kitchen. Xavier and Tony sit at the little kitchen table eating bowls of cereal. Xavier smiles at me, but Tony looks less enthusiastic about being awake.

As I prepare my own breakfast, I look over my shoulder at Tony. "You coming with us to Tiberius's?"

He looks stunned at the question. I don't know why he's surprised; I ask him to come with me all the time. "Why?"

"There's a little girl that needs our help," I remind him as I walk back towards the table with my own bowl of cereal.

"How would I be able to help?" he asks, like it's a ludicrous idea.

"We're probably going to need to go to France to do some scouting first. It'd be nice to have another set of eyes." Plus, I've been wondering if I enhance him, could he see through walls?

"I don't know," he says, eyes fixed on his bowl, spoon slowly swirling through the milk.

I catch Xavier out of the corner of my eye. His gaze keeps ping-ponging between us. I don't know how to explain Tony and myself. I also wish Xavier knew what Tony used to be like. How he was the funny guy. The ladies' man. Someone you wanted to be around. Someone who exuded life, but it's now been wrenched out of him.

We quickly finish eating and clean up. Xavier heads for the door and I join him, but I call out to Tony before he gets to the hall. "If you change your mind, we could really use you," I tell him.

He nods without looking at me and continues to his room. Xavier steps out and I follow suit.

Xavier gives me a sideways stare. I know he's got a million questions. I would too. And before he can ask any, I control the conversation. "I haven't been able to get him to leave Fordlandia since I brought him here," I tell him.

"Does he say why?" he asks, eyes scanning the surrounding houses.

"No, and he won't even tell me about his kidnapping," I say, kicking a stray rock down the dirt road.

"Well, maybe—"

Xavier stops abruptly and I turn and see his wide eyes and open mouth. What on earth—

Luca comes walking towards us; his shoulders rounded, hands tucked deep into his pockets.

"Hey, Luca," I call out to him.

"*Ciao*, Becca," he says as he heads over to us.

"Close your mouth," I whisper out of the side of my mouth to Xavier.

His jaw snaps shut, and his whole demeanor shifts to the proud FBI agent he is. And as soon as Luca is close enough, Xavier extends his hand. Luca hesitates a moment. Aside from me, Tiberius, and occasionally Lucy, no one has touched him. Or even come close enough to touch him.

They shake hands, exchanging names.

"Want to come with us to Tiberius's?" I ask him, because for some reason I think Eloise would really like him. "There's someone there I want you to meet."

"*Va bene*," he says and joins us.

We turn down a lane and walk up to Tiberius's front door. I reach my hand to knock, but it opens before my hand can reach it.

"Saw you coming," Tiberius says by way of greeting, and I let out a laugh.

I walk past him, Xavier close behind.

"Good to see you, Luca," Tiberius says.

"*Ciao*," Luca responds in a soft voice.

I walk into the living room. "I brought him to meet Eloise," I say as I take a seat on one of the couches.

"I'll go grab her and Lucy. We've got a place to investigate, but I'll let Lucy tell you all about it," Tiberius says, and then walks out of the room.

"Who is Eloise?" Luca asks, looking around the room before he takes a seat on the couch next to me.

"A little girl," I tell him.

He lets out a shocked hiss, a little too close to snake-like for my liking, and grabs my arm. I see Xavier tense out of the corner of my eye.

"You know how *bambini* act around me," he says in a harsh whisper.

I look down at his hand and he immediately removes it. I meet his gaze again and say, "I have a feeling this will be different."

"She has a feeling," he mutters to himself, along with a whole string of Italian that I've got no clue what it means.

The sound of footsteps causes all of us to look towards the hall. Eloise enters the room holding Lucy's hand. She smiles at Xavier and as she turns to Luca, I feel his whole body lock. But then her eyes brighten and a huge smile spreads across her face.

She drops Lucy's hand and rushes over to Luca's side. His body is still coiled, probably ready to flee the room. Eloise climbs onto the couch next to him, her face beaming. She reaches out a hand to touch the scales on his arm, but stops and looks up into his eyes, asking for permission without uttering a word.

"*Si,*" he says softly.

She lightly touches his arm, running her fingers over the teal scales. And I'm pretty sure I hear her whisper the word "*Joli.*" But it's so soft I might be hearing things, and she hasn't spoken once since we rescued her. But the awe and wonderment on her face soothes something in me. We found her in a cage, being experimented on, and yet she's able to put it aside and bathe in the joy of seeing a man with teal scales.

"Eloise, this is Luca," Lucy says, her voice light and happy.

"See. I told you she would like you," I tell Luca. He smirks at me, letting me know that I was totally right.

Tiberius clears his throat, breaking the little spell we've been under. Well, not Eloise; she's still touching the scales on Luca's arm. "Lucy, do you want to show them what you found?" Tiberius asks.

"Right," she says, and walks over to her desk, grabbing a tablet. "So, I cross-referenced some of the words that Xavier saw on the stone wall. Apparently Collégiale Saint-Laurent is a church in Salone de Provence of France. It says it's where Nostradamus is buried."

"Nostradamus?" I ask, because I have no clue who that is.

"He's the guy from the 1500s who made all these prophecies about the future. Some believe he predicted the French Revolution, Hitler, September eleventh, and a whole host of other events," Lucy tells me.

"Seriously?" I ask, because that's crazy.

"Well, some people believe in it, but there're a bunch of people who think his prophecies are a little far-reaching. Though his prediction on the death of King Henry II of France was pretty accurate, actually," she says, typing away at her computer.

"They're doing experiments at a church?" Xavier asks, probably wanting to get back to the whole point of this conversation.

"I'm not sure, but you're going to want to do a scouting mission first. This is all I've got to go on for now," she tells him.

"You're not coming with us?" I ask, because she's always been there.

"Who else is going to stay with Eloise?" Lucy says.

"I can stay with her," Luca tells us. Eloise is cuddled up to his side, her giraffe tucked under one arm, and her head resting on his shoulder. "She reminds me of my little sister I used to have, Filomena."

I hear the pain in the words "used to have." All of us can use that phrase, and I'm pretty sure all of us sound broken when we do.

"She seems comfortable with you," Tiberius says. "Eloise, would you be okay with Luca watching you for a little while?"

She nods, not moving from her spot against Luca. "Guess that settles that," Xavier says.

"We're making a trip to France?" I ask. I've always wanted to go there, but obviously not under these circumstances.

"Yes. We need to scope out the place. I think we should transport here," Lucy says as she turns her tablet towards us. "There's a park not too far called Parc Du Pigeonier. Time wise, France is about six or so hours ahead of us. I'm thinking after lunch?" She directs the question to the room, and we all nod.

"Sounds good. Let's meet back here after twelve o'clock," Tiberius tells us.

We get up to leave. "Walter wants to see you, Becca," Tiberius says when I reach the door.

"I forgot Walter was here. I'd love to see him," Xavier says from behind me.

"Did he say why?" I ask, hesitating, because lately he's been trying to get me to open up and I wish he'd stop.

"I think he wants to check your head again, and he mentioned Bronia," he tells me.

"Your head?" Xavier asks.

I wave away his comment. "It's nothing. Just a little knock on the head. No permanent damage. It's fine."

He lets out a startled whisper of, "What?"

"We'll go stop by," I tell Tiberius, ignoring Xavier.

And I hope it's just that, because I don't want to deal with anything else.

TEN

"Is your head okay?" Bronia asks from the swing next to mine.

"Yeah. Your *JaJa* said everything looked great," I say, slowly swaying in my swing.

I escaped out behind their home with her after Walter checked my head from the brawl the other night, and Xavier bombarding him with questions allowed me to slip out.

I watch Bronia out of the corner of my eye. It's been almost six months since Ania died, but she doesn't look any better. "What's eatin' at ya?" I ask her.

"Nothing," she says, dragging her feet in the grass.

I stop swinging. And twist the swing so I'm facing her. And I wait, because I know it's not nothing. It takes her a bit, but she finally slumps a little more in the swing.

"My birthday is next week. And this is the first one without *Mamusia*." Her voice breaks on the Polish word for mama.

I wrap my arms around her, squeezing her to me. Knowing she needs it. Especially because she's been hesitant to touch anyone since she received Ania's power of strength.

"I'm sorry," I whisper into her ear.

I let her silent tears soak my hair, but I don't pull away. I don't say any other words. Too often we try and say things like "it's okay," or "it'll get better." We try to get people to look on the bright side of things, when really all that person needs to hear is, "I'm sorry." But we don't need to find the words to make it better. Just be there, that's all they want.

She pulls away and wipes her face on her sleeve. We start swinging again, both lost in our own thoughts.

The back door opens, squeaking as it swings. "You guys want to come in for lunch?" Xavier calls out.

I look over at Bronia. "Ready to go inside?" I ask, not wanting to rush her.

She takes a deep breath, and then nods. I've never been more in awe of this kid, only ten years old and dealing with things most of the world will never have to.

We head inside and dish ourselves some leftover *feijoada* that Walter got from one of the restaurants in town. And for that I am eternally grateful, because with it being the end of fall in Brazil, this hearty stew hits the spot.

I watch Bronia a little bit. You can still see the gentle way in which she pulls out a chair or shuts the fridge. But she's gotten a lot better. And is probably saving Walter a lot more money now. The first time I met her, she ripped a door off its hinges like it was nothing. Now she's learning, and a heck of a lot faster than the rest of us took to learn our powers.

"Xavier tells me you're going to France," Walter says, wiping his face with a napkin.

"After lunch," I tell him.

"Is Tony going with you?" he asks, somewhat hopeful.

"What do you think?" I ask, not bothering to look away from my food.

He slaps his hand on the table, making everyone at the table look up at him. "That little *baran*. You could really use him on this."

"Preaching to the choir, Walter. You're welcome to go and try and talk him into it," I say, shoveling another delicious bite in.

"I'll swing by this afternoon," he says in his gruff Polish voice.

Who knows, maybe Tony will be persuaded by Walter.

We finish up our lunch, and after cleaning up, Xavier and I say our goodbyes as we walk out the door and head over to Tiberius's.

"You're different," Xavier says to me out of nowhere as we walk down the dirt street.

"Yeah. How's that?" I ask, not really wanting to have this conversation.

"Something's gone," he says, but doesn't elaborate.

"Cryptic much?"

"Sorry," he says, looking me over. "I can't explain it. Something is different."

We pass the turn for my house, but I stop and stare at it. "I'm going to go talk to Tony. Why don't you head over to Tiberius's and I'll transport there in a minute?"

"Think it's going to help?" he asks.

"Won't know till I try," I say. I close my eyes and, in a blink, I'm standing in front of my front door.

After we moved in here, Tony and I agreed I'd never transport directly into the house. The first time I did it, I ended up with a black eye and Tony refusing to come out of his room for two days. But now he can have the chance to hear the front door.

"Tony," I call out as I walk in the front door.

Surprisingly, he's not sitting on the couch, so I head for his room. I get to his door and hear mumbling coming from the other side. I raise my hand to knock, but lean closer when I hear him curse. What is going on in there?

"Tony?" I ask as I knock on the door.

Something heavy drops to the floor, and I hear him scrambling around the room. I turn the handle on the door, and it clicks open.

"No! Don't come in here!"

What the...

"What are you doing?" I ask, still holding the doorknob.

"Nothing," he says, but he sounds frantic.

I push the door open just a little, and then what I see causes me to push it wide. "Becca, no."

He stands frozen by his hamper, a towel crushed in his hand, wearing nothing but a t-shirt and briefs. His legs are covered in blood. It's flowing down his thighs, from long cuts above the knee.

My eyes make their way back up his body, and they stop on his hands. He's twisting the towel so tightly, but I doubt he even knows that. I connect with his eyes, but he averts his quickly to the floor.

I walk slowly across the room to him. And the closer I get, the more his muscles seem to tense. I stop in front of him, blood still dripping onto the floor, and slowly pry his fingers off the towel.

He reluctantly releases it, and I squat down in front of him and put the towel against his left leg. A whoosh of air leaves his lips, and I watch them start to tremble, but he fights it.

He clears his throat a few times. "You don't...you don't have to do this." He forces the words past his still trembling lips.

"I know," I tell him, doing my best to keep my voice even and normal.

Because inside I'm freaking way the heck out. I'm out of my depth here. He's cutting himself. And I know there's no way I can truly help him, aside from this. But I feel my frozen heart start to melt a little bit. Because my friend is hurting.

"I don't..." He's struggling for words, and I reach up to grab his hand.

He finally looks down at me, and that allows a tear to escape. He opens his mouth, but I interject before he can say anything. "You don't owe me an explanation—"

"Yes, I do." He rushes to interrupt.

"No." It's just one word, but the weight behind it is fierce.

I've been so wrapped up in myself, that judging by the healing scars, this has been going on for a while. And I know there's probably nothing I could have done, but I can start now by being there for him.

I lift the towel and move to his left leg. He makes a pained noise when I put pressure on it. "You gotta talk to someone." I say the words quietly.

"Don't think I'm alone in that," he says pointedly.

I press my lips together. I pull the towel away and stand up. He takes the towel from me. "I'm not ready," he says, looking at the bloody towel.

"You know where I am when you're ready. Or you might want to talk to Lucy." There are still horrors about Lucy that I don't know. And I think that's why she's latched on to Eloise, because unfortunately, they've got so much in common.

"Everyone in Fordlandia is broken in some way," I tell him.

He nods and then walks over and sits on his bed. "So, uh, was there something you needed?" he asks.

I let him drop the subject, because I know he needs to. "Just letting you know we're headed to France," I say, not bothering to ask him to come.

"Be careful," he says.

"You too," I tell him, and I look at his hunched profile for a beat longer.

I take a deep breath, trying to focus my mind for what's ahead. But it's hard. There's so much I want to do for him, but he's got to want the help too.

I blink and I'm standing in front of Tiberius's door.

ELEVEN

"This is the place we're going to transport to." Lucy points to a park on the map. "Satellite photos show lots of trees, and at the moment it seems pretty deserted. That could change, obviously." We all lean closer, looking at the computer monitor.

All the trees are green, and grass is sprouting everywhere. It's like a little medieval forest in the middle of a city.

"Shouldn't we wait until the sun goes down?" I ask, because even though it's late fall in Brazil, it's late spring in France.

"If we wait too long the church will be closed," Tiberius tells me from his spot leaning over Lucy's desk chair.

"I could just transport us into the church. Lucy could probably take care of their security."

She shakes her head. "This is just for scouting. We need to look like tourists. And I would need to disable the security from outside. I've never been in this building. Hopefully after today I'll be able to remotely access it."

"Lucy's right," Xavier says from beside me. "You haven't done enough missions yet to know how to blend in a crowd. This scouting mission calls for that so we can gather as much intel as possible."

I nod and turn my attention to the map and satellite photos. "Well, I think I've got it nailed down."

We all step back to allow Lucy to get out of her chair. "Heads up, Xavier, the first few long-distance transports might leave you a little dizzy, nauseous, and lightheaded," Tiberius tells him.

"Thanks for that," he says, and then he looks at me, determination written all over his face.

"Grab a hand, everyone," I tell them.

I concentrate on the image before me, focusing on a copse of trees along a stone wall. Hopefully that'll cover our transport.

I grip everyone's hands, and in a blink we're across the world.

The park is still lit by the sun when we appear behind a massive tree. "One of these days we're going to get caught," I say, hearing voices not too far off.

"Today's not that day, though," Lucy points out since we're alone.

Xavier's hand slips from mine as he drops down in a crouch against the tree.

"You all right down there?" I ask him.

"Give me a second," he says in between deep breaths.

After a minute or so he stands, shaking out his arms and legs.

"Let's head over to the church," Tiberius says.

We head out of the park and onto the busy street. "Tony didn't want to come?" Xavier asks as he walks beside me. Lucy and Tiberius walk in front of us, pointing things out and generally acting like tourists.

"Not this time," I tell him.

Part of me wants to tell him what I found so I'm not alone in this knowledge. But if I were going to tell anyone, it would be Lucy. And I don't think he wants to kill himself, but I know what he's doing isn't healthy. But he's not going to reach out until he's ready. Telling someone could derail that, but I don't think I can give him the luxury of time.

"Maybe next time," he says.

"Yeah, maybe," I say, but even I can tell that I don't believe it. I think it would take something crazy, like *me* getting kidnapped, to drag him away from Fordlandia.

People bustle by us on the street, some smiling as we pass, others looking at all the sites to see. The number of languages is astounding. The different cultures are so interesting it makes me want to explore.

After walking for fifteen minutes, we turn the corner and a large sand-colored brick church towers above us. It's adorned with gothic and medieval peaks, but for some reason I thought it would have more adornments. It's quite plain. People stroll around the grounds, others coming and going from inside, and a few sit staring up at the grand building.

"Let's get inside before we can't," Lucy says.

We walk through the large wooden doors, and I take in a huge breath. The place is stunning. The plain façade outside truly hides something striking within. The stonework is beautifully carved, and the paintings on the wall are amazing. The scent of incense hangs heavy in the air. "This place is super cool," I whisper, because it feels like the right thing to do.

"I think the tomb is this way," Xavier says.

We move closer to it and I come up alongside Tiberius. "You getting anything?" I ask.

"No," he says, sounding genuinely confused.

Xavier gets close to the wall and puts his palm on it. He bows his head as if he's praying, and I look around. There's a piece of paper on a nearby pew. I pick it up. *Nostradamus* is written across the top. I keep reading.

"Find something?" Lucy asks as she sidles up close to me.

"Yeah, apparently there's a curse on Nostradamus's tomb, and all the people that moved his body have died," I tell her.

"It does not say that." She snatches the paper out of my hand. Her eyes dart back and forth across the page. "Whoa."

"I know, right? No wonder what's left of his bones is secured behind a thick stone wall," I say, pointing towards the tomb.

I turn back to look at Xavier. His face is angled towards us and is pulled into a grimace. I head over and place a hand on his arm, hoping he'll see farther into the past. He gasps and steps back, his eyes shooting to mine. "What are you doing?" he asks.

He knows something is up with me, and I can't hide it from him for much longer, but this isn't the place. "Later," I tell him, lifting his arm back up.

He puts his palm back on the wall, and a small shudder works through him.

"Did you get anything?" Tiberius asks.

"Lots," Xavier tells him. His face looks haunted, and he keeps opening his mouth and closing it. Like he wants to tell us something, but not here.

"Good, let's get out of here and we can talk more at home." Tiberius looks over his shoulder, searching for his wife. "Lucy," he calls for her.

She's taking pictures on her phone like a tourist, but I watch her take the last one of a camera that's pointing at the wall the three of us are standing at. "I'm ready," she says.

We walk down a hall, giving a wave to the passing priest. As soon as we're out of the building, Tiberius leads us down a street and into a side alley. He looks up and I follow his gaze, searching for cameras. "Looks like we're good to go," I say.

I grasp their hands and transport us back to Tiberius's living room.

"YOU'RE NOT GOING to believe who I saw," Xavier says as soon as we appear in Tiberius's living room, his long raven hair streaming out behind him as he paces between the couches.

"Who?" I ask, having no clue.

"Chelsea," he says, practically spitting her name out.

"Who's Chelsea?" Lucy asks, taking a seat at her desk. She pulls up her computer and starts typing at a rapid pace.

"She's Mr. Rivers's personal assistant," I tell them, and then a memory from Gregory strikes, and my heart races. "Gregory was pretty sure she's one of us—"

"What?" Xavier cuts me off.

The words start coming quickly. "He read Mr. Rivers's thoughts about someone being a 'null.' And he could never read her or Mr. Rivers when she was around. He was thinking that she could nullify powers," I tell them.

Lucy stops typing and slowly turns to us in her chair, and Tiberius sits down heavily on the couch. "Does that mean she could block someone like Tiberius from finding people?" Xavier asks.

"I think it does," Tiberius says, his voice heavy with concern. "It would also render any power useless."

The severity of a null settles on all of us. What does this mean? "Do you think Mr. Rivers knows about her involvement?" I ask. "Is Mr. Rivers behind all of this?"

Xavier starts shaking his head. "No. No way. Mr. Smith would know right away since you can't lie to him." He keeps shaking his head.

"Yeah, but Mr. Rivers can control people, so couldn't he make it so Mr. Smith would always believe him? Or couldn't Chelsea block Mr. Smith's abilities?"

"Wait a minute. Someone can control people?" Lucy's voice rises at the end of her question.

"He has the power of suggestion. Not mind control," Xavier says.

"Same thing," I say, throwing my hands up in the air.

Tiberius holds his hands out, trying to calm us down. "Hold on a minute. We can't start jumping to conclusions without more facts. Did you see anyone else?" Tiberius asks.

"Not that I recognized. She was mostly walking past the tomb," Xavier says.

"Is there any way to know if that place has a basement or a tunnel underground connecting it to something?" I ask. "There has to be a reason she's at the church. I highly doubt it's to save her soul."

"I'll pull up the blueprints in a moment, but first I need to erase us from their servers. They had so many cameras around the area. And if someone like Mr. Rivers is involved, we don't want them to know we were there," Lucy tells us. She turns back to her computer and starts typing furiously again.

"What now?" I ask.

"We need a plan, because there's something big going on there," Xavier says. "We need to do it for Eloise and whoever else is involved. After what I saw happened to that little girl and her parents"—he takes a deep breath—"I'm more invested than ever now."

"Don't you have to check in with Mr. Smith? Isn't Raven wondering where you are?" I ask.

"In a few days I'll have to check in, but for now, it's fine. And even when I do, I won't tell them about this place," he says on a promise.

How can he promise that? Isn't he worried about them tracking him? I guess Lucy could help him make sure he's untraceable, but a lot more people's lives are at stake aside from us. And he can't even lie to Mr. Smith.

"We'll figure it out," Tiberius says. "For now, let's let Lucy do her job and we'll go from there."

I hate the waiting. The planning. But until Lucy gets the layout of the building, I can't do anything. I guess I could transport there and look around. Place is probably deserted anyways. A thought bursts into my mind. Maybe I should talk to Tony.

TWELVE

"I can't," Tony tells me for the tenth time, his arms crossed tightly across his chest.

"Please," I beg, stepping closer to him.

"Becca," he says, pleading me to stop.

I get that he's scared, but it just feels like something else is stopping him. And I can't put my finger on it, but maybe if I tell him what more I can do, it'll convince him. "What if you could see through walls?" I ask him.

He takes a step back from me. His face scrunches like he doesn't get what I'm asking.

"Just listen for a minute, okay?" I ask him.

He stands silent, waiting, and I take that as my go-ahead. "Tiberius is my dad's brother," I tell him.

His arms drop to his sides. "What?" So many emotions flicker across his face: hurt, confusion, anger.

I get it. I kept this from him on purpose. Aside from Lucy, Walter, and Xavier, no one really knows. We made that decision so it couldn't be used against us, but it's time to change that. So I tell Tony about my dad, how he's Tiberius's identical twin, about them being adopted separately. I tell him *everything*.

I take a deep breath. "I inherited powers from my dad too. He could enhance powers."

I wait for a response, but he just stands there, staring out into space, not saying anything. All the emotions I saw earlier are wiped clean, leaving nothing but a cold mask. "How long have you known?" he asks, his voice quiet.

"Not long. The day before we rescued you in Myanmar. I took a chance transporting you to Walter, but I had to try. It's why I can transport people now. And I think I could enhance your vision to look through walls."

His hand lashes out and grips my arm. "Does anyone else know about this?"

"What's wrong—"

"Does anyone know?" he asks, squeezing harder.

I transport a foot away from him and he stumbles forward. "What the hell's your problem?" I ask, looking at the fading handprint on my arm.

He fists his hands in his hair. "Do you know they want you? That they asked me repeatedly if I knew what made you special? They know there's something different about you."

He doesn't know that they sent a ransom offering to exchange him for me, but I'm not going to bring that memory up now. "I know they want me. But aside from Tiberius, Lucy, and you, no one knows. I think Xavier suspects something, but I haven't told him," I tell him, trying to calm him down.

"Don't tell him," he says, slicing his hand through the air. "The fewer people that know, the better. They want you, Becca, and if they know about this, they'll never stop hunting you."

I throw my arms out wide. "Then come and help me." I launch the words at him. "Help me put a stop to this. Don't let them hurt other people like they've done to you. Don't let them kidnap any more children and put them in cages. I don't want any more kids like

Eloise having to watch their parents be murdered in front of them. Help me so things like that don't happen again."

He puts his hands on his hips and stares at the ground. Moments of painful silence pass, but I wait it out and watch him war with himself.

"Okay," he says, and I could kiss him. "But first, let's see if you can even enhance my power."

I pace back and forth in front of the couch. How do we even test this? And then it hits.

"I've got an idea. Wait here," I say and head off down the hall.

I run to my room and look through my things. I need something that I can place on the bed. The only thing I have, other than clothes, is a bright green scarf that Maria made me. I ball it up and put it on top of my pillow.

I rush back out to the living room. "All right, I put something on my pillow, and I want you to tell me what it is."

"How do we do this?" he asks, looking at the wall where my room is on the other side.

"You're going to have to hold my hand," I tell him, and he looks at it for a moment before grasping it in his. "Now focus like you do when you use your powers. But try to see past the wall."

He stares ahead, and I try pumping in a little bit of enhancement into him.

After some tense moments, he lets out a low growl. "This isn't working," he says, and drops my hand to run his through his hair.

"Let's try it one more time," I say.

"Fine," he says and grabs my hand.

I pump a lot more enhancement into him and he staggers back a step. "Holy...how...? That's impossible." The words are whispered in a mix of horror, and yet promise.

He turns to me, his face drained of color. "There's a green scarf on your pillow."

WE STAND OUTSIDE of Tiberius's door waiting for him to answer. Tony fidgets next to me, kicking a stone with his foot. The door opens and the minute Lucy sees Tony, her face clouds with confusion, but it quickly clears into a bright smile. "Hey, guys," she says, stepping back to let us in.

We walk in and I can hear Luca and Xavier in the kitchen. "They're all in the kitchen if you want to head in there," she says, and we follow her.

I walk right in and take a seat at the table. Tony lingers in the doorway, his eyes locked on Luca. This can't be the first time he's seen him, can it?

"Have a seat," Tiberius says, pointing at the extra chair.

He walks over and sits in the chair. "Tony wants to help," I tell the group, and watch Tiberius's eyebrows shoot up.

"This is Luca," I say to Tony.

They eye each other for a minute, until Eloise bursts into the kitchen, breaking up any weird tension. She walks around the table giving hugs, and when she gets to Tony, she throws her arms around him, squeezing him tightly around his middle. He lifts his arms like he doesn't know what to do.

But just as quickly as she came into the room, she's running out of it.

"I'll go see what she's up to," Luca says as he stands from the table.

Tony's eyes follow them out. "Did you know we found both of them in cages?" Lucy asks him.

He turns back to the table. "Becca mentioned it."

"Eloise still won't speak. Whatever trauma she endured has made her mute. When they had me, the things they did to me..." her words trail off, and she clears her throat a few times. "As an adult I've had a hard time processing it all, but to go through that as a child...I don't envy her in the least."

Silence reigns around the table until Tiberius clears his throat. "Do you have a plan?" he asks me.

"I do. I want to go back to France. There's more there that we've missed. Tony can come with me, and Lucy can stay here and hack their camera system."

"Wait a minute," Xavier interrupts. "Why don't we all just go like last time?"

"I think I'll have an easier time transporting into a small corridor when the church is closed with only one other person, versus if the whole group of us is there."

"And what if Chelsea's there?" Xavier asks.

"I don't think she can block more than one person at a time, and we're both trained in fighting. Plus, if it's late enough, we might not even encounter her," I tell him.

"What if you transport all of us to an outside location, and then transport you and Tony into the church. Things can go south very quickly, and I'll be able to monitor those with powers coming and going," Tiberius says, always thinking ahead.

I tilt my head back and forth. "That could work."

"Either way, I want you all to have comms set up so we can be in constant communication," Lucy says. "I don't like that you two have no back-up within the church, but I get it."

Tiberius lays his palms flat on the table. "We've got our plan. Get some good sleep tonight. We'll leave late tomorrow afternoon."

THIRTEEN

"Nervous?" I ask Tony, because for the last ten minutes he's been acting like he drank ten cups of coffee.

"No, just peachy," he says, and I raise a brow at his sarcasm. "Of course I'm nervous. The last mission we did, didn't turn out so great." He doesn't meet my eyes, but I chalk it up to anxiety.

"Well, Sariah isn't here, and now you can see through walls. I think this is going to go a lot smoother."

"We'll see," he mutters. "Why aren't you more nervous?"

"She thrives on this," Lucy says, coming up from behind. She hands each of us a small earpiece. "Put these in. Becca, can I borrow you for a moment?" she asks.

I follow her into the kitchen. She stops by the door and motions me farther into the room. I open my mouth to question her, but she motions for me to walk over to the table. She shuts the door and reaches into her front pocket.

"I have something I want you to wear, but I don't want anyone to know about it," she tells me, and then she puts her hand out and on her palm is a small piece of—skin?

"What..." My head tilts to the side as I study what's in her hand.

"It's a tracking device," she tells me.

Whoa.

"Do you really think I'll need that?" I ask her, still staring at the small dot on her hand.

"You can never be too careful, especially when you're going to be near someone who could nullify your powers."

"Good point," I say, because I wasn't even thinking about that.

"I want to attach it under your arm so it's someplace no one would consider looking, and it'll blend in," she says, and motions for my shirt. "Lift that up a bit so I can put it on."

I pull up the side of my shirt. Her fingers press the small tracking device into my skin. "This should stick like a Band-Aid," she says, applying pressure. "And I tried to match it as closely to your skin color as possible."

She holds it down. "Okay, I just have to hold this for a minute to stick it to your skin well."

We stand side by side. "How's everything going with Tony?" she asks me.

I blow a breath. "You reading my mind?" I ask.

"Doesn't take a mind reader to see something is even more tense than normal with him," she tells me, dropping her hand and checking the patch.

I promised to give him time, but I can't do that.

I lower my voice. "He's not good."

She raises her brows, waiting. I look back over my shoulder, but I don't think they're too close. I shuffle closer to her. "He's hurting himself."

Her shoulders droop and a sadness fills her.

"I don't know how to help him," I say.

She grabs my hand. "Just be his friend, but he needs help, Becca. Help that's way more than you can give. I'll talk with Tiberius and see what we can do. He's not the first here who's self-harmed, and sadly, if we don't stop all of this, he won't be the last."

My stomach still twists in knots, but a little hope wiggles in there. They'll know what to do.

She squeezes my hand and then drops it to step back. "Your tracker is all set."

"Is this like GPS?" I ask as I fix my shirt.

"Yes. I should be able to track you anywhere in the world with this. It gets a little spotty underground, but it'll still be sending a signal."

"Is everyone getting one?" I ask.

She shakes her head. "Tiberius always wears one, but I only have one other for now. So we'll keep this between us."

"Got it," I tell her, and we both leave the kitchen.

"All set?" Tiberius asks as we walk into the living room.

Xavier nods, and Tony is still super jittery. "We're just doing some more scouting. It'll be easy," I tell him.

He turns towards me, and I don't understand the look that passes over his face, but it's gone too fast for me to completely read it. "Both times I've transported with you I've nearly died," he says with a choked laugh.

"She's much better at it now," Tiberius says, trying to be reassuring.

I walk closer to Tony. "It'll be fine," I say to him in a soft voice.

He nods, but I'm not sure he's convinced.

"Let's get this show on the road," Xavier says.

"Grab on to a hand," I tell them. "We'll drop off you two, and then Tony and I will head inside the church."

Tiberius and Xavier hook onto one arm, and Tony grabs my other a lot tighter than I expected. I look up at him, and his eyes are wide and darting around the room. "Close your eyes," I tell him.

Our stares connect, and after a beat he closes his eyes. I blink and we're across the world.

"NOT TOO BAD, RIGHT?" I whisper to Tony as we appear in the darkened church.

I didn't give him the chance to recover after we dropped Xavier and Tiberius off at the park we transported to the first time.

"Heart's still beating," he says softly back. "But give me a second." He leans against the wall.

The first time he transported with me he almost died, and the second time he was completely unconscious. Tiberius is so used to it, it doesn't even faze him anymore. But Tony will get used to it sooner or later.

"Don't take too long, this place is super creepy," I tell him.

For how beautiful this church was during the day, it's eerie at night. The stonework, pews, and stone statues cast strange-shaped shadows across the room. What light there is, is distorted from the ancient glass windows. Shapes form in the darkened alcove. I know they're just shadows, but I can't completely suppress the shiver of fear that's creeping up my spine.

"Ready to look through some walls?" I ask him, because I want to get going.

"Yeah," he says, but his voice sounds sad. I shake it off; we can deal with whatever is bugging him later.

We walk down the hallway that Xavier saw Chelsea leaving from earlier. It ends with four doors. I hold out my hand and he places his in mine. I pump a large amount of my enhancing power into him, causing him to shudder.

He clears his throat. "That's a closet," he says pointing towards the first door. "Office, office...this one is a stairwell." He points at the door closest to me.

He drops my hand. "Let's check it out," I say, heading for the fourth door.

I try the knob and it doesn't budge. "It's locked, let's just head back," Tony says.

"Hello, best locksmith ever," I say, and I grab his hand before he can protest and I transport us to the other side.

He stumbles into me as we appear on the other side of the door. "Warn me next time, will ya?"

"Sorry," I tell him, not really meaning it.

"Does your power help with seeing in the dark?" I ask, hoping it can because it's complete darkness in here. I guess I could transport us down the stairs, but what if someone's at the bottom?

"Kinda? I think my eyes just adjust faster and I can see the details in the shadows. There's a stairwell a few feet in front of you, and I think that's a railing on the right-hand side."

I put my hand out until I feel the cold stone wall against my hand. I start to shuffle a little forward, then Tony lets out a sigh. "Here," he says, and leads me to the railing.

"Huh," he says, squeezing my hand.

"What?" I ask, trying to scan the darkness.

"Guess you can help me see in the dark better."

I let out a soft chuckle. "Well that's handy."

"Yeah," he says, and places my hand on top of the railing. "Here ya go."

"Thanks," I whisper back to him. "Let me know if you spot something," I tell him.

As we make our way slowly down the stairs the air around us drops in temperature. A cool breeze gusts by us up the stairs. I wonder if that's a bad omen. There is that supposed curse attached to Nostradamus's tomb. I shake the thought off. We're here to do good things, to help people. I have no plans to steal someone's bones. Something scuttles across my hand and I squash the urge to freak out.

I'm pretty sure we've gone down three floors when a faint light illuminates the stairs. I stop us a few steps down and lean close to Tony. "Let's have you check to see if anyone is down there," I whisper.

He steps down onto the same stair as me. I hold my hand out and he grabs onto it.

"What do you see?" I ask, getting impatient, but I'm wondering if this is part of the catacombs. And if it is, I don't know how long I'll last down here.

"Lots of medical equipment, jars, tons and tons of jars," he says the word jars like it makes no sense to him why they're there. "But no people."

I give his hand a squeeze. "Let's go check it out, then."

We creep down the stairs, trying to make our footsteps light just in case someone suddenly decides to round a corner. Once we get to the bottom, the soft light has increased tenfold, and it's coming from a bulb dangling overhead.

"Double check that there's no one on the other side. Otherwise I'll transport us in."

He gives me the all-clear and we transport onto the other side of the door, and into a large spacious cavern. The walls and ceiling are made of a rough gray stone. It's not like the smooth sand-colored stone of the building, but more roughly carved. Metal tables hug the walls, each covered in different equipment, and one whole table covered in metal jars.

We walk closer to the table with jars, because each has a plaque with a small inscription. As we get closer, I start seeing names and dates. "Does that say 200 AD to 250 AD?" I ask.

Tony's gaze takes in all of the jars. "Yeah, like on a tomb. I'm pretty sure these are people's remains, like ashes, maybe bones."

We break off, each looking at different jars. "No way. No freaking way," I say, holding up one of the containers.

"What?" Tony asks.

"This says Joan of Arc," I tell him, turning the jar so he can see.

He picks up the jar in front of him. "This says King Arthur."

"I thought he wasn't real?" I ask.

"Uh, we have superpowers," he points out.

"Good point."

We keep going through the jars, naming famous people from history. "They've got Nostradamus down here as well. Good luck with that," I say.

He gives me a questioning look, so I tell him about the supposed curse I read from the paper earlier. He slowly puts the jar back down.

"What do you think they're doing with all of these?" I ask, and I'm pretty sure that says Cleopatra. Huh.

"If there are bones, then there is DNA."

I turn away from the jar and look over at him. "No way. You don't think they're experimenting with these people's DNA, do you?"

His hand sweeps out, pointing at all the containers. "These *were* all extraordinary people."

I look at Cleopatra's name again. "Yeah, but like us?"

"Maybe. They thought Nostradamus could see the future. King Arthur pulled a magic sword out of a stone, Cleopatra was revered as a god, Joan of Arc had visions too. It's really not that far-fetched to think that they had powers."

"Next you're going to tell me Merlin was real too."

He waves off my words, ignoring my comment. To most people, what we do is fantastical, and it was at first to me, but now it's commonplace in my life.

He points at the jar with Nostradamus's bones. "Could you imagine if you could see the future?" he asks.

I wish I could have foreseen my grandparents' deaths. I could have stopped Gregory from getting on that plane. Tony wouldn't be a shell of his former self. I might know who's behind all of this experimentation. But I might have driven myself insane, because what if I couldn't get to my grandparents in time? What if I couldn't have saved Gregory? My guilt already crushes me on some days; what would it be like if I failed in stopping something I knew was going to happen?

"We really need Xavier here," I tell him. "He might be able to tell us who's behind all of this. There's too much here, like this feels like it could be a main place."

As soon as I say those words, the quiet starts to sink in.

"I think we should leave," I tell Tony.

He puts down the jar he's holding and looks at me confused. "Why?"

"We've been here for ten minutes, and no one has entered this room."

"Maybe they're off for the night?"

"No." I shake my head vehemently. "Every place we've raided, they've been doing things at night."

I walk towards him, ready to grab him and get out of here. His eyes dart around the room, and his hands shake a little. Has he been this nervous the whole time?

"I want to check out one more thing," he says, pointing to the opposite wall.

"Let's do it quickly," I say, and grab his hand.

He stares at the wall, and then tilts his head and squints. "Not possible," he says so softly, that I'm not sure he knows he said it out loud.

"What?" I ask.

"He's supposed to be dead."

FOURTEEN

"Who—"

I don't get to finish my question, because Tony keeps ahold of my hand and rushes me to the door connecting us to the other room. He drops my hand and quickly whips the door open, rushing into the other room.

The smell of antiseptic hangs heavy in the air, and it's accompanied by the sound of beeps. I move around the door. Tony stops near the end of a hospital bed, and it's occupied.

"Tony," I whisper-shout his name.

He doesn't move, so I walk quietly towards him, looking around the room for someone hiding. Because there's no way they left this person alone in here.

"Tony. We gotta—" The sight before me robs me of all my words. This can't be real.

"Gregory," I say in an anguished whisper. My hands come up to cover my mouth.

He's alive. He's *alive*!

I wipe my eyes, but he's still there. I watch his chest rise and fall, and that almost brings me to my knees.

I walk closer to his still body laid out in a hospital bed. Wires and tubes run off of him. Machines softly beep behind him. I lift my hand, desperately wanting to touch him, but afraid that it'll be an illusion that will shatter.

My hand softly grazes his, and the warmth of his skin is what finally undoes me. My knees buckle and they slam to the floor, his hand still in mine. "What happened to you?" I say softly, holding his hand close to my face.

My tears moisten his dry skin. And it takes several moments, but I finally drag myself to my feet and stare into a face I thought I would only get to see in my dreams. His eyes are taped

closed and a breathing tube is coming out of his mouth. I bring up my free hand and gently run my fingers through his brown hair. I lean in and press my lips to his temple. I can feel the life in him, and my heart gives a hard thump. But he doesn't smell like Gregory. He smells like Band-Aids and antiseptic.

"I'm sorry I didn't look sooner for you." The words come out choked, forced. "I'm so sorry," I say, the guilt and pain almost unbearable.

"Becca," Tony says from behind me. He places a hand on my shoulder.

"We've got to call the others. We need to get him out of here," I say, not taking my eyes off of Gregory.

"I'm sorry," he says, sounding tortured. And I think he means about Gregory, but then he shoves a needle into my neck and plunges something into my body.

What?

I drop Gregory's hand and reach back for the syringe, but he's already pulled out the needle. I turn and face him, but I stumble to the side. A whoosh sounds to my left and I whip to find the noise. My eyes widen as I watch Chelsea walk through the door at the other side of the room. Her arms are crossed, eyes averted.

I try to transport, but nothing happens. I start to lose feeling in my legs, causing me to sway, and Tony catches me. I try to slap his hands away, but I can't lift my arms. "I'm so sorry," he says again, and I finally look at him.

"Why?" the word comes out garbled.

He gently lays me down on the ground. "Because they have my mom," he says.

"I would...have...helped..." I can't finish the words; my lips won't form them.

"I'm sorry," he says again.

His face starts to blur, and my eyelids start to droop. I hear the click of heels approaching, but I can't keep my eyes open.

"You know he's not going to let your mom go," I hear Chelsea say.

It's hard to latch on to what they're saying. Who's *he*?

"You wouldn't dare!" I hear Tony roar.

Something crashes near me, but an insistent buzzing fills my ears, and everything else fades.

***

THE SOFT SOUND of murmured voices reaches me first. What happened? Memories come rushing back. What am I going to do?

I go to move my hands, but they're secured by my sides. I try to transport, and nothing.

Footsteps stop near my feet. I hold my breath. "You're going to have to stay here the whole time. Did he tell you that?" a man says. His voice is deep, rough, like he's been smoking cigarettes since he was ten. But there's something eerily familiar about it.

But he's not talking to me, because the clack of heels walk across the floor. They don't know I'm awake. I try to stay utterly still.

"If I need to leave, I can just knock her out," Chelsea says, like it's not a big deal to have her blocking my powers, or keeping me chained to a bed, or injecting me with who-knows-what drugs.

Chelsea sounds like an *awesome* person. But what am I going to do? "Shouldn't she be awake by now?" the man asks.

"One way to find out," Chelsea says, and her heels click against the floor as she moves closer.

The sound of metal scraping against metal causes the hair on my arms to raise. What is that?

"Leave her alone!" *Tony?*

Tony. His name feels like a curse even in my mind.

"Little late to start protecting her, don't you think?" the man drawls.

Tony starts to say something, but I block out his voice at the feel of a hand trailing up my arm. I try my best to keep my breathing under control, but I want to open my eyes so bad. The hand stops just above my elbow, and then I feel the cool press of metal against my skin. And that wouldn't startle me, but the sharp edge slightly sliding across and cutting me does.

My eyes pop open and stare directly in Chelsea's. "Gotcha," she says, and if I could raise my arms, I'd punch her in her smug face.

"Are you really that surprised considering that you're holding"—I look at her hand—"a freaking scalpel to my arm!"

"Enough."

I turn my head.

Everything freezes at the smirk on his face. I've seen that before, that exact facial expression. But the last time I saw Henderson was in Myanmar. Something else is nagging me.

"It doesn't make a difference. No one will hear you." The way he says that makes my heart skip, like there've been plenty of people trapped down here screaming.

"Good to see you again," he laughs. "Well, maybe not so good for you."

It clicks. That voice. He's the man who kidnapped Gregory. Who "rescued" the kids.

"Where've you been, Becca?" Chelsea asks me like we're just friends having a chat.

Woman is unhinged.

I keep my mouth closed, because does she really think I'm going to tell her? My eyes stay on her hand; she hasn't put down the scalpel.

"Should be using a hunting knife instead, it'd hurt more," Henderson says like it's a common fact.

Chelsea stares at him, a slightly horrified look on her face. If that makes her nervous…

Fast, erratic beeps from behind me stay Chelsea's hand. She curses and drops the scalpel on the metal tray. Both she and Henderson rush from my side. I try to turn my head, but I can't see what they run too.

"Do we need the crash cart?" he asks, but he sounds like he wants her answer to be no.

Crash cart. Like the shocking thing they use to bring people back to life? What the hell is going on back there? I try to contort my body more, but it's no use.

"Don't you die on me, Gregory," Chelsea mutters.

Gregory.

"What are you doing to him!?" I scream at them, pulling against my restraints, but they don't even acknowledge me.

"What's going on?" I yell at them again. I jerk my body, trying to move the bed, but it's bolted to the ground.

The beeping slows. Is that bad? Is he okay? Someone lets out a long sigh. "Think he knows what you're doing?" I'm assuming he's asking Chelsea.

She scoffs. "How? Last I checked, people in medically induced comas aren't thinking."

"Yeah, but how many of those people are mind readers?" Whoa. He does not like her. They might be forced to work together, but from his tone, he thinks she's an idiot.

"Doesn't matter anyways. His vitals are fine now," she snaps back at him.

My body relaxes a little bit at her words, until her footsteps take her back towards me.

Her face comes into view and we stare at one another for a

minute. Real fear spreads through me. Not that I wasn't scared before; it's just that then I was coasting on adrenaline, but now...now things have sunken in. My heart is racing so fast that I swear I'm having a heart attack.

Tony starts thrashing from somewhere past my feet. Footsteps storm over in his direction. "Enough," Henderson commands, and the sounds of flesh pummeling flesh resounds in the room, cutting off Tony's cursing.

"Was that really necessary?" Chelsea asks, sounding more annoyed that he took so long beating Tony than him actually hurting Tony.

"He wouldn't shut up," he says matter-of-factly.

I'm being held by psychopaths. And I have no clue how I'm going to get out of here, never mind take Gregory and Tony with me. Even though part of me wants to leave Tony. He should have trusted me and told me what was happening. Too late now.

A buzzing fills the room. Chelsea takes a phone out of her pocket and turns away from me. "Yes, she's here. Fine. I'll be there soon."

She lets out an exasperated sigh. "We need to go. Grab me the syringe," Chelsea says.

She stands over me, and I start to struggle against my bonds. "There's no point," she says matter-of-factly.

Henderson walks over and hands her the syringe. Chelsea takes it and lifts up the sleeve of my shirt.

"I will get out of here." I look her dead in the eyes. "And then I'll come for you."

She gives me a patronizing smile. "Good luck with that." And she plunges the liquid into my arm, plummeting me back into a black abyss.

FIFTEEN

"Wakey, wakey," someone says next to my ear.

A low groan slips out and I try to turn away, but something won't allow me to.

"Open your eyes," Chelsea says, but my body just doesn't want to comply.

A loud whoosh sounds and then a resounding smack. The sharp burn on my face follows closely behind the sound. My eyes shoot open.

"You've got anger problems," Chelsea tells Henderson.

"And you take too long," he snaps back.

Did he just?

He hit me.

This grown man...hit me. My hands clench into tight fists. "What kind of man hits a tied-up woman?" I ask him.

He doesn't answer, but his eyes fix on me. There's my answer. Nothing but pure evil stares back at me. There is no light in this guy. No redeeming this guy.

My face throbs; any harder and I think he could have broken my cheek bone if he wanted to. Chelsea avoids looking at my face, like she doesn't care what happened. "I've got some questions for you," she says.

I don't answer her, but she doesn't seem to mind, yet. But I track Henderson out of the corner of my eye; he's the real danger in this room.

"We know you've been the one infiltrating our labs around the world." That makes my gaze drift towards her, but I keep my mouth shut. "What I want to know is who's been helping you find them?"

I stare at her dead in the eyes, lips sealed.

"And also, what have you done with the experiments you took with you?"

"Experiments? You mean the people, the kids, that you locked into cages? That you've tortured, treated worse than lab rats?" The unchecked words fly past my lips.

She looks at me, totally unfazed by my words. She doesn't care. She's probably dead inside. I can see it behind her green eyes: the intelligence, the ruthlessness, and the lack of sympathy. She doesn't care what's happened to those people.

We stare at each other, and I see the realization on her face that I'm not going to talk. "Henderson, bring in our other guest," Chelsea orders.

He walks out of view, but I hear a heavy door being pulled open. Two sets of footsteps approach the hospital bed I'm strapped to. I turn my head as far as I can.

One very pissed-off Sariah stands next to a manically grinning Henderson. Her body shakes with anger. Under her eyes are deep, purple smudges, and she still has healing burns covering the right side of her face.

We stare at each other, not saying a word. I wish I had Gregory's power right now. I'd love to know what's going through her mind. "Look, it's your old friend," Henderson says, draping an arm over Sariah's shoulder.

She shrugs it off. "Don't touch me," she tells him without taking her eyes off me.

He backs up a step, hands up in the air. "Sure, sweetheart."

"Sariah agreed to come and ask you some questions since you don't want to talk with me," Chelsea says. "But first, Henderson, would you mind securing her to the wall?"

His body splits into five, which is honestly downright creepy. As one they each remove one of my bonds. I start to thrash, but it doesn't even faze them. The fifth walks over to Tony, takes out a knife, and stares right into my eyes. Dread races up my spine. "You don't cooperate, we'll take more than a finger this time." His words are cruel, but they halt my movements.

Tony's eyes go unfocused, like he's not here with us anymore. He's gone somewhere in his head, and by the looks of it, this is an art he's mastered. My heart breaks for him. A sick feeling wells up inside of me. Henderson must have been the one to torture him in Myanmar. I can't let them do any more to him.

Henderson number five keeps his eyes locked on mine as the other four of him undo my hands and feet. "Good girl," he says, a smirk on his face.

I've never wanted to punch someone so badly.

They drag my limp body over to the corner, not too far from Gregory's hospital bed. His monitor starts going crazy, but Chelsea silences the alarm.

Dangling from the ceiling above my head are a set of cuffs. The two Hendersons holding my feet lift me, while the other two secure my hands. My toes barely scrape the ground. And when the four step back, the weight of my body pulls on my wrists. My shoulders stretch and burn. I try and grab purchase with my toes, but it's hard. My hands grip the chains above my wrists, and I know I won't be able to use that leverage for too long.

"Now, how about you answer some questions?" Chelsea asks.

I stare straight at her and keep my lips sealed.

"We've got time. You, however—" She points at my body. "How long until your shoulders pop out of their sockets?"

I still don't say anything. So, Chelsea pulls a chair over and takes a seat, primly crossing her legs like she isn't waiting to further torture me.

I don't know how long I hang there. It feels like hours—it's probably only minutes—but it's enough for sweat to start dripping down my back. My hands begin to shake, rattling the chains. I stay focused on Gregory, on his breathing, trying to use that to help block my mind from the pain in my arms.

My hands slip, allowing my body to fall a bit, and I let a low groan escape. But the pain, it's excruciating. I've lost feeling in my fingers.

Chelsea lets out an irritated sigh. "This is taking too long. Sariah, why don't you see if she'll talk."

Sariah moves from her spot against the wall and stands right in front of me. Her face is wiped of emotion, and that makes me more scared than Henderson's crazy.

A sick smile spreads across Henderson's face, and my stomach clenches in fear. Why is he so excited? These people are freaking unhinged.

Sariah takes a deep breath. "Becca." My whole body locks. There's no way. "I need you to answer Chelsea's questions."

The world stops at the sound of my grandfather's—my dead grandfather's—voice.

I shake my head back and forth. This isn't happening.

"Becca," I hear Sariah say in *his* voice again.

I close my eyes, trying to desperately be somewhere else.

"Who's helping you find the labs?" Grandpa asks me.

No. Not Grandpa. This isn't Grandpa. They brutally murdered him. Sariah is talking. Not Grandpa.

"You need to tell us."

A low moan slips out at the sound of my grandma's voice. Bile surges up my throat, but I choke it back down.

Something sharp touches the underside of my chin. "You can't escape," Henderson's hot breath whispers into my ear.

I turn my head away, trying to block them all. He puts pressure on the knife, and I hiss at the burn of the cut. My eyes snap to his.

"I want you paying attention." He grits the words out. "Now answer her questions."

I stare at him, not saying anything. I feel the knife move. My toes grab for purchase again so I can brace myself.

"No stabbing," Chelsea scolds him, and some of the fear abates. "Can't have you hitting an artery or something."

He grabs my chin and turns my face towards Sariah. "Better talk, or Sariah is going to have to be more...convincing."

I stare at Sariah, and it's the first time I see anything but coldness in her eyes. It looks like she's uncertain, but it's gone in a flash. Henderson steps away and makes a gesture for Sariah to take his place.

She clears her throat. "Where are the people you took?" she asks me, still using my grandpa's throat.

"Screw you," I tell her, and spit in her face.

She slowly wipes it away. Her gaze drops to her hand she used, like she can't believe I did that. She stares at that hand for a moment, and then suddenly pulls it back and slaps me across the face.

Pain explodes across my cheek, and my shoulders pull from the movement. "Answer the questions," she orders me in her own voice.

I grip the chains above my hands. If this keeps going my shoulders are going to dislocate. I keep looking at her, trying to breathe through the throbbing ache.

"Answer me!" she demands, but I stare right through her.

She brings her fist back and slams it into my ribs over and over again. My mouth opens, allowing the scream to rip through. Tears stream down my cheeks, and the air is stolen from my lungs.

I try taking a breath, but my lungs can't expand. I think she broke a rib.

"Answer!" Spit flies across my face, and I flinch.

I watch her arm pull back, ready to inflict another blow, but the shrill ring of Chelsea's phone halts her movements.

"Hello." Her whole body locks. "Fine," she says, but sounds anything but fine with whatever he told her.

Chelsea waves off Sariah. "He says to stop," Chelsea tells her.

Sariah looks down at her hand like she doesn't recognize it and takes a step back.

"Put her back on the table," she orders Henderson.

His clones undo my wrists and roughly take me down. I can't stop the moan of pain. I'm dragged back to the table. And when my body is tossed onto the surface, I scream at the pain from my ribs. "I think you did some damage," Chelsea says to Sariah.

"She should have talked," Henderson butts in. "Sariah went a lot easier on her than I would have."

Chelsea walks over with a syringe, and for once I welcome the oblivion, because I can't handle the pain anymore. Every breath is agony.

As she injects me, she leans close. "Might want to answer them next time or Henderson will start on Tony. And that poor guy's been through enough."

The world starts to blur, and I feel a sharp pressure applied to my ribs. My head turns to the side and I throw up from the overwhelming pain. "Sweet dreams," Henderson whispers to me.

The world spins, and finally goes black.

SIXTEEN

Mom sits on the boulder at the base of some mountain I don't recognize. It's craggy, with lots of fallen rocks and boulders. We usually meet near water, so this is different. I glance at her quickly, and her face lights up with hope when our gazes connect. I haven't dreamt of her in months. And I've been torn about my feelings concerning that. She's warned me in the past about things that were coming; why couldn't she have told me about Grandpa and Grandma? Why couldn't she have warned me about Tony leading me into a trap?

Maybe she sees the disappointment on my face. Or maybe it's the indecision. Whatever she sees causes her to slump down on the boulder.

I avert my eyes towards the sky. It's clear and a bright blue. No storm clouds in sight. No wind pressing in. Maybe now she'll have the time for more answers. I grudgingly walk closer to her. I don't look her in the eye yet; my anger is still too close to the surface.

I sit on another boulder close to hers. The silence is awkward and heavy. So much has happened since the last time I saw her in my dreams. So much has been lost.

She clears her throat and I take a deep breath before I finally lock *gazes with her. Her eyes fill with tears. "I'm so sorry, baby," she whis-pers, sounding tortured.*

I bring my hands up and cover my face. Through everything, I've been strong, but those four words cut me so deep. My heart squeezes so tightly and the tears I've kept at bay start streaming down my face. The anguished cries are ripped from my soul.

Arms surround me, and I do something I never thought I'd be able to do in this life. I cry into my mother's shoulder. And the tears don't stop. I've unplugged the dam and it keeps pouring out of me. The pain, the loneliness, the loss, and the uncertainty spill out in tears and tortured sounds.

I'm not sure how long she holds me while I soak her shirt, but eventually the tears subside and the cries cease. I pull back and wipe at my face.

"Why now?" I ask her, my voice hoarse.

"You've been blocking me. The drug they gave you allowed me in," she says, her voice still sounding concerned. She leans forward to search my face.

"Do you know?" I ask, not wanting to put it into words.

"Everything," she confirms.

My heart starts to pound. "Have you seen my..." I can't even finish the question, because I can feel my eyes wanting to tear up.

"Yes. I've seen your grandparents," she says so softly.

I rub at my chest, feeling the ache there, the missing pieces.

"They're with your dad."

"Good." I manage to croak out.

And it is good. I know how much they missed him. Especially Grandma. But I'd still rather have them here. I need them. I need them so, so much.

I lean forward, resting my head in my hands, and take deep breaths. I don't know how long we'll be here, but time is way too precious.

"How are you here, Mom? How are you able to come and talk with

me?" I ask her the same question I've asked her before. I know she's dead. I wouldn't have my powers otherwise.

"There's a man named Shemnon. His power is to link the dead with the living."

Whoa.

"He's part of a small group that monitors the world's Urotanmians."

"The what?"

"That's what we were originally called, the name of our people."

I don't think anyone knows that name anymore, but I taste the words on my tongue. And they resonate in me as truth.

"Shemnon and his group have been waiting for you to come into your powers. And they knew what the future held. So Shemnon crossed into the spirit realm and found me. But I wasn't allowed to tell you too much; they didn't want to influence the future."

"And now?" I ask, because this is more than she's ever given me.

"Now these people conducting these experiments are disturbing the dead. They're desecrating their resting spaces, and their bodies. Shemnon said if we didn't intervene, the atrocities would be insurmountable."

All right, no pressure or anything.

"What am I supposed to do about this?" I ask.

I'm already doing what I can, but I don't even know how I would stop any of this from happening. And when someone like Chelsea is blocking powers, it makes it hard to find out everyone involved.

"Fight back," she says with conviction.

I throw my arms up in the air. "That's real rich. How am I going to do that? I can't even tap into my powers right now. And why aren't these people like Shemnon coming and helping? I'd love more help than a few cryptic dreams."

Why can't people just tell you what you need to do, how to do it, and what help you'll get? It'd make my life a whole lot easier. And why couldn't they have stepped in when this first started happening?

"You are more than these powers," she says, anger threading her *words. "You have been trained in more than just how to use those gifts. And I did not birth a stupid girl."*

"So basically, what you're saying is 'figure it out.'"

"Use that excellent brain. And Shemnon said help is coming."

Of course, and is it going to come after we've all been killed? "How is help coming? Who's coming?"

"When you commune with the dead, you've got eyes everywhere."

So creepy.

A thunderous rumble starts in the distance. I turn towards it. Boulders are careening down the mountainside like they're tennis balls. "Guessing time's up?" I ask, keeping my eyes trained on the mountain as larger rocks start to slide.

She nods and grabs my hand. "Don't lose yourself to vengeance; it'll make you bitter and get you killed. But know that on both sides of the veil of life and death, you have people helping. Trust those around you. Open up to them. Heal with them. You aren't just an army of one."

"Wake up, Becca," someone says from a distance. "You need to wake up now."

The dream world with my mom disappears in a blink.

"Becca?"

I go to raise my hand to my head, but it doesn't budge, and I look down. I'm still chained. My head lulls to the side. Tony looks at me with wide eyes. "Transport," he orders.

I try to shake the fog from my brain.

"Transport," he says more urgently. "Get the hell out of here."

I close my eyes and think about the space beside the bed. I see myself standing there without shackles around my wrists and ankles. I open my eyes, but I'm still stuck in the bed.

"What's wrong?" he asks, his eyes constantly darting to the door.

"I can't do anything," I tell him, panic rising within me.

His face snaps back to mine. "What do you mean?"

"I can't transport. Why I can't I transport? She's not here."

"It's because my blood is mixed with the medicine," Chelsea's voice booms around us, and I let out a yelp.

"Glad to know it works so well," she says.

I scan the room; she's not here. "To the right," she says, super smug.

A small camera sits in the corner, just below the ceiling. "Be in soon to ask you some questions, Becca," she says and then she's gone.

But what she's left is panic like I've never felt before. "What are we going to do?" Tony asks.

"Well, talking about that seems stupid considering THEY. CAN. HEAR. US." I shout the words at him.

His head rears back, and I close my eyes.

"I'm sorry." I say the words softly to him.

"What do you have sorry to be about? I got us into this mess in the first place," he says, sounding thoroughly disgusted with himself.

"Why didn't you talk to me?" I ask. "I would have moved mountains to help you."

He looks down at his bound hands. He's still on the stone floor. Guess they don't think he needs be strapped to a bed. "I haven't been thinking really clearly lately," he says.

A harsh laugh slips out, which is followed by a groan because of the sharp pain from my ribs. "You and me both," I say.

"They never took my mom." He says the words so quietly, I'm not sure I heard them. "They told me that after they knocked you out. Betrayed my best friend for nothing." The last few words are said to himself.

"How did they even contact you?" I ask, because this seems so outta left field.

He takes a deep breath. "I've been emailing my mom every now and again, but never telling her where I was. She thought I was still working with the FBI. But yesterday there was a message from her, only it wasn't my mom sending it."

My stomach twists.

"They knew you had been here. They were banking on you

coming back and if I wanted to see my mom again"—his voice breaks —"I had to find a way to get you back here or come with you and keep you occupied."

Oh, Tony. I probably would have done the same thing if it was my grandpa. "It's okay," I tell him.

"No. It's not," he says sharply.

I roll my head and look up at the ceiling. "Well, we're in this together now," I say.

We both go silent. The only thing making noise is the beeping of Gregory's monitor. I haven't looked back at him again. I feel like if I let my mind go down that path, if I think about the things they could've done to him, then my mind will be so full I won't have a chance to escape.

I stare at the stone ceiling above us. What are Tiberius and Xavier doing now? I know they must have realized something went wrong. But if they come in here, they might be in the same boat I'm in.

"How long was I out this time?" I ask. Because I'm pretty sure I only slept for an hour or two.

"I think a day," Tony says.

"What?" I ask. "How is that even possible?"

"She came in and gave you another dose two hours ago."

Awesome. I've got no clue how long this stuff lasts, but I guarantee she does. The sound of something scurrying makes my eyes shoot towards Tony. He lets out a curse and tries to angle away from the very large rat that sniffs around him. The rat sits and looks between the two of, which is weird because rats don't do that.

My heart starts to race, and not because Tony looks likes he's going to freak out. I try to keep my facial expression calm. "Don't swat at it, it might bite you," I warn, but hope is blooming in my chest as I stare at this rat.

It scurries away, and my pulse races. "Ever since Myanmar, I can't stand rats," he says, his voice shaking, body shuddering.

"Hey," I say, and he looks back at me. "It's okay. It's gone now," I say. I want to tell him about who I suspect sent the rat, but I can't. Not with them watching us and probably recording us.

I'm praying that Lucy knows about the cameras in here. What am I thinking? Of course she knows.

"So, tell me about that video game you play all the time," I say to him, and he gives me an odd look. But I need him to not think about Myanmar right now. I need him to focus, but if I'm right, Raven sent that rat as a message.

They're rescuing us, and I'm thinking soon.

SEVENTEEN

Tony doesn't even have the chance to answer my question about his video game before the door bursts open. Tiberius and Xavier storm into the room, followed closely by Robert, Raven, and a few other people I don't recognize.

Raven and Robert survey the room. I can't believe they got him to come out of hiding. Last I saw him, he and Poppy were escaping England.

I turn my head at the sound of rats scurrying around, finding gaps in the wall and doors to squeeze through, probably scouting.

Tiberius rushes to my side, and Xavier goes to Tony. "I never thought you'd come," I say to him, my voice breaking.

I've tried to stay strong. Through all the things they've done. I tried not to break. But the sight of Tiberius's face is just too much. Sobs wrack my body, causing my broken ribs to scream in pain.

"Shh, I'll always come for you. We're family." He strokes my hair, making soothing noises while he undoes my cuffs.

I take a couple of deep breaths, trying to get myself under control. "I can't transport," I tell him.

He pauses but keeps going. "Doesn't matter, we'll figure it out."

"How are we going to get Gregory out of here?" I ask.

Tiberius and Xavier share a look, and alarms goes off in my mind. "No," I say. "We can't leave him here."

"We've got incoming," Raven warns.

"Send in the rats," Xavier orders.

She nods, and a moment later muffled screams filter in through the steel door.

"We've got to go," Tiberius urges.

I grab on to Tiberius's wrist, pulling him towards me with more strength than either of us thought I had. "Gregory has to come with us."

He covers my hand with his. "Becca, we don't know what they did to him. What if we unhook him and he dies?" Tiberius says.

I look over at Gregory's still form. He was healthy the last time I was with him. He has to be still. "Let me try transporting him," I beg.

"You just said you can't," he reminds me.

Shouts and gunfire increase outside the room. "We've got to go now," a man I don't recognize says.

I ignore the warning, not ready to give up. "I have to try," I tell Tiberius.

I slide off the table, my knees almost buckling from the pain, but I put it aside and do my best to rush over to Gregory. "Where are you going to take him?" Xavier asks. "We don't know yet if it's Mr. Rivers behind all of this."

I rub my hands over my face. I don't know what he needs, but I know Walter won't be able to handle anything like this. I look between Xavier and Gregory. "I'll take him to headquarters. Text Mr. Smith," I say.

"Becca," Xavier warns.

"I won't leave him!" My scream silences the room for a brief second.

"Someone's trying to breach the door!" Robert shouts.

I grab Gregory's hand and close my eyes. I picture the room where I had my very first physical at Project Lightning. I think of the hospital bed and computer. I picture talking to the older guy who's the resident doctor.

"She's flickering," I hear Tony yell.

"We've got to go, Becca!" Tiberius roars as the metal door starts to break.

I close my eyes tighter and pump as much enhancing ability into my thoughts, into Gregory, into our bond.

Metal screeches, and gunshots fire. My stomach drops and I feel the pull of our bodies across space.

ALARMS BLARE overhead and the feel of cool tile pressed against me seeps into my skin. My eyes pop open and I reach out a hand, searching. Gregory lies against me. We did it.

I turn my head and his still body pushes me into action. "Help!" I scream.

The doctor who gave me my original physical comes barreling into the room. His eyes widen at the sight of us. "Help him, please," I beg him.

Mr. Smith comes exploding through the door. He locks onto Gregory, and if I weren't watching him, I would miss the welling of tears in his eyes.

"We need to get him up on the table," the doctor orders Mr. Smith.

I stand up on my trembling legs. "Step back," Mr. Smith orders, but I don't listen.

"I don't know what they've done to him, but they put him into a medically induced coma," I say.

Mr. Smith lifts Gregory up like he weighs nothing and quickly moves him to the table. The doctor grabs a heart monitor and oxygen mask and rushes over to Gregory. They start hooking him up to all these different things. "Becca, pick up the phone on the desk. Tell the person on the other line we need nurses in here stat," the doctor says, and I hurry to follow his orders.

Not even a minute later, three medics come rushing in and I back up against the wall so they can work without me interfering.

Mr. Smith leaves Gregory's side and heads for me, and his eyes widen as he gets a good look at me. I know I look like a hot mess, but at the moment I'm still standing and that's all that matters.

We lock stares on one another as he walks closer, so many emotions crossing his face. Is he going to yell at me? Kick me out of here? I can never get a read on this guy.

He reaches for me, and I flinch, waiting for a blow, but he drags me in for a hug. "Thank you," he says softly into my hair. "Thank you for bringing my son back to me."

Whoa.

Wait.

What?

EIGHTEEN

I take a step back and look at him. "How?" I ask, because Gregory has powers.

"It's a long story, and we don't have time for that right now. But I didn't know about him until he was nine. After his mom died and his grandparents reached out to me," he says, his eyes unfocused like he's picturing her now.

"Does he know?" I ask.

"No," he tells me, his eyes drifting back to where they're working on Gregory.

He's going to freak out. "He needs to know," I tell him firmly. Lies destroy so much, and to keep this lie of omission is just as bad.

"He will," he promises me. "I thought I'd lost him." He looks as broken as he sounds.

"So did I," I say, my eyes running over the parts of Gregory's body that I can see.

"We'll talk soon," he says, and I nod, but I wonder if he'll actually tell me more.

We both watch everyone working, but my mind can't compute what Mr. Smith said. Especially since he's hammered into us over and over again that Gregory and I can't have any type of relationship. He always made it seem like it was my parents that caused the no-fraternizing policy, but it must have really been him. And a thought suddenly comes to me; he's going to be like me one day. He'll have two powers. Not only would he be able to read minds, but nobody would be able to lie to him. What is that going to be like?

The frenzy surrounding Gregory dies down a bit, and the doctor walks over to us. "He's stable for now." He directs his comments to Mr. Smith, but I step closer. "I want to keep him in the coma until I can run some blood tests on him. I've got no clue what's in his system or what's happened to him, and I'm afraid if we bring him out of it too quickly it could cause brain damage."

"Good. I want reports every hour. I'm going to be posting a guard on the door. No one is allowed in this room aside from who is in here now," Mr. Smith tells him, back to his usual authoritative tone.

The doctor nods and walks back over to Gregory.

Mr. Smith turns and levels me with a serious look. "We need to talk," he all but commands me.

I know he's got lots of questions, but Tiberius's face plays in my mind. I have to leave. "We will, but I need to check on everyone else I left. I don't even know if they made it out okay."

My heart starts to race. The last thing I heard before I disappeared was gunshots. Did they get out of there? Were they captured? I'm praying that Tony is okay. I don't know how much he can handle.

"Are you going to come back?" he asks nervously.

I know he's afraid to let me out of his sight. I disappeared off the face of the earth when everything happened the last time.

My eyes drift to Gregory. "I'll be back," I promise him.

He lets out a deep breath. "See you soon," he tells me.

I close my eyes and picture the living room in Tiberius's house. Lucy will know where they are.

"BECCA!" Lucy's voice startles me and I open my eyes to see her rushing towards me.

Before she can reach me, my body collapses to the floor. "Luca! Run for Walter!" she screams, and I hear the front door open and close on a bang.

"What the hell happened to you?" she asks as she drops to her knees at my side.

"Later," I tell her. "Where is everyone? Are they okay?"

"Still in France," she tells me as she studies my face. It's probably horrid shades of black and blue.

I try to get up and fail. "I need to get back to them," I tell her.

"You can't go anywhere yet. I don't even know how you're coherent right now," she tells me, reaching out a hand to touch me, but quickly pulls it back. She's probably afraid she'll hurt me.

The front door crashes open and Walter comes charging into the room, his black doctor's bag with him. He comes to an abrupt halt.

"What happened, *serduszko*?" he asks, full of concern, as he drops to the floor.

I try and fail to sit up again. "I'm pretty sure my ribs are broken, and possibly my cheek," I tell him, trying to remain indifferent about my injuries.

Polish flies out of his mouth, and from the tone I'm pretty sure he's cursing. He pulls a bottle and syringe out of his bag. At the sight of the needle I try squirming away from him. Lucy and Walter watch me, concern lining their faces.

"What did they do to you?" Lucy asks on a whisper.

"It's just ibuprofen. I promise. Here, look at the bottle," Walter says as he hands me the bottle.

I take it with shaking hands, reading the label. I hand it back to him and lie back on the floor. "They kept injecting me with this serum to knock me out and to block my power," I tell them without looking at them.

Someone inhales a deep breath, but I keep my eyes averted from them. "I'm going to give you the shot now," Walter tells me, a lot softer.

I clench my hands so I won't knock the needle away. "Lucy, can you call Tiberius so I can talk with him?" I ask her as Walter cleans off my arm.

I hear the rustle of fabric and then the ringing of a phone on speaker.

It only rings once before it's answered. "Is she okay?" Tiberius asks in a rush.

"Still alive," I yell to him from my spot still on the floor.

A huge huff of air blasts across the speaker. "Thank God."

"Did everyone get out safe?" I ask, my voice strained from feeling Walter pierce my skin with the needle.

"Tony is pretty banged up and won't talk. Thank goodness for Raven and those rats, though. They bought us time."

Tony. *How am I going to help you this time?* How does someone come back from this?

"Give me a minute and I'll come get you guys," I say through gritted teeth, trying to sit up.

Lucy rips the phone away from its spot next to me on the floor. "No, you won't," she says. "She's got a couple broken ribs, and a possible fracture to her cheek bone. She's been drugged and tortured."

"I need to get them back here," I argue, trying to muster myself into standing.

"They can grab a flight like every other damn person on the planet," she spits back at me.

I flop back down and then yell at the jarring of my ribs.

She points a finger in my face. "Right there is why you aren't going anywhere."

"Becca, it's fine. We're flying back," Tiberius tells me, probably glad he's not here right now to deal with Lucy and me.

I hear Lucy start to walk away. "Wait, he needs to know about Tony," I call out to her.

Lucy stops and turns back around. "What's going on?" Tiberius asks, sounding concerned.

"I don't think he'll do it again, and I already know he regrets what he did—"

"Spit it out," Lucy yells.

"He set up that trap," I tell them. "They said they had his mom, and you know how he's been lately."

Walter sucks in a harsh breath. "That's no excuse," he says.

"They broke him, Walter. They broke him in unimaginable ways. He was just trying to hang on to the only thing he had left. I won't fault him for that. I'd do the same thing if they had Grandpa Joe." It's hard to confess that. The words are brutal. But now having lost them, I'd do whatever was in my power to have them back and whole.

"I'll be watchful," Tiberius says carefully; Tony must be close by. "We'll see you tomorrow," he tells us.

Lucy walks out of the room, her phone off speaker and against her ear.

I look back at Walter. "What do you need?" he asks me just like Grandpa would, and it sends a bolt of agony to my chest.

I reach out and grab his hand, not answering with words. He clasps his hand in mine and stays like that for long minutes, filling the room with silence, but with the warmth of love too.

NINETEEN

Lucy walks back in the room some time later, a glass of water in her hand. "They're headed to the airport now. Mr. Smith is flying them to Peru. Tiberius won't tell him where in South America we are," she says as she makes her way over to me on the couch.

"Smart man," Walter says from his spot beside me.

"Too many leaks at Project Lightning," I tell them as I take the glass from Lucy.

We sit in a heavy silence. I know they have questions, and I know I need to fill them in, but there's so much. And what Mr. Smith told me about Gregory...how can I share that before he even has a chance to know?

"Gregory's alive," I tell them while staring at my water.

"We know, Tiberius filled us in," Lucy says.

Good, I'm glad he told them. "He's with Mr. Smith. I didn't know where else to take him. And I knew Walter wouldn't have what he needs to help him."

Walter lays his hand on top of mine. "It was the best move," he tells me. "I don't have the equipment to do blood tests or keep him in the coma. We could have lost him."

I tug my hand from under his and run my fingers through my hair. "I trust Mr. Smith to protect him. He'll be safe. I just wish I knew what they did to him."

"Don't let that fester. He'll wake up. Trust in that," Lucy says, and I nod.

"They kept asking where I was stashing all the people we rescued. And they wanted to know who was helping me find them," I tell them, eyes fixed to the wall. From the bruises littering my body they can see how that conversation went.

"Let them come," Luca says from the doorway, his Italian extra heavy and filled with wrath, causing us all to jump a little. "I won't let them hurt any of us again." His large shoulders shudder, and his hands clench and unclench at his sides.

"I don't know what the next move is. Project Lightning is involved now. Maybe that means we'll be able to put a stop to this," I tell him.

Luca walks into the room and sits across from me. "I want to keep working on shifting. I want to be able to go on missions to help you. They don't get to do what they did to you and Eloise and get away with it. *Non va bene.*"

"We need a plan. We can't go in there guns blazing," Walter says, being the logical one we need. "But we'll need to strike soon. They won't be happy that they lost Gregory, Becca, and Tony. Not to mention it seems that you found a major lab of theirs."

I haven't even had a chance to tell them about what we found. So much has happened. "They had all these canisters filled with bones and other things, from people long gone. Do you think they're trying to get DNA from that? I just don't know what their endgame is."

"Maybe they're building an army." Lucy says it offhandedly, but we all suck in a breath. Her eyes dart between us. "No...you don't think?"

"Why else?" I ask. It's the most logical answer. It's just none of us have thought of that yet. "We need Mr. Smith's helping us with this more than ever."

"Let's wait and talk to Tiberius. Once he's here we can get a game plan. In the meantime, Becca, get some rest. You can stay in one of the spare rooms here," Lucy says, and I'm glad she does, because I can't go back to that empty house right now.

"Thanks. Where's Eloise?" I ask, looking around.

"She's playing with the other girls in the village," Lucy says, and that makes me smile. It won't change what she lost, but it'll help find her home here.

I gingerly slide to the edge of the couch. Luca leans forward as if to help me, but I push away his hand. "I'm going to lie down. Let me know when they get here."

"It'll be awhile," she tells me, and I nod.

"I'M surprised to see you so soon," I tell my mom as I walk up behind her, tall grass grazing the tips of my fingers.

She looks over her shoulder at me. "There's lots you need to know."

Straight to business then. I walk through soft sand and stop by her side. "Where are we?" I ask.

A large lake stretches out before us. The water's a pristine crystal blue. Boats in the distance look like small dots floating on the horizon. She looks off to her right, where a lone pier juts out into the lake. Her face softens and her eyes brighten. "This is where you dad proposed to me," she says with reverence.

"Why is he never here?" I ask, fearing the answer.

"Only one of us could come. And it needed to be the one with the strongest connection. Your anger towards me has always been a thick thread."

I feel ashamed about that now. I feel horrible that the way my mother was able to get to me was through my hatred for her.

"I don't fault you for that anger," she tells me.

I look down at the sand coating our feet, too guilty to look at her face.

"Becca." My name is a plea from her lips.

I look up, and our eyes connect. "I was a horrible mother for a very long time. Towards the end...I was making my way back to you. There's nothing we can do about that now. I can't change the past. But maybe together we can make the future better."

"I'm so scared." I whisper my admission to her, the breeze taking it out to the ships kissing the horizon.

"How much more am I going to have to lose before this is over?" I ask her an impossible question.

She pulls me into her arms. And this time I don't even flinch. "I don't know. But I am so proud of you." She gently runs her hand over my hair. "You've endured more than I could ever imagine. Keep fighting, my baby girl. And I'll keep trying to do what I can from this side."

I step back, but she still keeps her arms around me. "What now?" I ask.

"You know who's behind this," she tells me, gripping my arms.

"Mr. Rivers," I say without hesitation.

Her arms drop and I feel her shudder at his name. "Yes." Her response is weak, timid almost.

"I just don't get why." I don't understand what he wants with all of this. He's spent years working with Project Lightning. And he knows what he's doing is morally and legally wrong.

She crosses her arms tightly over her chest. "Mr. Smith will have the answers."

Mr. Smith. That man is keeping a lot of secrets too. "Did you know about Gregory being his son?" I ask her.

"I did," she says.

I stagger back a step at her direct response. "Why didn't you tell me?"

She shakes her head. "It's not my secret to share."

It may not be her secret, but she's still my mom and she knows what's been going on between us.

I turn and follow the coastline with my eyes, trying to rein in the words that want to spill out.

I clear my throat a few times. "Do you think Mr. Rivers knows?" I ask her.

She lets out a soft sigh, most likely grateful that I didn't get on her for not telling me. "Probably not. He would have used that bargaining chip a long time ago. I'm pretty sure Gregory has no clue either. Mr. Smith is very good at hiding what he doesn't want known."

We stand there in silence, a warm breeze blowing our hair. "Things are going to happen—and soon," she tells me.

"I know you said there are people helping us meet, but how do you know all of this? How does anyone know what's coming?"

"Because it was foretold."

I give her a look, because that's so cliché. "Seriously?" I say, my voice thick with sarcasm. I spare her the eye-roll.

"Nostradamus kept most of his prophecies secret," she says, completely ignoring my question. "Only sharing certain ones to the whole world. But he and his ancestors kept impeccable records."

"Does Mr. Rivers know about these?" I ask.

"Yes, Gregory found them years ago." A memory pushes to the forefront of my mind. Gregory told me about that. When we were on the boat to North Korea, he told us about his mission retrieving artifacts and scrolls. I forgot he told me that.

"Do you think them finding those scrolls is what set this all in motion?" I ask.

She nods. "I believe so. One of the prophecies said that there would be a time where our people would again flourish and spread across the globe. I think Rivers wants to control that. If he can control those powers, think of what he could do."

I picture all the people at Fordlandia with powers that Rivers has no clue about. "He could topple countries."

She throws her arms up in the air. "He could crush whoever he wants. What if he had an army of people like Ania? What if he knew what you could do? What Gregory will one day be able to do?"

Flashes of utter destruction cross my mind. He would destroy our world. Scenes from The Hunger Games fly before my mind.

Mom steps back. Her face goes blank, and her eyes dead. "The time has come to stop putting restrictions on our people." Her voice is off, like it isn't her speaking to me. "We need to become a part of society. Use our God-given gifts to bless this world, not destroy it."

I step closer to her, but her body jerks back a step, like a puppet on a string. "Mom?"

"Join with Mr. Smith. Let him see what you are sheltering. Remember, we will help wherever we can."

She stumbles back another step, her feet entering the water. Slowly she continues to move backward, the waves now lapping up her legs. "You'll see her again soon," the voice tells me from my mom's mouth.

And in a blink, the water rises up and swallows her whole.

I stand there, waiting for the dream to end. But it doesn't, so I sit in the soft sand and let the lapping waves lull me into a calm I haven't felt in a long time.

I send a silent thank you to whoever controls this dream world, because this is a peace I've needed but couldn't find.

TWENTY

A knock at the door drags me from the calming waves and warm beach.

"Yeah," I call out, wiping the sleep from my eyes.

Lucy peeks her head in the room. "Tiberius and the gang are almost here. They just got on the boat."

I push up into a sitting position and quickly suck in a pain-filled breath. Lucy rushes in, putting her hands out to stop me. "You've got to take it easy. Broken ribs take a bit to heal. Last thing we need is you puncturing one of your lungs with that."

I wave her away, but she just moves around me and opens the drawer next to the bed. "Walter left these for you," she says, grabbing out pills and lifting a glass of water from the table.

I eye the pills in her hand. "Are these going to put me into a weird haze?" I ask.

She shrugs. "No clue, but you can't function if you're in constant pain."

She's right. I take them from her hand and swallow them down.

"You've got enough time for a shower. I grabbed some of your clothes from your room," she points to a bag on the chair against the wall.

A shower sounds awesome right now. "Thanks," I tell her.

I slide ever so carefully to the edge of the bed. My body jerks in pain at every movement, but the promise of warm water is too much to resist. I make my way slowly into the bathroom.

As the shower heats up, I lean against the sink and finally look at myself in the mirror. I look horrible, there's no way around it. My cheek is mottled in black, blues, and purples. My bottom lip has a cut in it, and my eyes are slightly glossy and bloodshot. I gently lift my shirt up and over my head, cursing the entire time and having to take frequent breaks. I turn my body so I can see my ribs. I look like I was in a fight and lost, which is pretty much the truth. Images play on a reel behind my eyes. It doesn't help that I can see the imprint of Henderson's hand on my wrist. I try to breathe through the pain and terror, but it's taking hold of me.

I'm safe now. We're all safe.

I walk on shaky legs to the shower and slowly climb over the edge. The hot water hits me, and I wince at the shock. I lean my head against the cool tile wall and let the warmth of the water penetrate my cold skin. And as it rains down on my body, I finally let the tears fall.

I know my mom wants me to be strong, but this is too much. What they're asking of me is too much. How do we stop someone who can compel people, who's been part of a government organization for decades, and has a secret weapon at his disposal named Chelsea? She can block anyone's power. Rivers could have lied to Mr. Smith and if Chelsea was there, no one would have ever known.

I stay in the shower long enough for my fingers to wrinkle and prune, until the sound of voices drags me out.

The sight that greets me when I walk out of the room is enough to bring me to my knees. Xavier, Tiberius, and Tony are all here and in one piece. "Hey guys," I say, and all of their heads snap up.

Tiberius walks over to me and tenderly enfolds me in his arms.

"I'm so glad you're okay," he whispers into my hair. "Never again are you going into a dangerous place without me."

"Here's hoping, right?" I ask on a sad laugh.

We walk farther into the room. Xavier curses low at the sight of me, and Tony goes completely white. He turns like he's going to walk out the door, but Walter stops him.

"You can't run anymore," Walter says softly, but we all hear him. "We *need* you now. You are in a room with people who have lost loved ones, been tortured, have seen unmentionable horrors. You are not alone in your pain."

"I don't belong here," Tony says to him. He grips his hair. "I betrayed Becca. The one person who has always been there. I *betrayed* her."

I walk across the room and grab his shirt, making him look at me. "I get it. We *all* get it. We all probably would have done the same thing if we were in your shoes. But now we need you to commit. We need you all in. I can't help you if you don't let me."

"I don't know what's worse," he whispers, eyes refusing to meet mine. "Being the one who's tortured or watching them beat you."

I swallow hard at his words. Because I don't think I could have handled watching what they did to him.

"It's done now," I tell him. "Can't go back. We just need to keep going forward."

"Why don't you hate me?" he asks.

"Some moments I do," I say, watching his throat bob as he swallows a thick ball of emotion. "But other moments, I think—if it were my grandparents, I'd do anything. I wish you had talked to me. I wish you had trusted in me. But you're my friend. And I saw how much it hurt you to watch what they did to me. Just don't do it again."

He nods once.

Lucy steps up next to us. "Let's go have our long-overdue chat," she says to Tony and leads him out of the room, Walter following closely on their heels.

I clear my throat a few times, turning to the rest of the room. "Where's the rest of the group?"

"They went back to headquarters," Xavier says, walking over to the couch, and we all follow, taking our seats. "I'm going to need to go there soon as well."

"We all need to go soon," I tell him.

"I agree, but we need to fly," Tiberius says in a stern voice.

"I can—" I start to say.

"No." Tiberius's voice leaves no room for arguing. "You need to rest and heal. I know how worn out you can get traveling long distances with a lot of passengers."

Not going to lie, I was kind of hoping he hadn't noticed that.

"We'll need your transporting skills soon enough. You're no good to us if you run yourself into the ground."

"How were things when you left headquarters?" Xavier asks, ever the peacemaker.

I take a deep breath and focus on Xavier. "When I left, Gregory was with Mr. Smith, and I don't think he'll let anyone get near him."

You can visibly see some of the tension lift from his shoulders. "Good. Did Doc say anything?" he asks.

"They were running tests when I left. But he was stable," I tell him.

"Thank goodness for that. It was so hard to tell when I first saw him strapped to that table." Tiberius says.

Thinking about Gregory makes me think about the chaos I left when we transported out of there. "How bad did it get in France?" I ask, searching both of their faces.

Tiberius sits forward on the couch, his hands clasped between his knees. "They almost broke through that door," he says, shaking his head. "If it weren't for Raven's rats and mice, things would have been different."

An awkward silence fills the room, and the guys share a look that I can only guess has something to do with me.

Tremors race up and down my legs as I watch some unspoken conversation. "What?" I ask, not handling the tension at all.

"We were wondering if you would tell us what happened?" Guess Tiberius pulled the short straw on asking *that* question.

But that question makes me hear my grandpa's voice coming through Sariah's vile mouth. It makes me shudder.

"Sariah and Henderson were there," I tell them. I look away, focusing on the floral curtains hanging in front of the window. "They hung me from chains attached to the ceiling."

Xavier lets out a stream of curses.

"Who's that?" Tiberius asks, and you can't mistake the rage in his question.

I look over at Tiberius, and he's barely containing the anger I see simmering behind his eyes.

"Sariah was recruited with me. Her power is to mimic anyone's voice. She's the one that questioned me."

Tiberius looks at me with such pain that I know I don't even need to tell him whose voice she used against me.

"Henderson," I soldier on, not wanting to hear how sorry they are, "his power is to clone himself about five times. He's the one that was on the plane, the one that kidnapped Gregory."

Xavier sucks in a sharp breath and leans back into the couch. He looks up at the ceiling. "All those men were him." He says it as a statement, not a question, but I nod anyways.

"Handy power," Tiberius says, virtually growling.

I nod. "When do we head back to the states?" I ask, desperately wanting to focus on something else.

Tiberius looks me over. Probably cataloging all the injuries he can see. "We'll have to leave in a few days," he says.

Can I wait that long to see Gregory? Do I really have a choice?

We sit in silence, the moment feeling heavy.

"I'm pretty sure Raven had the rats piss on the people on the other side of the door." Xavier says it so seriously that it takes a moment for the rest of us to catch on.

Tiberius lets out a surprised bark of laughter that I've never heard out of his mouth before, and I burst into laughter with him. "Oh no more, my ribs can't take it," I say between laughs.

"I'm serious though. Pretty ingenious on her part."

TWENTY-ONE

"I want to come with you," Luca tells us for probably the tenth time.

"I know. But I need you here to protect these people. Lucy is staying here as well," Tiberius says from behind us.

"He's right," I tell Luca. "And I can always come get you at any moment." Granted, the stir he'd cause might make it a bad idea.

He nods but doesn't look happy about the situation at all.

"The best thing you can do is work with Bronia. In your scale form you're almost unbreakable. She needs someone like you to help her learn to defend herself," Tiberius tells him, and that makes Luca stand a little taller.

We all want to be needed. We all want a purpose. Maybe Luca's is helping these people with powers they don't fully understand. Hopefully he'll realize that as he works with Bronia.

He grabs my hand and gives it a firm but gentle squeeze. "I will help her, but if you need me, I'm ready."

"Check in with Lucy when you visit Eloise. She'll keep you up to date," Tiberius tells him.

They do the universal handshake-backslap man thing, and then Luca gives my shoulder a soft pat and he's on his way.

"Are you really going to reveal yourself to Project Lightning?" I ask Tiberius as we watch Luca walk down the dirt road. Thankfully none of the kids run screaming at the sight of him. A couple of brave ones even run up and hug his leg.

"I'm not sure. One thing I won't budge on is giving away the location of Fordlandia, or what's here. These people have been through enough. I don't want them to be put through more."

"Agreed." My eyes drift to the kids running and playing. I won't let this sanctuary be taken from them.

"We need to leave in twenty minutes. Do you know where Tony is?" he asks me.

I look over to the water tower. "Yeah, I've got an idea. We'll meet you at the boat dock in fifteen minutes."

His eyes follow my gaze. You can just make out Tony's legs dangling over the side of the high walkway running around the tank. Tiberius gives my shoulder a soft squeeze and then heads off for his home.

In a blink I'm standing over Tony. The only sign he gives of being startled is his hands gripping the rails.

"Never going to get used to you just popping in out of thin air," he says, sounding a little breathless.

"Sorry," I tell him as I sit down next to him. "I was just below you talking to Tiberius. Figured it was better just to pop in than have to climb that never-ending ladder."

"Don't blame ya. The climb sucks," he says, looking down at the faraway ground.

I stare at his profile, trying to categorize all the changes in him. It's almost too many to count. "I miss your laugh." The words fall out without me meaning them to.

He turns and connects his eyes with mine. "I miss yours too."

"Think we'll ever get back to that carefree place?" I ask him.

His whole demeanor turns desolate, and his mouth drops a little. "I don't know. But living this way is so draining. Something has to give."

A thought occurs to me. "What if Mr. Smith offered to get you help? Would you take it?"

He releases a sad sigh and looks back over Fordlandia. "Do I really have a choice?" he asks, sounding resigned.

"That depends. What kind of life do you want after this is all done? The fear is crippling. And I know there are so many things that *I'm* not dealing with right now." I shake my head. "And sometime soon, that's all going to rear up and level me. But one day when I look back at this point in my life"—and hopefully I'll get a chance to do that—"I want to tell my kids that I had the strength and courage to help myself. That I didn't wait for someone to tell me what to do. That I went and searched out the help I needed. That I was an active part in working to get better. I want to look in a mirror and see someone who won't stop."

"Guess with that speech I've don't got no choice, huh?" he asks, a little smirk lifting his lips. "After all, can't deprive the women of the world this handsome face."

I want to weep at the small glance of the Tony I've come to know and love, but I'm afraid if I do that it could undo whatever is going on here.

"Ready to head back to headquarters?" I ask.

He lets out a huff and looks out at the jungle surrounding us. "No, but I need to do it. I've got a lot to make up for."

I grab his hand, forcing his attention back to me. "You can't keep thinking that way. It'll eat you alive."

"I'll get there, but right now guilt is what is motivating me."

I stand up, shaking out my jeans. I don't want to push him anymore, but I'm glad we got this far today. "Let's transport over to the docks; they're waiting for us. Plus, Mike is probably dying to see you, so we gotta hurry. And wait till you see Dex's lab."

I know I'm babbling, but I feel like he needs it. He stands and grabs my hand. "How long is it going to take to get there?" he asks.

"If I could transport us all, only a blink, but since I can't, it'll take a day. Get ready to hold my hand on the plane like you did on our trip to Japan. I hate flying."

He smiles a genuine smile, and in a blink we're gone.

"WE'LL BE THERE IN AN HOUR," Xavier says from the driver seat of the rented SUV we picked up in New Jersey.

"What are you going to do, Tiberius?" I ask him from the back seat looking at his disguise. "I don't know if Lucy's tech will work inside the building. I have a feeling they scramble signals in there."

Tiberius is using the same disguise as the first time I met him when he was at my grandparents' house. What Lucy is capable of doing with some wires and circuits is beyond amazing. How she was able to basically "cloak" Tiberius I'll never understand, but it's freaking cool.

"Didn't you have a cell phone? Shouldn't any technology work in there?" Tony asks from beside me.

"Yeah, but Mr. Smith gave that to me. What Tiberius has is something completely different. I don't know if it makes a difference."

"What I'm really worried about," Xavier says, not taking his eyes off the road, but the way he wrings the steering wheel is telling enough, "is if it fails, Tiberius is Becca's dad's identical twin. Mr. Smith recruited your dad. This could turn bad fast."

"I'm going to have to reveal myself to him eventually," Tiberius tells everyone, looking in his mirror and adjusting his hat that controls the disguise. "But this situation is going to be tense as it is. We really need to get Mr. Smith away from headquarters so you guys can really fill him in without worrying about who could betray us."

We all nod.

"Under no circumstances do we disclose or mention Fordlandia," Tiberius says, but we all hear it for the order it is. "The people there are victims. I won't subject them to more pain and anguish if I can help it."

"Agreed," Tony says forcibly.

I lean back and look at him, surprised at this much anger from him. "What?" he asks, probably seeing my open mouth. "You get to know people when you can read lips from any distance. Most of them are just trying to figure out their role in life now, and how to help the kids."

The car falls into a stunned silence. "That's what you've been doing up on that water tower?" I ask.

He shrugs like it isn't a huge revelation. "It sounds a lot creepier than it really is. But I can't help my powers, just like the rest of you."

"True," Xavier says. "You can't imagine the gross things I've seen when I walk into a public restroom. No one, and I mean no one, should have to see those things when they go into a stall. I don't want to know about anyone's bathroom issues. That's a hard and fast line."

I wince. "I am so, so sorry," I tell him honestly. "But I have never been so thankful that I can't do what you can."

"That's awful, man," Tony says, completely disgusted.

"Yeah. If I could bleach my mind, I would," Xavier says, and Tiberius chuckles softly.

The air in the car is much lighter, but we're still getting closer to headquarters. "In thirty minutes, I'll direct you off the freeway to where you can take me," Tiberius says. "I'll stay there until you three can get a read on Mr. Smith and see if it's time for him to meet me."

The next thirty minutes are filled with talk radio and the sounds of passing cars on the freeway until Tiberius directs Xavier off the highway.

As Xavier continues to follow instructions, things start to look recognizable. And as we pull up in front of a huge familiar home, my heart starts to race.

I unbuckle and scoot forward until I'm right next to Tiberius. "How do you know about this house?" I ask him.

I can feel the others' eyes on me, but I stay focused on my uncle.

"A friend of mine owns it," he says, looking super confused.

I point at the house. "I've been here. I've stayed here," I tell him.

Everyone freezes. "When?" he asks me.

"Grandpa brought us here the night before I went to Project Lightning for the first time. He said it belonged to a friend of his."

The front door of the house opens, making us all turn and watch Daemon run for the car, his hands outstretched. "Go!" I scream. "They're here!"

Xavier puts the car in drive and punches the gas. My body flies back, slamming into the seat and then the door. Tony tries to grab a hold of me, but I watch his eyes widen in horror. A large ball of fire slams into the SUV. It rocks to the side, throwing me into Tony's lap.

"Keep going," Tiberius orders.

The SUV drops back down onto all four wheels. I scramble off Tony and look out the back windshield. "Get down, Becca!" Tony roars as he dives on top of me, right before the back window shatters.

"They're shooting at us," Tony yells.

"Kind of figured that with the window shattering," Xavier says. He jerks the steering wheel and we fly around the bend. "Becca, get buckled up; I've got to get us out of here."

More shots hit the back of the car. "We've got two cars coming up hot behind us," Tiberius says.

Xavier takes a couple more turns and I don't know how the car doesn't flip onto its side. "They're gaining," Tony yells at them.

"I know," Xavier says through gritted teeth.

A field comes into view on our right. "Xavier, head for the field. I've got an idea," I tell him.

"What? Why?" he asks.

"I'm going to transport us to headquarters," I tell him, still trapped under Tony.

Tiberius looks back at me, his eyes wide. "Have you done that from a moving vehicle?" he asks.

Tony pushes my head back down, saving us from a spray of bullets. "It doesn't matter. We're going to die or get kidnapped if I don't. I won't let them take me again," I tell him with as much venom in my voice as I can muster.

There's a beat of silence before I catch Tiberius's nod. I grab Tony and we wedge ourselves close to the front. "Grab my arm, Tiberius," I tell him, and he does.

I lay my hand on Xavier and as I'm closing my eyes, a car barrels into the side of us.

TWENTY-TWO

"What the hell?"

I never thought I'd be so happy to hear Mr. Smith's voice, even if it sounds like he's ready to murder one of us. I open my eyes to see him staring in complete shock at the four of us sprawled across the ground.

I look at the guys, making sure we all made it, and suck in a sharp breath. "Tiberius, you're bleeding."

"I am?" he turns to look at his arm and Mr. Smith comes crashing from behind his desk.

Mr. Smith tackles Tiberius to the ground, causing all hell to break lose. Xavier tries to grab Mr. Smith, but he's kicked backwards. Tony stands there, his mouth dropped open. If I didn't think my uncle was about to be killed, I'd laugh at the ridiculousness of all this.

Tiberius and Mr. Smith roll around the ground until Mr. Smith pins my uncle to the carpet.

"Who the hell are you?" Mr. Smith roars the question.

I rush over and hop onto Mr. Smith's back, making me yell out a pain-filled curse. "Stop," I tell him, panting through the pain.

Mr. Smith looks up at me. "He's my uncle," I tell him.

"How?" he demands.

I fall to his side, jarring my ribs again. I'm never going to heal at this rate. "Dad had a twin brother," I rush out the words.

He relaxes instantly because he knows I can't lie to him; no one can. He pushes himself off of Tiberius and stands, brushing off his suit.

Tiberius takes a little bit longer to get up. That's when we notice the blood everywhere. "I think a bullet nicked you," I say, crawling over to him.

He looks at his sleeve. "Looks like it's just a graze," he says.

"Just a graze!?" I want to shake the man. "Can we please go at least one week without someone getting hurt?"

"I'm fine," he says, placing a hand on my arm to calm me down.

"Still might need stitches," Xavier says, coming closer to look at it.

"Will someone please tell me what is going on?" Mr. Smith demands, throwing his hands up in the air.

Tony moves closer to us, startling Mr. Smith. "Tony?" he asks, like he just realized Tony's there.

"Hey, boss," he answers, rocking back and forth on his heels.

Mr. Smith walks closer to him, and all of us tense. Tony's eyes widen and find mine. I bite my lip, not sure how this is going to go. "I'm so glad you're okay," he tells Tony, reaching out and gripping his shoulder.

"Getting there," Tony replies, eyes averted.

"We were on our way here. And we were stopping at a safehouse when we were ambushed," Xavier says, breaking the tension. "We almost didn't make it here. Guessing Tiberius got hit right before we transported."

Mr. Smith opens his mouth, but he snaps it closed. His eyes flit around us, calculating. "Wait, why aren't you all on the ground from Becca transporting all of you?" he asks.

I rub the back of my neck. "A lot has changed," I say.

"That's an understatement," Tony says from beside me.

Mr. Smith keeps looking at Tiberius. He rubs a hand over his face. "I can't deal with all this right now."

My jaw drops. This is the second time in a week I've seen Mr. Smith lose his cool, and I've got no clue how to handle it.

So like we all have learned to do...I change the subject.

"How's Gregory?" I ask. "Can we see him?"

"They're bringing him out of his coma today," he tells me. "We were waiting for you all to get here. Let's head over there now," he points at Tiberius. "They can fix him up while we're there."

"Will anyone recognize him?" Xavier asks.

That makes Mr. Smith pause in his tracks. He shares a long look with my uncle. "Not much we can do about that now."

Tiberius raises a finger. "Actually, we might." He pulls out his hat and puts it on. He hits a button on the side and his face completely transforms. Mr. Smith takes a surprised step back.

"I've never seen technology like that," he says in awe.

"My wife is pretty handy," Tiberius says with pride.

Mr. Smith studies him and then shakes his head before he moves for the door.

We all file in behind him. "Do you think Gregory will be okay?" I ask Mr. Smith softly.

"I hope so," is his response.

We follow him down the stark white hallways until we reach a set of double doors. Mr. Smith puts his hand on the scanner to the right on the wall. He leans forward and a red laser scans his eye. The door swings open and we continue through to another set of doors. Two guards stand on either side. They both stand a little taller when they see who's coming, except one falters. Mike.

He moves away from the door and steps in front of Tony. I don't know what he sees. Maybe he notices the weight Tony's lost, or the black smudges under his eyes. Or maybe he can sense some of the light that's been snuffed out of him.

"Hey, Mike," Tony says, crossing his arms tight over his chest.

He blinks a couple times, like he doesn't trust his eyes. "Where've you been, man?" Mike asks, not bothering to hide the hurt in his voice.

We all stand there in the overwhelming awkwardness, but thankfully Mr. Smith puts a swift end to that. He puts a hand on Mike's shoulder. "They'll be here for a while, so you'll get to talk soon. But Gregory is being brought out of his coma and we need to be in there."

It's like Mike just realized there're a bunch of us standing there. "Uh, yeah. Sorry. Of course," he rambles.

Mr. Smith heads into the room, and we file in behind him. But I still see Tony stop, lean close to Mike, and have a quick, quiet conversation.

I turn back around and brace myself. I've been trying to put thoughts of Gregory to the side, because there was nothing I could do. And the more I would think about it, the more anxious I'd get.

We walk on silent feet into the room. I can't see anything yet. And then the guys part, and there he is.

Gregory.

His face looks thinner, and his arms have lost a lot of muscle. He looks so much younger lying in that hospital bed. And the guilt of not finding him sooner starts to engulf me. What if I'd gone back to Project Lightning instead of fleeing to Brazil? What if I'd kept having Tiberius search for him? What if I'd gone to Mr. Smith sooner? So many questions and scenarios swarming around in my mind, making my stomach clench in agony.

"Stop," Tiberius orders me, and it halts the overwhelming feeling threatening to suffocate me. "I can see the guilt written all over your face. You didn't know. There's no way you could have known. Even if I had looked right away, we wouldn't have found him because Chelsea was blocking his power."

I take a deep breath and try to let his words set in. It helps, but only a tiny bit. So I push it to the back of my mind and focus on the doctor talking with Mr. Smith.

"There's no telling how long it'll take him to wake up. Some people come to quickly, and others take a while. From our scans there's plenty of brain activity, so I'm confident that he *will* wake up. I just can't tell you when."

Everyone in my group deflates at the news. Mr. Smith continues talking with the doctor, so I walk over to Gregory's side.

I reach for his hand, and the warmth of his skin eases some of the tension crippling me. Dr. Wilkens said he had lots of brain activity; hopefully that means he can read my mind.

I really need you to wake up. There's so much going on, and we need you. I need you. I miss you. These last several months have been hell thinking you were gone. But now you need to come back to us.

I squeeze his hand and watch the rise and fall of his chest. It's hard, because he looks like he's sleeping and I just want to shake him to wake him up, but I know that won't work.

Tiberius walks over to my side and leans down to whisper in my ear. "Have you ever tried to use your other power with him?" he asks.

A memory flashes in my mind, of Gregory crouched down next to me in the stairwell in Myanmar. I heard his thoughts that day, and I shouldn't have. "Yes," I whisper back.

I turn and look up at him. His face just shows concern, so I do my best to school my features as well.

"Try it now, but be careful," he warns. And I know why; we're still keeping it secret that I can enhance powers.

I grip Gregory's hand again and close my eyes. I push my enhancing ability into him.

Gregory? Can you hear me? I ask the question in my mind, hoping he'll hear it, but I doubt this will work. He's technically still in a coma.

Becca?

I drop his hand.

"Everything okay?" Mr. Smith asks from across the room.

"Yeah. Just want him to wake up, ya know?" I say, using the truth to cover what I'm doing.

He nods and turns back toward Xavier. I pick up Gregory's hand again. *You still there? Sorry for dropping the connection earlier.*

I'm here. How is this even possible?

That's for later. Are you okay? Do you even know what's going on? I don't know if he can hear the desperation in my thoughts, but it's there and it's strong.

My brain feels foggy.

I'm not surprised. They're bringing you out of a coma right now.

Where am I?

At headquarters. I found you in France.

France? He sounds so confused, but I won't tell him more. He needs to be clear-headed for that conversation.

We'll talk more when you wake up. Just please wake up. I need you.

I'm trying. I take that promise, and I hold it close to my heart. If he tells me he's trying, then I believe him.

I'll see you soon.

I drop his hand and move away from his bedside. Xavier walks up next to me. "Did you feel him twitch or anything?" he asks, sounding so hopeful, and I wish I could be honest with him, but it always has to be half-truths.

"No twitching, but I talked to him. I'm confident he heard my thoughts."

He stares at Gregory and I hope he doesn't touch the chair I was just sitting in, because he'll see the conversation I just had with Tiberius. I didn't even think about that until right now. For all I know he already knows I have another power and is keeping my secret. Even if he does, I'm praying he won't understand what it is.

I step away from Xavier and Tony walks up to me. "Anything?" he asks. "I lipread your conversation with Xavier."

I tilt my head to the side and look him square in the eye. "You give me a hard time for popping in places, and you just basically eavesdropped on my *private* conversation."

He waves away my comment. "Well?" he asks.

"He's trying to wake up," I whisper to him.

He nods, but I watch his fingers continually tap the side of his leg. "You doing okay?" I ask him.

"Yeah, I'm fine."

I raise my brows at him. "I promise," he says.

We stand against the wall for the next two hours. Not talking, but neither are Tiberius or Xavier, or anyone else in the room. Occasionally Mr. Smith will ask the doctor questions, but other than that, and the beeping of machines, it's quiet.

"He's moving," Xavier says, waving us all over.

We rush over to Gregory's bed. "What did he just say?" Mr. Smith asks.

Did he just...?

"I'm not sure," Dr. Wilkens tells him.

"Becca," Gregory murmurs more clearly, and everyone turns to face me.

<h1 style="text-align:center">TWENTY-THREE</h1>

My cheeks catch fire. "What?" I ask, lifting my shoulders.

Mr. Smith shoots me a look, letting me know we'll talk more about this later. But whatever, the guy obviously had a relationship with another person of power, otherwise Gregory wouldn't even be here. So he no longer has a leg to stand on.

"Gregory? Can you hear me?" Dr. Wilkens asks as he leans over Gregory with his stethoscope.

Gregory's head moves back and forth a little on the pillow, his face pulling in a grimace. The doctor grabs Gregory's hand. "If you can hear and understand me, I want you to give me a squeeze," he says.

We all zero in on their joined hands, and I swear everyone in the room holds their breath. It's not much of a squeeze, but we all watch Gregory's hand slightly flinch. Everyone lets out a collective whoosh of air. I *knew* he was going to wake up, but the fear that he wouldn't kept creeping in.

Dr. Wilkens pats Gregory's arm. "Good. Now don't worry about opening your eyes. Your body has been in a coma for a while. But when you're ready, there are a lot of people eager to see you," the doctor tells him, and then he places Gregory's hand back on his chest.

We all watch, waiting for Gregory to do something else, but it's like he's back in the coma. The doctor turns and addresses all of us. "Even though he's been in a coma for some months, his body is exhausted. He'll be in and out of sleep for a bit. His muscles are also severely diminished. He's going to need some physical therapy and probably occupational therapy."

"I'll arrange all that," Mr. Smith tells him without hesitation.

Dr. Wilkens nods. "Good. I suggest you all get something to eat and rest. He probably won't really be able to talk with you until the morning."

Mr. Smith ushers us all out of the room and stops us on the other side of the double doors. "You heard the doctor. Get some food and then let's meet back in my office so we can figure out who's behind this."

"We already know it's Mr. Rivers," I say, totally not caring about the two guards standing behind us manning the door. They must have changed shifts, because Mike isn't there anymore.

"What on earth makes you think it's him?" he asks, leveling me with a lethal glare.

"Uh, Chelsea, his assistant, who tortured Gregory and me. She kept talking to someone on the phone. Who else do you think is behind all of this?" I wave my hands around.

"Until I have concrete proof, I won't accuse him of anything." His voice is deathly calm, and it has zero effect on me.

"Are you freaking crazy?" I yell my question, and Tiberius and Tony both grab one of my arms. "Open your eyes. This whole organization has been infiltrated—"

"Enough," he says firmly, slashing his hand through the air. He runs an agitated hand through his hair. "We'll wait for Gregory," he says and then leaves our group standing there.

I know my jaw is hanging wide open. "How can he be in denial about this?"

"Mr. Rivers has been his mentor for years, decades even," Xavier says.

I turn to Tony. "Did you ever see an old guy in Myanmar?" I ask him, just realizing he's never even met Rivers.

"No," he says, his fists clenching and unclenching. He clears his throat a few times. "They talked with someone in charge on their cells, but they never used names when they were on the phone."

I know he's uncomfortable telling us all this. We really haven't been able to get him to talk about what went down in Myanmar. The others might not realize it, but this is a huge step for him.

"Let's hope Gregory can clear everything up," Tiberius says.

"Let's hope that happens before another awful thing can occur. I can feel it coming; we don't have much time," I tell him.

WE WALK INTO THE CAFETERIA, and just like every other time I've come back to headquarters, everyone turns and stares. It takes a moment, but all the other people Tony and I were recruited with stand up and walk over to us.

"Hey, Tony."

"Tony, where've you been?"

"Man, we missed you around here."

"Got some cool stories to tell?"

Tony takes a step closer to me at the bombarding of questions—whether that's a subconscious thing or not, I don't know.

"Give the guy some room," I snap at the group.

"Becca! Hey," I hear from behind everyone.

I push my way through and thankfully they part, and I'm greeted by Dex's smiling face. As soon as he lays eyes on Tony he rushes forward and wraps his arms around him. *Huh, didn't know Dex was a hugger.* And by the looks of it, Tony wasn't prepared for that either.

Dex steps back but leans in close to Tony. "I'm so glad they found you," Dex says to him quietly, but it's not quiet enough, because Mike immediately butts in.

"Found you?" Mike asks, his eyes looking us all over.

"I, uh, I was kidnapped," Tony tells him, eyes looking anywhere but at the guy in front of him.

Someone lets out a startled gasp, but my eyes stay glued to Tony.

"Are you okay?" Mike asks carefully.

Tony lets out a sad laugh. "Gettin' there, man."

Mike looks him over, and I don't know him well enough to understand that look. But he steps forward and Tony visibly deflates. "Let's get some food into you. Your scrawny self needs some beefing up," Mike tells him and throws an arm around him, leading Tony to the buffet.

I watch them walk away, noticing Tony's tense shoulders that I'm sure Mike feels. But he needs this. He can't keep hiding.

And apparently, I can't either, because I'm suddenly engulfed in Dex's hug. "Hey, Dex," I say, my voice muffled by his chest.

He steps back but keeps a hold of my shoulders. "Where the hell have you been? And what happened to your face?" he asks in all seriousness.

I give his shoulder a little shove, and then gesture towards my face. "It's fine. But, hey. How come Tony got a warm welcome and I got that?"

"You up and disappeared off the face of the earth," he says, his voice rough.

I look down at my feet, trying to steady my breathing. It takes a moment, but I finally look up into his eyes. "After what happened to my grandparents...I had to run. I couldn't deal. I couldn't...I couldn't be here."

"I missed you," he tells me.

A throat clears from beside me. "Oh, sorry. Dex, this is my...this is Tiberius," I tell him. I don't know why I hide the fact that he's my uncle, but it feels right to keep that hidden for a bit.

Dex side-eyes my stumble, but thankfully he ignores it. Tiberius extends his hand, and Dex clasps it in his. "Nice to meet you, Dex."

Dex's eyes widen a bit, I'm guessing at the thick Russian accent. It's even more pronounced than Ania's Polish one.

"We going to eat or what?" Xavier asks from over Tiberius's shoulder.

"Oh, yes, sorry. Would you guys like to join me?" Dex asks.

"Sure. I want to hear what you're cooking up in that lab now," I tell him.

He laughs and walks back to his table while we approach the buffets. Four different sections are lined up. The selection is always all over the place. But I guess that happens when you've got people from all over the world here. At least this place has good food.

I grab a salad and some baked ziti. I look over my shoulder and scan the room until I find Tony. His body still seems pretty rigid, but he's got a small smile playing on his lips. "It'll take time, but he'll learn to conquer this," Tiberius says, leaning into me.

"How are you so sure?" I turn and ask him.

"Because I know," he tells me.

I open my mouth, but he waves his hand. "A story for another time. Let's go and talk with this Dex friend of yours."

We take our trays and sit down at Dex's table. "I thought you usually ate after everyone else?" I ask him before I dig into my food.

"Mike said he saw Tony, and I was hoping that meant you were here too," he says in between bites. "Are you guys back for good?"

I look at Xavier and Tiberius. Everyone here needs to be on guard, and if Mr. Smith isn't going to do something about it, I am. "There's some bad stuff going on. More than you were even aware of. People are being kidnapped and experimented on."

"Geez, Becca. Not much of a lead-in," Xavier says, sounding pissed, but I completely ignore him.

"We found Gregory in a tomb in France. They had him in a medically induced coma. But we've also found children locked in cages. Tortured and DNA manipulation forced on them."

Dex's fork drops from his hand, clattering to the table. His mouth hangs open and his eyes are wide.

"Enough," Xavier tries again with more force, and Tiberius grabs his arm, cutting him off.

"No." My voice is guttural—I barely recognize it—but I push on. "These people killed my grandparents. They beat me. They did horrible things to Tony for weeks. Keeping them secret helps no one." I know my voice has risen. I can see everyone staring at us, but I don't care anymore.

"People from Project Lightning are behind this too. People we've trusted. They're the ones who kidnapped those three agents' kids that we rescued. They took Sariah's grief over her mother and used that to lure her in. She's now helping them. She helped them kidnap that little girl in England."

Xavier puts a hand on my arm, but I rip away and push to my feet. My heart feels like it's pounding out of my chest. "I went into that burning house. I saw my murdered grandparents in their bed. And then I had to watch my home burn. I had to see the photos of them shooting Gregory in the head. I won't be quiet anymore." I point around the room. "They all need to know. Because they could be taken next."

Arms wrap around me from behind. I go to raise my leg to kick out, but Tony's voice stops me. "We won't let it keep happening," he promises me. "We will stop this."

I sag against his chest. "We've rescued so many kids," I say softly.

"I know," he tells me, still holding me tightly.

"So many raids, and it's like nothing we've done has helped," I whisper my failure to him.

He turns me around. "They're getting desperate. They wouldn't have done what they did to you in that underground room if they weren't. We're going to figure this out. Together this time."

I wrap my arms around him, soaking up some warmth. "But maybe next time when you tell everyone, let's not do it when we're eating. Let people enjoy their meal first, yeah?" He says it jokingly and I let out a bark of laughter.

"Deal," I tell him.

I turn back to my table. Dex still has a shocked look on his face, and the awkwardness is so thick that I've got to get out of here. "I'm going to sit with Gregory for a bit if you guys need me. Xavier, can you help Tiberius find a place to sleep?"

He nods.

I squeeze Tony's hand one last time and in a blink I'm back in the hospital room, causing one nurse to curse and another to throw her notes in the air.

"Sorry," I tell her, cringing at her scowl.

TWENTY-FOUR

"Any change?" I ask completely nonchalantly, like I didn't just appear out of thin air.

One of the nurses bends over with her hands on her knees, taking deep breaths. The one that cursed just shakes her head.

"Sorry," I tell them again and walk over to Gregory.

His body twitches, and a low, quiet moans escape past his lips, like he's having a bad dream. "Has he been like this a lot?" I ask the nurse closest to me.

She looks up from one of the machines attached to him. "Yeah, but it's to be expected. Tomorrow should be a better day."

"Here's hoping," I say, more to myself than to her.

I take the seat beside him and grab on to his hand. I wish he could wake up now and talk to us. He's got to know who's behind all of this. Even if he couldn't read Chelsea's mind, there must have been others around.

I try talking with him again through our minds, but nothing. Maybe when he's dreaming, he can't. I lean forward and rest my head on my folded arms, still keeping a hold of his hand. I close my eyes, letting the constant exhaustion wash over me and drag me under.

DARKNESS SURROUNDS ME. My heart rate picks up. I reach out with my hands but it's like a dark abyss. Where am I? I put my hands on the ground, feeling the gritty stone beneath my fingertips. I crawl across the floor, afraid to lose purchase of the only tangible thing I can feel.

"Two more feet," a voice I don't recognize rasps out, and I barely hold in my scream.

"Where are we?" I whisper.

"My cell."

"Gregory?" I ask. Is it really him? What is going on?

"Hey, baby." Two words, but the way he says them are filled with such love and yet such sadness too.

Emotions threaten to swallow me at the sound of his voice.

"You're going to have to come to me. I'm chained to the wall," he says and my head drops.

I take a breath and follow the sound of his voice, tears silently slipping down my cheeks.

"Where are we?" I ask as I crawl closer.

The chains scrape across the stone floor. "My cell. I think you're stuck in my dream with me."

I reach out a hand and finally feel his leg. I grab it tightly and move closer to him. One of his arms hooks around me, dragging me up his body. He buries his face in my hair. "I can't tell you how much I've missed you." His voice is rough, like he's trying to keep himself from crying.

I can't see him, but I trace my hands up his arms until I'm cupping his face. "I thought you died," I tell him, sounding as tortured as I felt.

"I know. I'm so sorry. They thought if you believed I died, it'd make you vulnerable and easy to capture."

I wrap my arms around his neck. Hugging him as tightly as I can.

"There's so much I need to ask you. Do you know who's behind all of this?"

He starts to make a sound, but it's cut off by the cell door crashing open, bathing our dark spot in harsh fluorescent light. Gregory gently grips my chin and lifts my face to meet his. "The dream is going to play out regardless. Saying or doing anything won't change it. Believe me, I've tried. I'd rather you stay here or wake up, but I know you won't."

Henderson saunters into the room. The light catches the cruel smirk on his face. "Ready to talk yet? Or do you need more...convincing?" The way he says that last word makes all the hairs on my arms stand up.

Gregory's lips stay firmly closed, but his grip on me tightens to the point of it being painful. His chest rises and falls quickly, and his breathing increases at a rapid pace.

"Still not talking? Well, at least I know I can make you scream," Henderson says with something akin to pride. My stomach bottoms out and a sick feeling fills my chest.

I look back at Gregory. His eyes are locked in terror on the sadistic man approaching us. I put my palm on his face, my heart breaking even more at his flinch. "Keep looking at me," I tell him. His eyes drift to mine. "Stay with me, okay?"

Henderson walks through me like my body is smoke. "I'm really here," I rush to tell Gregory, afraid he'll think he just added me into his dreams. "You're asleep in the hospital and I fell asleep beside your bed. I'm here. I promise you, I'm really here."

I watch him take some steadying breaths.

"That's good. Keep breathing. You aren't alone." I keep my voice steady, trying so hard to give him some calm.

Henderson grabs Gregory's tattered shirt in his meaty fist. "Guess we'll have to be even more creative this time, huh?" He releases Gregory's shirt and unlocks the heavy iron shackles I hadn't even noticed on Gregory's feet and one arm. What are we, in a freaking dungeon?

Henderson grabs him by the arm that's wrapped around me and starts to drag him by the arm towards the cell door. I watch Gregory's *face go completely blank. Why is he giving up? "Fight. Why aren't you fighting?" I call after Gregory as I scramble off the floor and rush after them.*

"It doesn't do anything. The dream keeps going," he says, sounding utterly defeated. "The worst is I always knew what he planned. He'd make me listen to his thoughts before he followed through with them in reality."

I feel like a part of my soul breaks at his matter-of-fact confession. "Why can't we just wake up?" I ask him, desperate for a way out for us.

"I never get to wake up until I'm chained back up in my cell." He says it's just the way things are, and it causes a sick feeling to almost stop me in my tracks.

I keep up with them, not wanting to leave Gregory alone for even a moment. We enter into a stone hallway, like we're in some ancient castle's dungeon. Are we in France? Has he been under this church the whole time?

"Keep talking to me," I beg him. "If it doesn't matter what you do, talk to me."

I watch his face twist in agony. "You need to just go. I don't want you watching this."

I shake my head and set my mouth in a firm line. "Not going to happen," I tell him.

"So stubborn," he says, looking wistful until we reach an ancient-looking wooden door, and then it's like he's completely forgotten I'm here.

Henderson drops him to the ground like discarded trash. He tugs on the door's iron handle with both hands. A loud groaning fills the stone hallway as the door slowly opens. "Gregory," I say, looking away from the door to his body on the floor.

His face has gone stark white, and his breathing is fast and erratic. I squat down next to him and gently place my hand on his chest. "I'm right here," I remind him.

It takes so much not to burst into tears at his fear. I've never seen him like this. And I can't imagine what's happened on the other side of this door.

Henderson pulls harder and the door opens fully. He grabs Gregory by his already torn shirt and drags him into the room. Bile rushes up my throat at the first glimpse of what's on the other side of the door.

It's a medieval torture room, and it's filled with the smell of fresh blood, which must have spilt recently.

TWENTY-FIVE

I tried talking to him. I tried telling him stories. I told him about Luca and his teal scales, but I don't think he heard a word I said. I was able to keep the tears at bay, but after the first sound of the whip hitting his back, I lost the battle. And after what felt like an eternity of Henderson's continual questions and Gregory's silence, aside from his screams of pain, I've been all-out bawling.

How long did they do this to him before they put him in a coma? How long did this go on? How's he going to come back from this?

I keep trying to talk to him through my sobs and tears, but he's gone somewhere in his mind that I can't reach. I don't know what's worse, watching what they did to him, or knowing I can't wake him up from this.

I don't know how long we've been in this room now. Or how many torture implements they've used on him. But Henderson grabs Gregory, now shirtless, and drags him back to his cell. He's passed out now, either from blood loss or exhaustion. I didn't know that one body could endure that much.

I walk behind them, leaving a part of my heart back in that room.

He tosses Gregory back against the wall and chains him back up. The cell door slams closed and we're plunged back into complete darkness.

I want to hold him in my arms, but I don't know if that'll hurt him. I keep forgetting we're in a dream. Things are too real, too raw. The pain on his face could be echoes of memories, but either way, the terror I saw in his eyes was real. I run a hand over my face. We're all going to need some serious therapy after this whole thing is said and done.

I grab Gregory's hand because that seems to be the only thing not hurt. I lean my head back against the stone wall and listen to his stilted breaths. I close my eyes and let myself drift, hoping that this will all be over soon.

"BECCA. BECCA, WAKE UP," someone says from beside me. As soon as a hand touches my shoulder, I throw a fist at the noise and then transport across the room.

"Son of a..." Xavier says, holding his face. "What the hell was that for?"

A nurse rushes over to him with some gauze and he presses it to his face. "I think you broke my nose," he says, sounding shocked.

I look across the room at Gregory. He's still asleep. I back up until I'm against a wall, and then I slide down it, my butt hitting the ground. I bring my legs up and bury my face in my knees.

"Becca?" Xavier asks, sounding lost.

The tears pour out of me, and there's nothing I can do to stop them. He walks closer to me, but I hold up a hand. "Where's Tiberius?" I manage to get the question out through my tears and ragged breaths.

"He's in the room next to yours," he says, inching closer like I'm a caged animal.

I scramble farther away from him. He holds one hand up in surrender, because the other is still holding gauze against his face. I take one last look at Gregory's sleeping face and transport out of there and to the door of my uncle's room.

I knock repeatedly until I hear him yell that he's coming. As soon as the door opens, I fall into his arms. He maneuvers me into his room. Once the door is closed, he grabs me by the shoulders and pushes me back a bit to see my face. "What happened?" he asks, eyes frantically searching me.

"I think I broke Xavier's nose," I say, pacing in front of his door.

"What?" he asks, his face scrunched up.

"I went and saw Gregory. Somehow, I got pulled into his dream. His nightmare, really." The words are rushed, choked.

Tiberius leads me over to his bed to sit with him.

My eyes stay fixed on a spot on the wall, completely unseeing anything except for the constant barrage of images from Gregory's dream. "The things they did to him. I can't even…"

Tiberius lightly touches my chin, and I turn to look at him. "He's here now. He's not in that place anymore. He's safe."

I shake my head. "But he's not even safe from his dreams."

So through tears and anguish I tell him everything I saw, everything that Gregory went through, all the questions they asked him. I leave nothing out, *nothing*.

Tiberius leans forward, bracing both elbows on his knees. He drops his head between his hands, and I listen to him take deep, controlled breaths.

Finally, he sits back up and brings me into his arms again. "I'll kill him." The unbridled rage in his voice startles me. "No one should have to endure that. *No. One.*"

"I don't know what to do for him," I tell Tiberius, desperate for him to give me guidance on this.

"The only thing you can do is be there for him. He's going to need a professional to get through this. But from what I've heard, he's a strong man, and he'll conquer this as long as he has support from those he loves."

I wipe at the tears falling down my cheeks. "I need him to wake up. We need to put an end to all of this. I feel like I'm falling apart, and I can't do that, but I don't know how much more I can take."

"He will, and *we* will end this." He grips me tightly. "I'm so proud of you. You've been so strong. Stronger than any seventeen-year-old I've ever met. But it's okay to fall apart. You're human. You have suffered more trauma than anyone should. And yet you keep fighting. You keep moving forward. Give yourself this chance to mourn. Mourn the lives that are lost, the ones that have been changed forever, and the future that will be different than what you hoped."

I look down, but he gives me a little shake. "But you, my dear, you get to decide your future. Let no one take that from you. You fight with everything you have to gain the future you want and deserve. You have to make your dreams come true; they don't just happen."

His words surround me like a comforting embrace and a reminder. I know I haven't mourned my grandparents properly. I know that I can't keep putting that off. And I know I need to realize that Gregory, Tony, and I will never be like we were at the cabin in the woods. But maybe we can be something better, if we fight for it.

"Dig deep, Becca. You're going to need a lot more strength to get through all of this. You'll need all you can give."

I hear him, and I want it, but... "I don't know how."

He gives me a little shake. "Yes, you do. You could have fallen apart after your grandparents, but you didn't. You found a problem and went about solving it."

"More like avoiding stuff," I mutter.

Tiberius shakes his head. "Yes, you avoided dealing with the pain. But that's normal. That's part of the process. Now you're feeling everything."

How true those words are. "It sucks."

He lets out a low laugh. "I know it does. You and me, we've got a lot in common. More than anyone should."

"Yeah, we're part of the 'whole family is gone' club."

"Unfortunately yes, but you also make your own family. And for the most part you've built a loyal one. Luca wanted nothing more than to be here helping you."

I think about Luca, and how he didn't have a single person when we found him. "Should have brought him, would have scared everyone."

We both laugh, because we know how much of a softy Luca is, but those teal scales scare the crap out of everyone.

"What do you want to do now?" he asks me.

I take a deep breath and wipe the residual moisture off my face. "We need to talk with Mr. Smith. We need to come up with a game plan. And we *really* need Gregory to wake up so Mr. Smith knows that Rivers is behind all of this."

Tiberius stands from the bed and grabs his hat to camouflage his appearance. He reaches his hand out towards me. "Then let's go pay a visit to Mr. Smith."

TWENTY-SIX

Thank goodness for Tiberius's power or we'd be looking all over the place for Mr. Smith. He's always in his office, so I head that way, but Tiberius stops me, and we head back to Gregory.

I don't bother with all the security measures. I grab Tiberius and we transport straight into the room, right next to the door.

Mr. Smith doesn't jump this time at my appearance. "I'm glad you're here. I just sent someone to get you. Gregory's awake," he says, sounding like he's desperately trying to choke back his emotion.

I rush around him to Gregory's bed. His eyes are closed. "I thought you said he was awake?"

"I am, I've just got my eyes closed." The most amazing sound I have ever heard hits my ears. And I can feel the tears pooling, but I do my best to keep them at bay.

His eyes blink open and look straight at me. So many emotions flitting through them. I want to fall to my knees and thank God, because I never thought I'd get this chance again. I thought they took him from me forever. I want to dive on him and hug him tightly, kiss him, but I'm afraid I'll hurt him, or he won't be able to handle that right now.

"I can take it," he says to me.

"Guess I need to start wearing my earrings again, huh?" I say with a watery laugh, trying to fight back the tears.

I sit on the edge of his bed and lean closer to him. He raises a hand and softly touches my face. "Can that wait a little bit?" he asks as his eyes move over my face. "I've missed hearing you in my mind."

How can I say no to that?

"Guess you didn't stop seeing each other, did you?" Mr. Smith asks as he approaches Gregory's other side.

"No, we didn't," Gregory says, his eyes trained on me. "And I don't think we're ever going to follow that rule." His eyes leave mine and he spears Mr. Smith with a look of complete seriousness.

Mr. Smith sighs. "We'll talk about this later."

Tiberius steps into view, and Gregory tenses.

"This is my uncle—"

"Uncle?" Gregory asks, looking confused and a little wary.

Tiberius takes off his hat and his true face shows.

"It's a long story, but the short of it is that my dad had an identical twin that I didn't know about until recently," I tell him.

Gregory's eyebrows raise at that.

"I know, it's like a bad soap opera. But he's answered so many questions. He's a good guy. I promise."

Gregory squeezes my hand.

"We've got a lot to talk about," Mr. Smith interrupts.

Gregory turns his head on his pillow, spearing Mr. Smith with a serious look. "You've got a lot of traitors in your midst," he says, sounding sad.

Mr. Smith hangs his head. It's one thing to think it; it's another to have a mind reader confirm your fears. He puts his hands on his hips and takes a couple of deep breaths before he looks up again.

"Where do we start?" Mr. Smith asks.

"Mr. Rivers is the puppet master of this whole mess."

Mr. Smith curses and kicks out at a stool next to him, and my whole body tenses.

"And this thing stretches the globe. He's been working on this for years," Gregory tells him, eyeing the stool he just kicked. "He's trying to build an army. And these experiments"—his voice shakes on the word, and I wonder how much they did to him—"some have been successful."

"It's true," I say, turning to Mr. Smith.

Mr. Smith motions with his hand to tell him more.

"We've been ambushing his facilities and rescuing the captives for the past couple months," I tell him.

"And burning them to the ground?" Mr. Smith asks.

I shrug, not really caring that those buildings burned. "Seemed fitting," I say, my voice deadly calm.

"What happened?" Gregory asks beside me.

I look down at him and I watch his face crumble at whatever he's reading in my mind, but I voice it anyways. "When I left you at the tarmac, I got a text." I let the tears fall. I can still see the flames climbing the walls. The scent of smoke still lingers in my nose. And the image of them in their beds...that's always in my mind when I fall asleep at night. "They killed my grandparents and set their house on fire with their bodies inside." There's so much more to that story, but I still can't talk about it in detail.

"I'm so sorry, Becca," Gregory says. He pulls on my hand to get me closer, and I bury my face into his neck. "I'm so sorry."

He holds me for a bit, and the room stays quiet, until I pull back and wipe at my eyes. "We didn't leave anyone in those buildings," I tell him and Mr. Smith. "I know I've caused hundreds of thousands of dollars in damage, but I can't begin to care."

"She's been a one-woman army in many respects," Tiberius adds, pride lacing his words.

"How did you even find them?" Mr. Smith asks, looking between Tiberius and myself.

We share a look. I'll leave this up to Tiberius. It's his power, his secret. "I don't think we should disclose that here," is the answer Tiberius settles on.

"Too much at risk to let that kind of information slip here. Too many ears," I add in. "We'll need to take you somewhere remote for that chat."

"You're going to need me to ferret out any moles," Gregory says, trying to sit up in his bed.

I put my hand lightly on his chest. "You've been in a coma for who knows how long, and I don't know if anything is even broken. But you need to rest before you start dismantling the entirety of Project Lightning."

Gregory grits his teeth. "We don't have the luxury of time right now. Henderson kept taunting about some big plans they had."

I put a little more pressure on his chest, and he lies back down. "Where we found you. They had these canisters with names on them. I think they've found others with powers that have passed away. I think they're going to try to merge the powers of the dead with the living."

"You think they disturbed graves?" Mr. Smith asks.

I nod. "When we found Gregory, he was under the church where Nostradamus is buried."

"They want someone to tell the future," Mr. Smith says, sounding horrified. Which he should be. Because if Mr. Rivers get his hands on that power, we might not be able to stop him.

And if he finds out about my other power...game over.

TWENTY-SEVEN

"I've got to get back to Lucy," Tiberius tells me in a low voice. We left Gregory a few minutes ago so the doctor could run some tests on him and also so he could get more rest. "I can take you back now," I tell him.

He nods and I grab his hand. In a blink we're standing in his living room.

"You're back," Lucy yells before she throws herself into Tiberius's arms.

He bends down and she goes up on her toes to meet him. His arms engulf her, and he holds her close to his chest. They don't say anything, as if they don't need words to communicate. It reminds me a lot of my grandparents. How I would find them some mornings in the kitchen, their arms wrapped around each other, swaying to a song only they could hear. I'd forgotten about that, and I smile at the memory.

Tiberius pulls back, but his hands don't leave Lucy. "Did you hold down the fort while I was gone?" he asks her.

"Like there was any doubt," she says, smiling up at him. "And I'm happy to report that the U.S. government was not about to scramble my technology. I was still able to track you, even in the building." She sounds totally smug, but she should be.

He steps back, dropping his arms. "Gregory's awake," he tells her.

Lucy's shoulders drop, and she looks at me. "I'm so glad."

"Yeah. But Lucy, the things they did to him…" I take a deep breath. "I don't know how he's going to come back from that."

She steps away from Tiberius and walks over to me, taking me by the hand and leading me to the couch. I sit down, and she positions herself in the corner so she can face me.

She folds her hands in her lap, and then unfolds them. Her eyes look at something over my shoulder, but I don't think she's actually looking at anything particular. But I wait, because I can sense something heavy is coming, and after witnessing Gregory's dream, I don't want to force anyone to live their own hells.

Tiberius comes and sits on the arm of the couch behind her and lays a hand on her shoulder. She takes slow, steady breaths and then finally focuses on me. "I can't speak for him, but it was almost like they forgot I was human. Or maybe they just called me experiment twenty-five to dehumanize me to themselves."

She shakes her head. "It doesn't really matter. But for them I was a human test rat. They starved me. They would lock me in a room alone for hours. They burned me. They fed me all sorts of drugs. All with the purpose to try and activate my powers after they had injected me with something to try to merge my DNA with someone who had powers."

I want to rage at the man who kidnapped her. He isolated her, he groomed her for this. She was already an orphan, but he pushed out her friends too. She was just a young, naive girl in love.

"But what I never let them know is that the day after they had changed me, my powers started emerging. I think they believed if they made life awful enough, it would be a trigger like when a person with powers' parent dies. But I wouldn't let them know it had worked. Because I was afraid they'd either kill me or grab other people off the streets like me and subject them to the same thing."

Tiberius rubs her arm gently, and she takes another deep breath. I watch her hands shake a little as she brushes her hair off her face. "I wanted to die for a while. I couldn't see a way out, and my body just couldn't handle it anymore. But I think it was when they brought in this new guy, that my mind shifted. I watched them do to him what they did to me."

She looks me dead in the eye, and I brace myself. "He didn't survive. And I decided then that I would live, and I would escape, and I would find a way to make sure this never happened again. And that's when your uncle found me."

She looks back at him and her whole face lights up, like she put aside all the horrible things that happened.

"I got sucked into his dream," I say, and she looks back at me. Tiberius's face loses all its warmth, and I experience a twinge of guilt for darkening that moment.

I squeeze my eyes shut. "He relives his time captive in his dreams."

Lucy sucks in a breath.

My hands grip the edge of the couch. "I had to sit there and watch them torture him. I tried so hard to talk him through it. It was a dream, so he knew I was there, but the fear overpowered everything. When Henderson came and got him, Gregory tried so hard to stay with me, but he couldn't do it. And when his screams started..."

Tears streak down my face, but I don't move to wipe them away. "It's already horrendous what was done to him, but now he has to relive it constantly. How can someone survive that without going insane?"

She reaches out and pries my fingers away from the couch, clasping our hands together. "For the most part, the Gregory you know is gone," she tries to tell me gently.

I try to tug my hand away, desperately wanting to cover my ears, but she holds firm. "No. You need to listen. This experience changed him. Just like your grandparents' deaths, and what we thought was Gregory's death, changed you. But we get to decide how we live now. We get to decide to take back our power. These people do not control us anymore. They do not get to take our powers from us.

"Gregory's going to need counseling, just like you will. Tony desperately needs it too. But you are all strong. I know that. I've seen it. This fight is not over. But we aren't alone anymore. It isn't you against the world. It isn't me locked in a room like a lab rat."

"It's why I've called the people here the Blessed Many." I turn at the sound of Tiberius's voice. "What we all have gone through was a nightmare. But now we can take what was given, either forcibly or from the loss of our parents, and bless those around us. Make this world better."

He's right. And I'm pretty sure those principles are what Mr. Smith believes Project Lightning was founded on.

Lucy squeezes my hand one more time and puts it back down on the couch. "Right now, we don't have the luxury of time. And that might help Gregory not to dwell on what's occurred. But someday soon, it'll need to be dealt with," she cautions me.

"I know," I tell her, rubbing my hands up and down my thighs.

She shakes her hands out. "All right. Heavy feelings pushed aside for the moment. What's the plan now?"

Tiberius stands from his spot. "I think we need to fill Mr. Smith in on my power."

"If we do that, we're going to have to tell him about me too. There's no way around it; he'll know my dad had one."

"We could tell him you don't know," Lucy offers.

I shake my head. "That won't work. Mr. Smith's power is that you can't lie to him."

"Do you trust him?" Tiberius asks me, his voice deadly serious.

Do I? I lay my head back on the couch and stare at the ceiling. "Gregory would have read his mind the minute he woke up," I say, voicing my thoughts out loud. "And if Mr. Smith was behind this at all, Gregory would have told me. He would have warned me." Plus, my mom vouched for Mr. Smith as well.

"Would he have said anything with Mr. Smith in the room?" Lucy asks.

I shake my head. "When Gregory and I touch, we can talk mind-to-mind."

Her eyes widen. "That's handy."

"Yeah, as long as I'm not wearing my earrings it is."

They both look at me with identical confused faces.

"So, there's a stone that can protect from mind reading. And this guy Dex at headquarters can enhance any stone or mineral. He took the stone called carnelian and made me earrings. When I put them in, Gregory can't read my mind."

Tiberius and Lucy share a loaded look. "What?" I ask both of them.

"This whole area is filled with carnelian," Tiberius says, arm sweeping out.

My eyebrows scrunch together. "Fordlandia?" I ask.

"Yes. They used to mine it here a long time ago," he says.

I stand and start pacing, my mind going in a million directions. "Does that mean he won't be able to read minds if he comes here?" On one hand, I think he'd like that. He talked to me once about the horrid things he would hear. But on the other, since he's had this power for so long, I wonder if it would be like losing a limb.

Tiberius rubs his chin. "No clue. If this Dex guy had to enhance the stones in your earrings, I'm not sure. But since there's such an abundance here, then maybe."

"I wouldn't worry about that now," Lucy adds in.

I take a deep breath. "Anyways, back to Mr. Smith. Gregory trusts him with his life. And even though the guy can be kind of a jerk sometimes, I think he truly believes in Project Lightning. And I can only assume he's feeling crushed right now that his mentor and friend is betraying him."

Lucy holds up a hand. "Okay, wait a minute. If you can't lie to him, then how didn't he know about this Rivers guy?"

She makes a good point, but I think I know how Rivers did it.

"Two things. Rivers's assistant is Chelsea. And with her being a null, Rivers could lie all day and Mr. Smith would never know as long as she was there. Also, there's a way to lie without lying. Like if you asked me if I like this couch. I could say it fits the room without saying I hate it."

"You hate the couch?" Lucy asks, mouth dropped open in horror.

"No," I say smacking her in the arm. "It was just an example."

She runs her hand over the cushion. "Good, because it's not easy getting furniture when you live in the Amazon jungle."

She's got a point.

"We need to tell Mr. Smith," Tiberius says, bringing us back to the subject at hand.

"When?" I ask him.

He looks at Lucy. "Tomorrow. Tonight, I want to spend with my wife."

That's my cue to leave. "All right. I'll come get you tomorrow."

I step farther away from the couch, ready to leave, but Lucy jumps up, stopping me. "Hold on. I want to put a new tracker on you just in case." She runs over to her desk.

She rushes back and has me lift my shirt. "This one is waterproof," she says while sticking it to the skin underneath my bra strap. "There. Even if they see the area, they won't pick it out with it being flesh colored."

I pull my shirt back down, and Lucy drags me in for a hug. "Be careful," she warns.

I squeeze her back and she hands me off to Tiberius, who engulfs me too. "I'm going to see you tomorrow," I say, my words muffled by his chest.

"You never know what tomorrow can bring," he says.

"Cause that's not ominous or anything," I say as I step back.

"Whatever. Go get some sleep," Lucy says, waving me away.

I step back farther and close my eyes. I probably should sleep, but there's only one place I want to be.

TWENTY-EIGHT

I pop into the room, scaring the crap out of the nurse again. "Sorry," I say, sounding sheepish. "Next time I'll do it on the other side of the door."

She's got a hand to her chest and a dirty look on her face. I slink by her and head for Gregory's bedside, where I hear his soft chuckles, which warms my heart.

"Think that's funny, huh?" I ask, sitting in the chair next to his bed.

His head turns slowly toward me. "You're going to give someone a heart attack one of these days," he tries to chastise me, but I can hear the laughter in his voice.

"Probably," I say and grab his hand.

He squeezes it and I give him a bright smile. *I can't believe you're really here. I missed you so much,* I send the thought down our link.

He stares at our joined hands. *I knew they sent those pictures to you.*

Unwarranted, the images flash in my mind, and his hand shakes in mine.

Sorry. I build walls up in my mind, only allowing him to "hear" what I want him too.

He gives me a sad smile. I don't know what to say, what to think.

When are you going to tell me how this is possible? He uses his free hand and gestures between our heads.

My dad had powers. And his was to enhance. Apparently, that's why I can transport. And why I can enhance other people's powers too.

He drops my hand and covers his face with both of his. "If they find out—" he says the words out loud.

My hands drop to his bed, and I play with the sheet between my fingers. "I know."

He drops his arms and his whole body tenses. "It would be bad."

"They won't find out." I try to stress the words.

He grabs my hand again. *I haven't told Mr. Smith any of this yet,* I let him know.

Both of his brows shoot up.

I'm going to tell him tomorrow when I bring my uncle back. Tiberius wants Mr. Smith to know what his power is. Tiberius's power is to track anyone in the world with powers.

He lets out a low whistle. *That'll be helpful.*

Yeah.

"We couldn't find you." I say the words out loud, dropping our mental link. The nurses have been giving us odd looks. "Because of Chelsea. We couldn't find you." I can hear the torment and the guilt in my voice. All those months that I could have saved him.

"Can't change the past," he says in a somber tone. "But we're going to stop this."

I hope so.

He moves around in the bed, like he's trying to get comfortable. "Tell me about things I missed. Only good things."

I look at our joined hands. Trying to wrack my brain. "Honestly? There hasn't been much good in the past several months."

His face falls, and I rush to think of something. "I, uh...oh. I made a new friend. His name is Luca." Gregory's sharp eyes lock on mine and a laugh escapes me. "Just a friend. But he's covered in teal scales."

His jaw drops, making me laugh even louder. "Yeah. Kind of crazy. Experiment gone wrong. But he's a good guy. You'll like him."

I tap my chin. "What else? Oh, I've got amazing aim with a gun now. I bet I can outshoot you."

He chuckles at that.

"How's Tony?" he asks.

"You already know," I say.

"I want to hear it from you," he says.

I debate on what to tell him. I take a deep breath. "Honestly? Not good."

He looks at me questioningly. "Can I show you?" I ask, like Robert's daughter Poppy did when we rescued her in England.

He nods, his eyes still wary. I grip his hand tightly and flood him with memories. Times on the water tower, Tony's isolation, his unwillingness to leave where we were, what happened in France, and his guilt now.

The more I show him, the more Gregory grits his teeth. His eyes narrow and his breathing picks up speed. I stop the memories and lay my palm against his cheek. He flinches at the first contact, but then turns into my palm.

"I know you're angry. I can see it. I almost feel it like it's my own. But I don't know if I blame him. If they said they had my grandpa, I'm pretty sure I would have done the same thing."

He shakes his head repeatedly. "No, you wouldn't have."

I open my mouth, but he cuts me off. "If it had been reversed, you would have gone to Tony for help."

I rub his arm. "Well, I'm glad you think that highly of me," I say ruefully.

"Trust me."

I nod. "I do."

His stare stays ahead. I can see the anger still riding him. "You've got to drop it," I tell him. "It's done with now. I think having to watch what they did to me was the worst punishment he could ever get."

"It sickens me to know that Henderson and Sariah had their hands on you."

"I know," I tell him, because I feel the same rage he does.

The door behind us opens and Mr. Smith walks into the room. If I wasn't watching his face, I would have missed the way his eyes brightened at seeing Gregory awake.

"Clear the room," Mr. Smith orders the nurses.

I forgot they were there. They hurry and put down what they're doing and rush out the door he just came through. He joins us at Gregory's bed and sits on the other side.

"How are you feeling?" he asks Gregory.

"I want to say fine, but that won't work. I'm getting better though," Gregory says.

Mr. Smith nods once. "Good. The doctor got your tests back." Gregory stiffens. "Aside from being malnourished, you've got four broken ribs and a fractured tibia."

"Really?" Gregory asks, looking genuinely surprised. "I hurt a little, but not to that extent."

My eyes volley between the two. How do they sound so calm about Gregory's injuries?

Mr. Smith makes a humming noise. "Dexter has you on some pretty potent stuff. He found a mineral to block pain receptors."

"Dex is amazing," I say in complete awe at the things he's been able to do.

"That he is," Mr. Smith says, looking directly at Gregory.

"No," Gregory says, shaking his head, and he starts moving like he's going to get out of the bed.

"What are you doing?" I ask, trying to push on his shoulders so he'll lie back down.

"I don't believe it," Gregory says, and I finally realize Mr. Smith wasn't talking about Dex; Gregory's reacting to whatever he read in Mr. Smith's mind.

"I'm sorry," Mr. Smith says, and it's the first time I've ever heard him sound...vulnerable.

"Wait a second. What's going on?" I ask, looking between the pair.

"I told him who I am," Mr. Smith says to me, still looking at his son.

"Ooooh."

Gregory does his best to scoot away from me. "You knew?" he asks, accusation heavy in his voice.

"Yes." I kinda want to lie, but there's no point. He already knows.

His eyes cut away from me, and he clenches his hands on top of the bed's sheets.

"Don't be angry with her. She just found out when she brought you here," Mr. Smith says sternly.

I cringe, because that totally sounds like a dad lecture.

Gregory keeps his face averted, so I reach out and place a hand on his arm, but he yanks it away from my touch.

I get that he's angry. I get that he just had a huge bomb dropped on him, but we don't have the luxury of time. He can't break down on me now. I *need* him.

I stand from his bedside, and make to touch him again, but I drop my hand to my side. "I'll leave you guys alone," I say.

I step back and before I can transport, Mr. Smith's voice stops me. "Where are you going?"

"To my uncle," I say.

To someone I know won't pull away from me.

Gregory lets out a low groan, but before he can say a word, I transport out of the room.

IN A BLINK I'm in front of Tony's door at headquarters. My heart is still racing, and every breath I struggle to take in is an effort to control my hurt and anger.

I can't believe Gregory pulled away from me.

I need to go to my uncle's, eventually, but I better check if Tony wants to come with me. I raise my shaky hand and knock on the wooden door.

It slowly opens, and I get a glimpse of his face. Recognition dawns and he pulls the door open all the way.

"Hey," I say, feeling somewhat awkward because aside from the talk on the water tower, we haven't been alone lately, but I need my friend. "Can I come in?"

He looks over his shoulder, and my body tenses. Is someone in here? Is he doing stuff he's not supposed to? And just those thoughts alone let me know I'm not completely over what happened in France between us.

"Uh, yeah. Mike's here too," he tells me, and now I feel dumb and like a horrible friend.

"I can come back if you want," I say, not wanting to intrude on what's going on.

"Nah, come in. It'll probably be good for Mike," he says and steps aside to let me through.

I brush past him into the room. It's set up identical to mine. Bed against one wall, empty desk in the corner, and a door off to the right for the bathroom. The walls are beige and unadorned. But neither of us have spent much time here. I've actually slept here more than Tony has. We haven't gotten a chance to put our stamp on it. Then again, we haven't really done that in Brazil either.

Mike's sitting in the chair next to the desk. His massive body practically makes it look like it belongs to a doll. I swear he just gets bigger every time I see him. His red t-shirt stretches across his shoulders and molds to his chest. As I get closer, his eyes flick between Tony and me. I don't know how much Tony's told him.

"Hey, Mike," I say as I sit down on Tony's bed.

"Becca." All right...I can't really tell if he's cool with me being here.

Tony takes a spot against the wall. No one says anything, and it's *just* starting to dip into an uncomfortable silence when I finally break first. "Guys just catching up?"

They share a look. "I kind of gave him a run-down of the past several months," Tony says, not looking me in the eye.

I cringe, because that was probably a hard conversation to have. "It hasn't been pretty," I tell Mike.

"I'll say. I thought it sucked being here," Mike says. "Not gonna lie, I was super jealous that you all were out on missions. Part of me still is, but after hearing Tony's story..." He trails off, but he doesn't need to say anything else. Only someone with a death wish would want to be repeatedly captured and tortured.

I wonder how much detail Tony gave him. And I wonder if he knows why I've been gone. Because I doubt Mr. Smith informed them of everything.

"How's it been here?" I ask.

He folds his massive arms across his chest. Did he just intentionally flex his pecs? Probably. "Honestly, boring. I got to go home for Thanksgiving and Christmas, so that was awesome. But it was really weird being home. Like I hung out with some friends, but it was hard because I couldn't tell them about what was going on in my life. I couldn't show them my power either."

I hold my hand up. "Wait, what is your power?" We never got to know, or at least I haven't seen anything because I've been gone so long.

He puffs out his chest a little. "I can manipulate shadows."

Tony and I both stare at him blankly. Mike holds up both hands. "Okay, it might sound lame, but it's not. Just watch."

He closes his eyes. Tony and I share an I've-got-no-idea-what-he-means look. But we watch him take deep breaths.

Goose bumps cover my arms as I see shadows start to slowly slither across the room. Tony pushes himself off the wall and walks closer to me. The shadows pull from the corners, from under the bed, wherever there is darkness they come. And they start to crawl over Mike. In under a minute, he's completely engulfed in darkness.

I cover my mouth with my hand. Tony starts cursing from beside me.

"Pretty cool huh?" Mike says, but his voice is distorted and eerie.

It's taking all my willpower not to run from the room screaming.

"Uh, you guys okay?" he asks, still sounding creepy, but concerned.

I stand from the bed and walk closer to the black void. With my arm outstretched I say, "It's like you disappeared."

I stop my hand just before it can break the shadow barrier. But a hand darts out and grabs mine, causing me to scream bloody murder.

The shadows instantly disperse across the room, going back to where they came from. Mike holds his hands up in surrender. "Sorry, sorry. I didn't think you'd freak out like that."

"Dude, you just vanished into a black hole. Plus, it's like you're a shadow whisperer or something," Tony says.

"It's like camouflage," I say, thinking out loud. "No wonder your ancestor with this power survived. You can hide in plain sight. Can you cover other people too? And why didn't you use this power that first time you fought Ania?"

It's probably one of my favorite memories of her. I'll never forget how Ania wiped the cocky smirk off Mike's face when he realized she would always best him in a fight.

Tony laughs from beside me. "Man, she took you down in like ten seconds."

Mike waves away the comment. "Yeah, yeah. I had no understanding of my power. But mark my words, if I had, I could have won.

"Now, I haven't tried bringing someone in the shadows with me. Been so focused on covering my whole body. For a while it would look like I was a floating head."

"Tony, go stand next to Mike and see if it'll work."

Tony's eyes shoot to mine. He starts waving his hands in the air. "What? No. How 'bout you go try?"

I look at him with my best beggar's face. "Please, I just want to see something and then I'll try."

We share a look, and I see when it dawns. I'll enhance Mike if he has to touch me to do this. And we need to see if he can do it without me.

Tony shoulders droop. "Fine," he relents and walks across the room and stands next to Mike.

The shadows converge on Mike again. Tony goes completely still except for the widening of his eyes. Mike's completely covered, but only Tony's feet have disappeared.

I lean closer but stay sitting on the bed. "Hey, Mike, try focusing on really covering both you and Tony," I instruct him.

"Okay," he says from the void.

The shadows move a smidge up Tony's legs but stop there. "Tony, try putting your hand on Mike's shoulder."

Tony looks down at the darkness and then back up at me. "Just stick your hand in there," I say, motioning to where Mike should be sitting.

"You come and stick your hand in that," Tony mutters, but I ignore it.

I look to where Tony's legs should be. "Can you still feel your feet?" I ask.

"Of course," is his response.

"Well then," I say, motioning towards, hopefully, Mike's shoulder.

He lets out a grunt of frustration and thrusts his hand into the shadows.

"Hey," Mike yells. "I'm still right here."

"Sorry," Tony mutters and I start to laugh.

"What's it feel like?" I ask both of them.

"For me," Mike starts in that odd distorted voice, "it's like being wrapped up in a blanket."

"Uh, I feel cold and like my feet are smothered," Tony adds.

I watch the shadows but nothing changes. "Hmm. Here, swap with me, Tony."

I walk towards the darkness, and even though I know it's just shadows, and I know Mike is still sitting right there, I still feel uneasy. It's almost like when you feel like there's something behind you, but every time you look, no one's there.

I stop right in front of Mike. "People always feel uneasy in the dark, on edge. Even though it feels brighter in the room, just staring at this wall of shadows makes me want to run from the room."

"Great. So now I'm creepy," Mike says, sounding completely put out.

More like intimidating, but he doesn't need to know that; his ego is already big enough. I walk to the spot Tony was, and immediately my feet disappear. "Put your hand in," Tony taunts from the bed.

I discreetly flip him off as I scratch my hair, causing him to let out a surprised laugh. Man, I've missed that sound coming from him.

I shake off the memories and slowly ease my hand into the dark. As my hand falls through, it feels like I just plunged it into freezing cold mud. Pins and needles attack my fingertips. "Crazy," I mutter to myself.

"Can still see you," Tony tells me.

I reach farther until I touch Mike's warm shoulder. I grip it tightly and close my eyes to focus as I pump enhancing energy into him.

"Holy—" Tony stutters.

"What?" Mike asks.

"She's gone." Tony's voice shakes somewhat.

I open my eyes and it's like looking through smoke. Everything is hazy and surreal. "Is it cloudy for you?" I ask Mike.

"Not really. Like I know we're shrouded in darkness, but it's clear for me. Does that make sense?"

"Yeah." Maybe because it's not my power I can't really see through it. But Mike's power could be crucial for us.

I drop his hand and step away from him. The shadows go back to where they were. "How many people know about this?" I ask him.

He tilts his head to the side. "A couple, I think."

"Does he know what's really going on?" I ask Tony.

"*He's* right here," Mike interrupts, hitting his chest.

I ignore him, keeping my gaze on Tony. "I think he knows some," Tony tells me.

Mike huffs again, and I get it. I'd be pissed too if I was in his spot. I turn towards Mike. "People are being kidnapped. Some with powers, some without. They're experimenting on these people. Doing horrid things to them. They don't even call them by their names. You need to be careful. Don't trust anyone outside Mr. Smith and us. There are traitors within Project Lightning. We just haven't found them all...yet."

Mike stares at me, not saying anything. And I wait, hoping he'll understand the gravity of this.

"Is she serious?" he asks Tony.

"Deadly."

"Is Sariah being experimented on right now?" Mike asks.

The sound of her name makes rage explode within me. I want to lash out. I want to yell. But it takes all my control to speak through gritted teeth. "Sariah's the one who kidnapped Tony. She's taken children. She's tortured people. She's made choices that you don't come back from. She chose a side, and it was the wrong one."

I take a deep breath and run an agitated hand through my hair. Time to go. "I'm going back to Tiberius's. Did you want to come or stay here?" I ask Tony.

He looks at a shell-shocked Mike. "I'll stay here."

"Okay, but I've got a gift for you from Lucy." Technically, she gave it me, but I'll be safe with her and Tiberius in Fordlandia.

I motion him towards the bathroom.

He follows me in and shuts the door. I lift up my shirt a little and this stupid smirk spreads across his face. "Really?" I say as I peel off the GPS tracker.

I shove the tracker near his face, so he'll see what it is. "Here, lift your shirt so we can hide it," I tell him, holding the skin-colored sticker.

He hesitates but lifts his shirt and it takes all my self-control not to gasp. His body is riddled with old scars. We still haven't talked about Myanmar, but this alone gives me a good idea of what happened.

I place the sticker on the underside of his arm and step back. He won't look me in the eye. I softly touch his hand and I watch his stare shift to where I'm touching. "We're all covered in scars, either hidden or visible. You are far from alone."

He nods, still not looking at me.

I want to hug him, but I don't. "I'll be back in a couple hours," I tell him. I step back and in a blink I'm back in Fordlandia.

TWENTY-NINE

The sun spills in through the slats in the blinds, taking me out of a dreamless sleep. But that's fine. The last few dreams I've had have left me dreading falling asleep. Still, I wouldn't mind some direction from Mom or whoever this dream walker guy is. I wonder, though, if it's time to tell the others about this. It feels like ages since Ania told me to keep it secret. Who knows if anyone would believe me? I think Tiberius and Lucy would, but the rest might think it's all in my mind.

I swing my legs out of bed and let the quiet of the house settle within me. There's a peace I've felt in Fordlandia that I haven't felt since my grandparents' house.

Voices call out in greeting from the street outside the window. Guess that's my cue to get a move on. I only talked to Tiberius for a few moments last night when I got here. One look at my face and he knew something was up. I briefly told him about Gregory, but by that point I just wanted to sleep.

I know I need to get back to headquarters. I know we need to plan. There's so much to figure out. But I keep seeing Gregory's face in my mind. I keep feeling his anger like a tangible thing. What am I going to see when I go back? And are we going to tell Mr. Smith about my other power? Are we going to tell him about Tiberius's?

I rub my hands over my face. I'm seventeen, but I swear I'm going to develop an ulcer soon from all this stress.

I walk into the empty kitchen. At least everything in the fridge is still fresh. I'm pulling out a chair when there's an urgent knock at the front door.

I rush over and quickly open it. A calm Tiberius and a haggard-looking Lucy stand there. "Why aren't you wearing your tracker?" is her way of greeting me.

"Oh. Sorry. I gave it to Tony last night. He wanted to stay at headquarters, and since I was coming back here, I thought it'd be better if he had it."

Lucy takes a steadying breath. "Okay, next time give me a heads-up."

Tiberius wraps his arm around her. "I told her you were here, so I'm not sure why she was so worried," he says to me.

"Sorry," I say again. I step back. "Why don't you guys come in? We need to talk anyways."

They follow me into the kitchen, and we all sit around my small table. "What's the plan?" I ask.

"We've got to go back," Tiberius tells me.

"Are you coming with us?" I ask Lucy.

She shakes her head. "I have to stay. They need me here. And all my equipment is here as well. It's too dangerous for me to be anywhere else right now."

I nod. I get it. Plus, the government doesn't know about her. And Mr. Smith doesn't know about her either. It's better if she remains anonymous.

"Are we going to tell him about this place?" I ask them, gesturing around.

They share a look, one born of being in a relationship for many years. "I think we need to wait on that. So far there's no reason for them to know about it," Tiberius says.

"What about for protection?" I ask. If Tiberius and I aren't here, I don't know if there are enough people to fight.

"Do we need it?" Tiberius asks, like he's probing if I know more.

"When we were in France, they kept asking me what happened to all the people we rescued. What if they come looking for them?"

"They'll have a hard time finding us," Lucy says smugly.

I lean closer to her. "I never thought I'd be captured," I say. "Look how well that turned out."

Lucy casts her eyes down and Tiberius lays his hand on top of hers. "I think it'd be a good idea to put some things into place. Like plans in case of attack," Tiberius says.

"I know most everyone here is terrified of these powers thrust on them, but what if Luca starts helping them work on them?" I suggest. "He's been wanting to help. Let's see if he'll do this."

"That might be a good idea," he concedes.

We're all lost in thought, realizing that we essentially need to prepare to defend Fordlandia. Because there's this sick feeling inside me, and if I had the gift of premonition, I might think it was seeing the future. But my gut is telling me Fordlandia is not going to stay the safe haven that we need.

AS I WALK DOWN the front path, a voice calls out my name. Luca comes rushing over. "Becca," he says in his thick Italian accent. "I didn't know you were back."

I smile, glad to see him. "Only for a bit, and then I'm gone again."

"Ah," he says, but his disappointment is visible.

I know he feels he owes me for finding him in that cage, but there's no need. "There's so much going on. I've got to get back to the U.S. We need to find a way to stop all of this, and I think we might have the ally we need. But there's something I need from you."

"*Si*," he says without even hesitating.

"I need you to help train these people to use their powers. Lucy will be here, and she can help too. But I really think we need to be prepared. And I think the best way to do that is for everyone to work on these powers they have now. Not just on how to control them, but how to manipulate them as well. Can you help with that?"

I hold my breath and study his face. It's hard to read him with his reptile features.

He stands a little taller and nods once. "*Si*. I think I can do that. I want to help."

"Good. Lucy will help you more with this." That takes some immense pressure off me. "I'm headed over to my uncle's."

"I am as well. I promised Eloise we would have a tea party." He says it in all seriousness, but I can't stop the smirk on my face.

We walk side by side until we reach their front door. I knock, and the excited sounds of a little girl rushing to the front door is what greets us. She rips it open and flashes Luca her blinding smile.

"Hey, Eloise," I say.

Her happy stare leaves Luca and focuses on me, suddenly becoming a little shy. I wish I could have spent more time with her. Hopefully soon. No, strike that; definitely soon.

We walk into the house and Eloise wraps herself around one of Luca's legs. He smiles down at her and then picks her up. "Where is this tea party?" he asks, and she points towards the room she's staying in.

I walk farther in, towards the voices in Lucy's little techno lair.

"All set?" I ask Tiberius.

"Yes—" he starts, but Lucy pushes herself in front of him, waving a GPS patch in the air.

"Here, we're putting this on you now. And this time"—she gives me a reproachful look—"don't take it off."

"Yes, ma'am."

I follow her into the kitchen, and she places it on my back in a concealed spot. "How much are we going to tell Mr. Smith?" I ask Tiberius as Lucy attaches it.

"We'll tell him about my power. And we need to tell him about yours. But I'm afraid to tell him at headquarters. I may be a bit paranoid, but I think you need to take him out of there so we can inform him."

Lucy fixes my shirt and we walk out of the kitchen towards Tiberius. "I agree."

"Let's wait on telling him about here. And I know you might not agree, but it's for the best," Tiberius says.

"Deal."

He gives Lucy a long hug and an even longer kiss. He decided it might not be super convenient to keep coming back here every night —which I know is going to suck, but I can bring him back any time he wants.

He steps away and Lucy rushes over, giving me a quick hug. "You need to be more careful. You're starting to give me gray hair." We both laugh at that, but I can feel in her stare that, for her, I need to be more careful and more aware.

I grab Tiberius's hand, give Lucy a wave, and, in a blink, we're standing in front of Mr. Smith's door. I lift my hand and knock three times. The door opens immediately, Xavier standing on the other side. Raven sits in a chair in front of Mr. Smith's desk. And the man himself slowly stands from his seat when he sees who's come knocking.

We step into the room. "We've got a lot to tell you," I say, getting to the point right away. "But it can't be here."

Mr. Smith's brow raises at that.

"Will you let us take you somewhere?" I ask, and maybe I didn't realize it initially, but now I see how much I'm asking him to trust me.

Mr. Smith looks between the two of us. I know we're asking a lot. I know we're also asking him to leave Gregory here. But this is too important to risk being overheard.

"I think it would be a good thing for Raven and Xavier to accompany us as well," Tiberius says.

Mr. Smith strokes his chin. "All right. Where are we going?" he asks.

I think for a moment, trying to pick somewhere we can go. And it comes. "Some place safe, but we're going to need coats."

THIRTY

"You know, I love the beach and all, but being at one in Connecticut during the winter isn't that fun," Xavier says, his hands shoved in his coat pockets.

The cold sea breeze fills my lungs, but I love it. Spring is in full swing in Brazil, and the humidity has been killing me lately. The last time I was here, it was in a dream with my mom. Thankfully for us, no one is really hanging out at the beach this time of year.

"We're here, and we're freezing," Mr. Smith says as a way for me to get talking.

I turn from watching the waves crash against the rock pier. "Tiberius?"

Tiberius steps closer to me, most likely for body heat. "I wanted to tell you what my power is," he tells him.

Raven and Mr. Smith stare at him, eyes somewhat wide.

"I can find anyone in the world with powers," he tells them.

I'm watching Mr. Smith carefully, so I don't miss the widening of his eyes before he completely schools his features.

"I either have to know the person or have met them before,

though it also works if I walk by someone. But with Becca now…" He trails off, giving me the chance to fill in.

Everyone turns to look at me. "Did you know my dad had powers?" I ask Mr. Smith.

He shakes his head, his brow furrowing at the seemingly impossible question. "That can't be. There's no way. I would have known. Someone at Project Lightning would have figured it out."

Well, my mom did, but I don't think I'm going to bring that up now.

"He wore special gloves after the accident," Tiberius says, reminding him of the fire that burned my dad's hands. "They would have blocked any chance of you feeling the zap."

Mr. Smith shakes his head and takes an unconscious step back. "But I knew him before that all took place," he says.

Tiberius steps closer. "It was soon after the fire that our mom died. Neither of us knew the other existed, never mind that we would inherit powers."

"And when my dad died, before I was born, I inherited his," I tell the group.

"But we would have known. Someone would have known." The denial is thick in Mr. Smith's voice, even though he *knows* I'm not lying. It's a hard pill to swallow.

"I've always excelled, whether in sports or academics. I never thought anything of it. Then I met Tiberius for the first time, and he dropped a huge bomb in my lap. When I learned my dad's power is to enhance, it all made sense. It's why I can transport instead of just running really fast like my mom."

Raven lifts a hand, halting my words. "That time in the stairwell in Myanmar with the rats—that was you, wasn't it?" She may ask the question for everyone else, but she seems to already know the answer.

"Yes, that was one of the first times I ever tried to actually use it."

Mr. Smith turns around and faces the sea, giving us his back. We all watch him tilt his head to the side and place his hands on his hips.

"What other things have you been able to do?" Xavier asks me.

I tear my eyes away from Mr. Smith's back. "I helped you see farther into the past," I tell him. He sucks in a sharp breath. "Tony can now see through walls with my help." Raven's jaw drops. "I've been able to help countless ways. Just, whatever a power is, I can help it do more."

"You must understand how important it is to keep this quiet," Tiberius implores the group. "If Rivers finds out about what she can do, he'll never stop hunting her. Her life will be forfeit."

Everyone looks at me, like it's really just dawning on them how perfect of a weapon I really am. I've tried not to think about it too much.

Mr. Smith turns back to us, his face set in stone. "I won't let that happen," he says, full of conviction. "I won't let him take any of you again."

I'm glad he feels that way, but we've moved past what we *want* to do and now we need to focus on what we *have* to do. "We need a game plan, because he won't stop until we make him," I say to the group. "And I know he was your mentor, but that can't matter anymore. Especially with what was done to Gregory."

His whole body stiffens. I know that was a low blow, but now knowing that Gregory is his son, I expect so much more out of him. I don't know what it's like to have a kid, but I think if my dad was still alive, he would do anything to keep me safe. I'd bet he'd lay down his life for me. I know Grandpa did that for me. And I hope one day I can do something like that for my kids.

"What we need is more intel," Mr. Smith addresses us. He stands taller, and I can see him shift back into the role of director of Project Lightning. "The more information we can gather, the better. With Gregory awake, hopefully he'll be a wealth of knowledge. Tiberius, can you track Rivers now and tell us where he is?"

Tiberius nods. "With Becca's help, yes, but if Chelsea is with him, I won't be able to find him."

"Give it a try," Mr. Smith orders.

Tiberius grabs my hand and I think of Mr. Rivers. I picture the way he resembled a typical grandfather. His wrinkled hands, the cane he carries, his sweater vests, everything he used as a ruse to fool the rest of us.

Tiberius's grip tightens and I keep pumping enhancing power into him, hoping we caught Mr. Rivers alone this time. After a minute or so, I watch his shoulders fall.

"Unless he died suddenly, he's with Chelsea."

Xavier curses and kicks at the ground.

"Damn it," Mr. Smith mutters.

"We'll keep trying," Tiberius assures him and everyone else. "In the meantime, we might want to start searching for those who've helped him aside from Chelsea, Sariah, and Henderson."

"Daemon," Raven says.

"The fire guy?" I ask. "What's going on between you two? Because the last time we saw him, he was shooting a fireball at us outside of D.C."

She lifts helpless eyes to Mr. Smith. But he stays silent. "He was recruited the same time I was," she finally tells us. "He left Project Lightning around five years ago. Myanmar was the first time I've seen him since."

An arctic gust of wind slams into us. "We need to hurry this along before we all freeze to death," Xavier says, his teeth chattering.

I want to know more about this Daemon guy, because there's a connection there and I wonder if Raven can use it to get him onto our side. But I'm thinking I'll have to wait to get her alone to talk about him.

"First off, no one talk about Becca's other power, her father, or Tiberius being her uncle," Mr. Smith says, laying down the law. "Secondly, we need to talk with Gregory about things. He's our best shot at finding out what's going on. I'll do a sweep of his room and make sure it's secure.

"Tiberius, I want you and Becca to keep searching for Mr. Rivers. Let's plan on meeting again in two days, but next time how about a little bit of a warmer place?"

We all nod, and I'm ready to do whatever. Because this needs to end. "Everyone grab on," I say and put my hands out. They all grab on and I close my eyes, picturing Mr. Smith's office.

I HAVEN'T SEEN Gregory in two days. And it's not for a lack of trying. But I was told not to transport into the room. Every time I've gone to see Gregory, Mike has had to tell me, awkwardly, that he doesn't want to see me. I've had enough, and when I go to visit him in an hour, he better see me or I'm not giving him the option.

I walk to Dex's laboratory, curious as to what he's up to today. Yesterday he was going on and on about quartz and how it could be used to heal. I just sat at a table, desperately trying to have him distract me, but it was hopeless. Tiberius and I have tried finding Mr. Rivers, but Chelsea hasn't left him. So instead of following along with how clear quartz is better than rose quartz, I kept trying to think about where Rivers is and what his next move could be.

My thoughts stray there now too. It's taking over my every waking thought and my sleep too. I reach Dex's door and lift a hand to knock, but the sound of voices stays my hand. *Maybe I should come back.* The voices rise in irritation, so I press my ear to the crack in the double doors like a five-year-old.

"That's just not possible," Dex says, completely exasperated. "I'm pretty sure it goes against the laws of nature."

Against the laws of nature? What *are* they talking about?

"But this is what you do." It feels like everything stops at the sound of that voice, like the world quits turning.

I shove the doors open, not caring anymore that I'm interrupting. Dex sees me first, his cheeks turning a bright red. But I only give him a cursory glance, because my glare is centered on Gregory leaning against one of the worktables. "Can't talk to me for *one minute*, but you'll drag yourself all the way down here? How nice."

He finally looks at me. It's obvious he's in pain even if he's trying to hide it. Does Dex not see the sweat beading across Gregory's forehead, or the way his brows are scrunched? I don't even know how he's supporting himself on that table. The guy has broken ribs and if he isn't careful, he could puncture a lung. What is he doing out of the infirmary? And what is he doing here?

"You should be in bed." I scold him like he's a kid. Did no one say anything when he got up and left?

"I'm not asking for your help," he tells me, his voice short of breath.

Dex makes his way towards the door like he can't get there fast enough. "I'll just...be back in a minute," he says and then bolts.

"What is wrong with you?" I ask Gregory.

"Nothing," he says, looking anywhere but at me.

"Bull," I spit out.

He runs a shaky hand through his hair. "Can we not do this right now? I'm tired."

"Too bad."

He finally looks at me. "What?"

I throw my arms up in the air. "You heard me. And too bad. I'm not letting you hide behind some guards who, newsflash, can't actually keep me out of there. I want to know what your problem is. I want to know why you refuse to see me. What changed? Why are you acting like a jerk? I know it's not because of Mr. Smith."

He shuffles a few feet over to a chair and slowly lowers himself into it. His face pulls in a grimace. And part of me, a teeny tiny part, feels bad for pushing him right now, but he needs to answer my questions.

"You should have told me." The words rush out guttural, either from the pain or anger. Probably both.

"When? During the time you were in a coma? Or when you and I shared a dream?" He shudders at the mention of his dream, but I press on. "Or how about the fact that he asked me not to tell you? He asked me so he could be the one to tell you. It wasn't my place."

"It damn well was!" He swipes an arm out, knocking test tubes to the floor. I jump back from the shattered glass aimed my way. Poor Dex. I hope that wasn't important.

"What are you actually mad about?" I try to keep my voice neutral, but it's a strain.

He pounds a fist into the table. "I can't do this with you."

My heart rate speeds up and fear dances up my spine. "Do what?" I ask cautiously.

"We were never supposed to be together in the first place."

I walk over and get right into his space. "Don't. You. Dare. You *do not* get to make that decision now, after everything."

He puts a hand up in a helpless gesture, but I knock it down. "You don't get to be a coward now."

All the anger rushes out as fast as it came. His shoulders curve in and everything else about him seems to deflate. "I've changed, Becca. I'm not the same guy I was before."

"And you think I'm the same? You think I didn't change when I saw my grandparents murdered? How about when I rescued those people? Or when I was tortured? Do you think it didn't affect me watching what Henderson did to you? Well, guess what. Neither of us are the same. Now we need each other more than ever. And considering that both our parents broke the rules, I don't care about them at all."

"What is that supposed to mean?"

I grab him, and before he can protest and before I back out, I transport us straight into the packed cafeteria.

A room full of voices hit me right away. Gregory looks around, face scrunched up. "What are you—"

I cut him off by grabbing him by the shirt, going up on my toes, and pressing my lips against his. For a second he doesn't react and my stomach bottoms out. The noise in the cafeteria has completely vanished and I can feel my face flaming. But after only a brief hesitation, he kisses me back.

He threads his hands through the hair at the nape of my neck. I grab onto his shoulders, looking for better purchase. His lips move against mine and my heart for the first time in months feels light and free.

I fall back down onto flat feet and he leans his forehead against mine.

This is what we need. When are you going to realize we're better together than apart? I let my mind whisper the question. Hoping it can convey everything I can't say in words.

I don't want to disappoint you. I'm broken, Becca.

We're all broken. We just need to find the right people to help piece us back together.

We stand there, breathing each other in, but a tap on my shoulder breaks the spell. "So, that was quite the show. But, uh, Gregory, you're looking kind of pale," Xavier says to us.

Gregory lets out a strained laugh. "Got to shake things up now and again."

"Well, they're all definitely intrigued," Xavier says motioning around.

I peek around Gregory's shoulder, and sure enough there are plenty of jaws on the floor. Probably because not all of them knew I could transport, not to mention the whole non-fraternization rule we're supposed to abide by.

I feel Gregory sway a little. I pull back so I can look at his face. Xavier's right; we need to get Gregory back to his bed now. "Let's get you back to the infirmary," I tell him.

He nods and I close my eyes, picturing his temporary room for the past several days.

"HEARD you put on a bit of a show in the cafeteria," are the first words out of Mr. Smith's mouth when he sees us.

Man, news travels fast around here. We've only been back in the infirmary for like five minutes. "I'm not going to apologize," Gregory tells him, and I kind of want to high five him, but that might be a little inappropriate right now.

Gregory laughs lightly beside me.

"We've got a lot of bigger things going on right now other than your relationship. I want to talk about Mr. Rivers."

Gregory lets out a strained breath.

"It's time," Mr. Smith says in a gentle tone.

I gently push Gregory back so he's lying in his bed, hoping he'll at least relax.

Gregory runs his hands over his face. He doesn't want to tell us, but what if he could show us? "If I help, do you think you could show us your memories?"

That makes both men pause. Usually it's others showing Gregory, but why wouldn't it work the other way around? "It might be easier for you. And I think it'll let us know a heck of a lot more," I tell him.

Aside from his one dream, we haven't done anything like this. He grabs one of my hands and I grab one of Mr. Smith's. "How should we do this?" Gregory asks.

I squeeze his hand and offer him a small smile. "Just picture it in your mind like a movie you want to show us. And hopefully I'll be able to let us view it," I tell him.

"You're going to see things I wish you hadn't," he warns.

I give him a small smile. "You hear things all the time that I wish *you* hadn't."

He smirks. "I suppose so."

I turn to Mr. Smith. "Close your eyes. I don't know why, but it helps."

THIRTY-ONE

We're in the room underneath the church, where we found Gregory in France. But instead of Gregory being in a coma, he's awake and strapped to the bed I found him in.

Footsteps slowly walk closer to his body. "You know, Mr. Smith always talks like you're going to be his successor, but I just can't see it." Rivers bends down so he's eye-level with Gregory. "Maybe it's because you screamed a lot quicker than I thought you would."

Gregory spits into Rivers's face, and that earns him a powerful slap across the face. "That was not very nice," Rivers says while he takes a handkerchief out of his pocket and wipes his cheek.

It's weird being in Gregory's mind like this. It's like watching a movie, but also being inside of it too. But it's nothing like the dream of his I stumbled into.

Mr. Rivers sits down on the edge of the bed Gregory's strapped to, acting like he's getting ready to have a pleasant conversation. "You know, I thought Becca would have found you by now. Maybe she just didn't care enough about you. Or maybe she's with Tony instead."

His hands stay perched on top of his cane. His face is the perfect mask of concern, but his eyes show the malice lurking underneath, and that's something we've all missed. "Are you okay with her moving on? I don't think I would have appreciated my sweetheart forgetting me so quickly. Would make me think there wasn't much there to begin with."

Gregory grits his teeth, but he doesn't utter a word.

"I don't really need you to talk right now. But you better listen. Because I'm going to find Becca, and when I do, she'll be one of my prize experiments. I'll keep her alive, but I will take whatever I need from her body. She'll feel pain, she'll be in agony, and she'll be alone. But I'll let her know you led me right to her. She'll get to keep that memory until she dies."

The images Gregory's showing us shift, and soon we're watching Chelsea talk with Sariah.

"Any luck bringing me more kids?" Chelsea asks.

Gregory watches the two from his bed across the room.

Sariah's face pinches in disgust. "Yes." She practically spits the word out.

"And where is the child?" Chelsea asks, looking down at her tablet.

"She's in the other room with her parents."

Chelsea's head snaps up. "You took a family? What is wrong with you? I told you children. We don't need any adults."

Sariah runs an agitated hand through her hair. "Doesn't matter now, we have all three."

"Well then, take care of the parents. We don't need them." She says it so nonchalantly, like it isn't a big deal to go ahead and kill someone.

Sariah starts shaking her head and backing up with her hands in the air. "No. I'm drawing a line. You want that done, then you need someone else to do it."

"Fine. Henderson won't care."

Eloise's face comes into view as she and her parents are dragged into the room. Tears are streaming down her face as she clings to her *mother's leg. Her mom keeps trying to say things to her in a soothing voice, but Eloise just grabs on to her mom's leg tighter, screaming in denial.*

Gregory and Eloise watch what becomes of her parents. And my heart shatters. How does she go on from this? How do any of us?

The scene shifts again, and Gregory is being dragged down the hallway I saw in his dream. But this time must be one of the firsts, because he's fighting back. Only he's not strong enough when Henderson multiplies. The scarred wooden door looms ahead, and I can't take anymore.

I break the connection, dropping both of their hands. I stand up and pace the room, trying to calm my nauseated stomach.

"That's not the man I know," Mr. Smith says, his voice hardly above a whisper.

"Yeah, well, that man is pure evil," I say, still pacing back and forth.

"He wants *you*, Becca," Gregory practically growls.

"It doesn't matter that all he knows right now is that I can do more with my power than I should be able to. He can't have me." I hold my hand up, halting whatever is going to come out of his mouth. "They caught me once, but not for long. I got rescued from that. We both did. We have more information now, and we don't go against them with such small numbers again. And no more playing the martyr."

"Who was a martyr?" Mr. Smith asks.

I point at Gregory. "Pretty sure that's what happened in Myanmar."

Mr. Smith's face snaps towards Gregory. "He told me that if I didn't come with him right then, he would shoot everyone in the room," Gregory says, leaning towards me.

I plant my hands on my hips. "Obviously, that was a lie."

"You didn't have to see the plans in his mind. I did," he says pointing at his head.

"It's the same thing I told Tony. You aren't alone in this. You're part of a team. We start going off alone and we're all going to die. You need to trust us."

Mr. Smith raises his brow at that and makes a *tsking* sound.

"What?" I ask him, completely annoyed.

He straightens the sleeves of his suit jacket. "Nothing. Just the way I heard it, you were doing some vigilante activities in relation to those labs you all found."

I avert my eyes. "Yeah, well, I've got my head on straight now," I say and Gregory scoffs, but I ignore it.

"Good to know," Mr. Smith says.

"So now what?" I ask, not wanting to fight with Gregory anymore.

Mr. Smith stands from his chair. "I need to speak with Tony about his time in Myanmar. We need to visit this location in France again, see if it's still active. I'm assuming not. Gregory, I want you to try to list all the people that were working *for* Mr. Rivers. Sound good?"

We both nod.

"Excellent. Be at my office tomorrow at noon," Mr. Smith says as he moves away from the chair.

We watch him leave the room and then I'm walking over to Gregory and sitting on his bed next to him. "I don't know if I can ever watch you go into that place again," I tell him.

He wraps his arms around me, and I carefully burrow my face into his chest. "I don't really like reliving those memories either."

I tilt my head back so I can look into his eyes. "We're both going to need serious help. You know that, right?"

He lets out a puff of air. "Let's just see if we survive the next week, and then we can figure that all out."

"It's a plan," I promise him.

We stay in each other's arms for a while, letting the warmth of our bodies settle us somewhat. "We saved Eloise," I tell him, remembering that bit.

He pulls back and looks at me. "You did?"

"Yeah. We found her in a cage in Spain. Xavier saw everything that happened to her and her parents."

"Is she okay?" he asks.

I shrug. "As okay as she can be." I debate for only a second, but he's probably already seen the thought flash through my mind. "Do you want to see her? I can take you there."

He takes a step back, keeping his hands clasped to my arms. "Can I?"

"Yeah. Let's just double check with Tiberius. Make sure he thinks it'll be okay."

I grab Gregory's hand, and in a blink we're in front of Tiberius's door at Project Lightning. Gregory places a hand on the wall.

"Sorry. It takes a bit to get used to."

He shakes his head like he's trying to clear fog. I raise a hand and knock on the door. It takes a few moments, but Tiberius opens it. "Can we come in?" I ask.

He looks between Gregory and me. "Of course," he says and steps out of the way.

We walk in the room and I wait for Tiberius to close the door.

"What's going on?" Tiberius asks.

"He was there when everything happened to Eloise, and he wanted to check on her. And I thought I'd introduce him to Lucy," I tell him.

Tiberius looks between the two of us. "And we can trust him?" He looks over at Gregory. "I'm sorry, but this is no small thing."

"I get it," Gregory says. "I can see in your thoughts that you're unsure about me."

Tiberius's face loses some of its color.

"Sorry, I can't help reading your mind. And I know you don't know me, but Becca does, and I wouldn't do anything to harm her or her family."

They stare at one another, not saying a word out loud but having a conversation with their eyes and whatever he's saying in his mind for Gregory. "Then let's get going," Tiberius says.

I give him a small smile and grab his hand and Gregory's. In a blink, we're back in Fordlandia.

THIRTY-TWO

Gregory stumbles to the side and clutches his head the moment we appear in Fordlandia. "Are you okay?" I ask, reaching out a hand to steady him.

He crouches low to the ground. "Where are we?" he asks, his head tucked down towards his chest.

I get down next to him and rub a hand up and down his back. "We're in Brazil. Basically in the middle of the Amazon jungle," I tell him. "What's going on?"

He grips his head. "It's all gone."

I look up at Tiberius, hoping he might have a clue, but he just shrugs his shoulders, not understanding. "What's gone?" I ask Gregory.

"The voices," he mutters to himself.

Out of the corner of my eye I see Tiberius come a little closer. "Ahh. Our small town happens to be built on an area filled with carnelian," Tiberius says.

"Like the stones in your earrings?" Gregory asks me, still sounding pained.

I want to smack myself in the head. I forgot. "Yeah. Are you going to be okay?" I ask, still hovering next to him.

"It feels like when I was with Chelsea." He looks tortured, and I hate that the first time he's here it's making him think of his time in France.

I look down at the dirt road underneath our feet. In a way, I get it. Not being able to transport was like losing a limb. It was agonizing being stuck in that room, but I was only there for a day. He was a pris-oner for months.

I stay crouched with him, watching him take deep breaths. "I'm okay," he says. "It's just the loss took me by surprise. And it...yeah..." He shakes his head.

He starts to stand, and I move away to let him. I grab his hand. *Can you hear me still?*

His whole body relaxes, and he squeezes my hand. *Yeah. Guess we'll just have to be touching to talk mind-to-mind.*

"Let's go see if Lucy's at the house," Tiberius says.

I nod, and I watch Gregory's face as he finally looks at where we are. "Whoa," he says, staggering back a step.

I look around at our little village, smiling. "It's not as scary as it seems, I promise. I know it looks abandoned, but look closer and you'll see it's not," I tell him.

He turns in a slow circle, taking everything in. I wonder if he sees what I saw the first time I came here: buildings being reclaimed by the jungle, kids running in the tall grasses, people moving the curtains in their homes. "When I first came here, I thought it looked like a dystopian movie from the fifties."

"I can totally see that," Gregory says, looking up at the water tower.

"That was Tony's spot," I say, gesturing towards the tower. "It's a great spot to see everything that's going on."

He turns his back on the water tower. "When are we going to talk about him and everything that's happened?"

I'm pretty sure I see Tiberius wince. "Soon, but right now I've got some people for you to meet."

Tiberius leads the way and we follow behind him. "How many people live here?" Gregory asks, waving back to a man sitting on his front step.

Tiberius tilts his head like he's counting in his mind. "I think around forty-five."

Wow, I didn't even know that. "And you've rescued all these people?" Gregory asks in awe.

"Just about. Some of the really little ones were actually born here."

"Wow. Do you think their parents' powers were passed down in their DNA?" Gregory asks.

That makes Tiberius pause. We've never talked about that, but if that parents' DNA is changed, then maybe? "I'm not sure. We could probably run blood tests, but not only do we not have access to that here, I don't really want to put these people through anything else."

We keep walking down the dusty road until we reach Tiberius's home. He walks through the front door and we follow close behind.

"Lucy," he calls out.

We head for her work area, but she rushes around the corner and wraps her arms around Tiberius.

"You know you saw him yesterday," I say, laughing.

She peers around Tiberius's shoulder. "I don't care."

I laugh, but it's cut off when I watch her zero in on Gregory.

"Lucy, I'd like you to meet Gregory. Gregory, this is my Aunt Lucy."

She steps forward and holds out her hand. He shakes it and I swear he's blushing. He steps back and I lean into him. "Power working?" I whisper.

"Yup," he says, eyes avoiding my aunt.

"Heads up, Lucy. He can read minds," I tell her.

"Can you hear us now?" Tiberius asks.

Gregory tilts his head to the side, like he's trying to hear better. "A little, but it's like a bad phone connection. When she shook my hand, it was clear."

"Good to know," Tiberius says.

The sound of quick footsteps has us all turning. Eloise runs into the room, a huge smile spreading across her face as she sees Tiberius standing with Lucy still wrapped around him. She runs towards him but stops abruptly when her gaze catches Gregory. She rubs her eyes, almost like she can't believe it.

Gregory steps away from me and closer to Eloise.

"Hi, Eloise," he says to her softly.

She keeps looking between him and Lucy. She points toward me and then to herself. "Yeah, I saved him like you," I tell her, hoping that's what she's asking.

She grabs Gregory's hand. And his face pales. He reaches behind and grabs mine.

I'm so sorry they did that to you and your parents, Gregory says to Eloise.

Her mouth forms a perfect o.

"It's okay," I tell her. "This is his power."

We can talk this way if you want, he tells her.

Tears fall and splash against her chubby cheeks.

I miss Mama and Papa, she says, and the sadness laced in those words creates a tightness in my throat.

I know, sweetheart. I miss my mom and dad too. But I think they're always with you, even if you can't see them or hear them. You can always talk to them. Even if they can't respond, I know they're listening, he tells her.

Did you get the bad man? she asks.

He takes a deep breath. Neither of us want to worry her, but she needs the truth. Who knows what can happen if we don't end this soon?

Not yet, he tells her, and her body starts to tremble. *But we will, and soon,* he tells her with the most conviction I've ever heard from him.

She stares into his eyes, taking his measure, it seems. I guess she believes him, because she wraps her arms around him. I drop his hand and walk over to my aunt and uncle, leaving those two to have some alone time. "She talked to him mind-to-mind."

Lucy puts a hand to her chest and takes a deep breath. "That's wonderful," she says.

"He was there." I lean closer to them and drop my voice. "When her parents were killed. I don't think she got a good look at him though, because Xavier didn't see that in her memories."

"But they have a connection, and that's important," Tiberius says.

"Yeah, though, an unfortunate one," I reply.

Tiberius's eyes stay focused on the two of them. "Lucy and I met under horrible conditions. You met Luca when he was locked in a cage and unwilling to come out. These relationships will be the ones that will last, because no one else will ever understand."

I turn and watch Gregory and Eloise. She's smiling up at Gregory. I don't know if they're still able to talk without me holding his hand, but it doesn't matter. Eloise found another hero outside of Luca. Speaking of him—"Is Luca at home?" I ask.

Tiberius closes his eyes. "He's at the range right now with Dante. Probably helping him learn to handle a gun."

"We'll head over there. I want to introduce him to Gregory."

I hate to break up their conversation, but we're on limited time here. And I need to pick his brain on the walk to Luca. And I *have* to walk. Transporting and firearms do not mix.

"Hey, Gregory. There's someplace I need to take you," I tell him, leaving out Luca's name so Eloise doesn't beg to come with us.

He looks at me and nods, and then he turns back to Eloise and cups her face. Whatever he says makes her give him a sweet smile in return.

We walk out the door and I give his arm a nudge. "What?" he asks, looking genuinely confused.

"Doesn't matter the age, all the girls are charmed by you."

He lets out a loud, surprised laugh.

"It's totally true," I tell him.

"She's a cute kid," he says, still chuckling. "Where are we off to anyway?"

"I want you to meet Luca," I say, stepping back onto the main road.

He looks at me and lets out a huff of air.

"Sucks not being able to read my mind, huh?" I ask.

"Sorry. I know you hate it, and that's why we got you the earrings, and why I was trying to find ways for you to block—"

I grab his hand in mine. "I get it. Your power was suppressed for months, and you've only just gotten it back. Then we come here...I get it. And right now, I'm not mad. But that doesn't mean I'm not going to put those earrings back in."

He squeezes my hand and gives me a grateful smile. "Tell me about Luca."

I tell him all about finding him in Rome, what his power is, and what to expect when he meets him. And I also tell him what happens when I enhance his power.

"They just left him there? In a cage?"

"I don't think they expected him to permanently have the scales. I'm pretty sure he would have died in there if we hadn't found him."

We turn down a street on our left and I point out the gun range in the distance. "I can't hear anything," Gregory says.

"All of the guns have suppressors. Even though Lucy basically has us hidden from satellites and most of the world, it wouldn't do us any good if people start reporting sounds of gunfire."

We get closer, and I watch from a distance as Luca works with Dante. I don't approach yet. I want Gregory to get used to the sight of Luca, and I also want to wait until Dante puts the gun down.

I lean close to Gregory and gesture to Luca. "The kids used to run screaming from him, but now they flock to him. He's a good guy. I told him that everyone just needed to get used to him, and they have."

Gregory looks around. "You've built a sanctuary here."

"Oh, I haven't done anything," I say, waving away what he's said.

"This was all Tiberius and Lucy's doing. They gave me a place to go when I lost everything. Helping these people with them, it gave me purpose when I had none."

He grabs me and pulls me close. "I'm glad you had that," he says and then kisses the top of my head.

"Becca?" Luca calls out walking, over to us.

"Hey," I say, stepping out of Gregory's arms, but keeping a hold of his hand.

Luca and Gregory have a little stare-off. Is this a normal guy thing?

Gregory leans down near my ear. "No, it's just he's been able to be here for you when I haven't been. And I think he's making sure you're okay," he whispers to me.

"Good to know," I whisper back. "Anyways, Luca, I wanted to introduce you to Gregory."

They shake hands, and I'm so happy that Gregory doesn't stare. "Holding down the fort?" I ask Luca.

He gives me a small smile. "Trying."

"Good. How's it going with working on your powers?" I ask him.

"It's hard to test the full strength of the scales. Working with Bronia has helped in seeing how strong they are. But the idea of hurting myself doesn't sound appealing. I've been able to shift my arm back to normal, though."

"That's awesome," I say, smiling from ear to ear. "Can you show me?"

He holds his arm out and takes a few steadying breaths. We watch the teal scales slowly turn back to his natural Mediterranean color. It's just tanned skin all the way up to his sleeve. I reach my hand out but stop. "Can I?" I ask, and he nods.

I place my fingertips lightly on his arm. It feels like normal skin, like how my arm feels. "I want to try something," I tell him, and he raises a brow at that. "Can you turn it back to scales?"

He does, and it's a lot quicker than when it was the other way around. I grab his other hand. "Okay, try it again."

His face scrunches, but he does it. I pump him with as much enhancing power as I can. My eyes become wide as I watch the scales disappear, and his face is finally revealed to me for the first time. He's got beautiful caramel eyes that have specks of gold. His nose looks like it might have been broken a few times, but it makes him more rugged. His high cheekbones and square jaw make me wonder why he wasn't up in Milan modeling.

"Whoa," I hear from behind me.

My thoughts exactly.

We all turn at the new voice. Dante stands off to the side, thankfully without a gun, and his mouth is wide open. "What?" Luca asks, his eyes darting around the three of us.

"Didn't know there was a good-looking Italian guy under all of that," Dante says, pointing at him.

Luca takes his free hand and slowly raises it to his face. His fingers skim his cheek, and as it touches scale-free skin, he starts moving his hand all over the place. He turns towards me. "You," he says. It was only a matter of time before he figured something out.

"We'll talk about that later," I mutter to him.

He nods, still touching his face. I drop his hand and he slowly turns back to the Luca I know. His expression falls. "Hey," I say, grabbing onto his shirt sleeve. "It's still you either way. With or without scales doesn't change how any of us think about you. But if what you truly want is to be scale-free, then I'll do whatever I need to, to help you."

He puts his hands on his hips and looks at the ground for a moment. I wait for him, because I don't really know how hard this is for him. This was forced onto him, but hopefully he'll keep finding the will to turn it around and make it work for him. "It'd be a lot easier to go out into the world and not have teal scales," he says, looking at his arms.

"Yeah, I can see that. So, we'll keep working until we figure that out."

Gregory clears his throat. "Can we try something else?" he asks.

"What?" Luca asks, somewhat wary.

Gregory keeps looking at Luca's arms. "Becca said that your scales are basically like body armor?"

He stands a little taller at Gregory's question. "*Si*. At least as far as we can tell."

"Is it still like body armor when it's not covered in scales?" Gregory asks.

Luca looks down at his arm. "I don't know."

"Your skin felt just like mine a moment ago," I tell them.

Gregory's eyes drift towards the range. "Can we test it though? Maybe see if you need the scales for it to be effective?"

I follow his line of sight. "What do you want to do? Shoot him?" I ask, horrified.

His jaw drops and Luca curses in Italian. "What? No. I was thinking about if we cut his arm a little."

"I'm okay with trying to cut my arm," Luca butts in quickly.

Gregory pulls out a pocket knife I've never seen before. "Have you always carried that?" I ask.

"No, but I do now," he answers. Probably not a bad idea.

Gregory hands the knife over to Luca. He opens the blade and slowly drags it across his scales. Nothing happens. There's not even a line from the knife. "All right, now if you can change your arm," Gregory instructs.

Luca closes his eyes tightly. We all watch as his scales slowly change to skin. He opens his eyes, grips the knife tightly, and takes a deep breath. The blade slides across his skin. His face pulls in a grimace as blood beads on top of his arm. He drops the knife and puts a hand over the cut.

"Guess that won't work," I say, grimacing. "But you know if we can get you to learn to completely transform, it won't take much for you to start doing it fast. Maybe you'll be able to change in the blink of an eye."

"I'll keep working," Luca says.

"Good. We're going to get back to Tiberius and head back to the U.S. You need to hurry to Walter and see if you need stitches."

He lifts his hand and the skin turns back to scales, stopping the blood.

"Amazing," I say in awe, examining his arm. The cut's gone. I grab his arm, turning it over, but it's like it was never there. "Can you turn it back to skin again?" I ask.

The scales disappear, and the only evidence left on his arm is a faint, pink line.

Gregory and Dante lean in. "Magic," Dante says.

Gregory lets out a low whistle. "That's pretty impressive," he says. "Could come in handy someday."

Luca keeps staring at his arm, and I don't really blame him. But we don't have time to delve into this. Gregory and I have to get back before someone notices we're gone. But I need to warn him first. I lean closer to Luca, still holding his arm, and lower my voice. "I've got this fear that the fight might come here. Keep training people, keep working on controlling your power, and be vigilant."

He clasps his free hand with mine. "I won't let you down," he says, and we lock eyes, making a promise without words.

I step back and Gregory comes forward to shake Luca's hand. I wave to Dante and we leave them to keep working on his training.

THIRTY-THREE

"There's one more place we need to stop before we head for Tiberius," I tell Gregory.

He follows me as we make a couple of turns until we're walking up the path to another home. As soon as I knock, footsteps run for the door. I wait for the door to be ripped open, but there's a pause, and then it opens slowly.

"Gregory!" Bronia yells as soon as she sees him.

She goes to throw herself into his arms but stops at the last moment. But Gregory goes the rest of the way and scoops her up in his arms. Thank goodness Dex found that mineral to help his healing accelerate. He squeezes her tight and I can see her wanting to do the same, but she controls herself. He drops her to her feet and holds her at an arm's length. "You've gotten so big, bug," he says in surprise.

She gives him the brightest smile, seeming so proud of growing up.

"I've missed you, kid," he tells her.

I don't know if she can hear the strain in his voice, but I can. I can only imagine how much a part of her life Gregory was with Ania being his partner. Considering how young he was when Mr. Smith recruited him, he might have known Bronia her whole life.

"Gregory, my boy," Walter says as he walks out his front door.

Gregory steps away from Bronia and lets Walter grab him by his face and kiss his forehead. "You don't know how glad I am to see you alive." Walter barely rasps the words out.

Gregory grips Walter's shirt sleeve. "I'm so sorry."

"Not your fault," Walter tells him. "And I know this lady here must have thanked God when she found you."

They both look over at me. My cheeks heat from their intense stares. "Why don't you guys catch up? I'm going to head to my place and get a couple of things," I say.

Gregory steps away from Walter and grabs my hand. "You sure?" he asks.

"Yeah." I lean closer. "I think Bronia needs it most."

He leans in and gives me a chaste kiss on my lips, but it still makes my heart race. I lightly touch his face, and then step back, transporting to my room in my house here.

I STAND in the doorway of my room, examining it more closely than usual. Even though I've found peace here in Fordlandia, there's no life in this house. And maybe because it's not filled with the people I care about. It's not filled with warmth. There're no real memories here except for sleeping and the first time I tested enhancing Tony's power. It's just a place. I walk into my closet and grab a bag and throw the small amount of clothes I have into it. I lost almost everything in the fire, except for the picture sitting on my nightstand.

I pick it up and run a finger around the frame. Grandpa, Grandma, and me standing in front of our favorite pizza place, Pepe's. That was such a good night. I had just been contacted by several universities about playing basketball for them. Two months after this picture was taken, I ruined my knee and ruined my chance at a scholarship. But that night was still awesome. Grandpa was so proud and kept telling random people about all the colleges talking to me.

I stare at the picture one more time, drinking in the love I can see in their eyes. I'll have to get Lucy to copy it, just in case. I slide it into my backpack and throw the bag over my shoulder. I close my eyes and, in a blink, I'm standing outside of Walter's front door.

Gregory and Bronia's voices carry from the back, but I leave them be and knock on the front door. I hear the creak of Walter's recliner and then his soft footfalls.

"Hey, Walter," I call out to him, leaning into the screen door.

His smile greets me and I step back so he can open it. "They're in the back," he tells me.

"I know, but I'd rather come and talk with you."

He smiles. "Then come on in."

I follow him into the living room and sit in the matching recliner. We both start rocking; I swear it's a subconscious thing. You can't sit in something that rocks and stay still. He doesn't start pestering me with questions, and for that I'm grateful. But Walter has this thing about him where you just vomit words whether you want to or not.

"Tony was the reason I was captured," I tell him, surprised that that's what comes out of my mouth. But it's probably what I need the most guidance with.

Walter's chair stops rocking, but I keep my eyes trained ahead and keep going. "They told him they had his mom. And honestly, I know he's not in the right head space. Because he didn't even think to come to me and ask for help."

I keep rocking, letting the chair help churn my thoughts. "They didn't have his mom. Apparently, Mr. Smith had her under surveillance when they thought Tony was a traitor, and then kept her under watch after they learned he was kidnapped and didn't know who did it."

I keep rocking, eyes focused on watching what's going on outside. "Becca?" Walter says.

"Yeah," I say, still looking out the window.

"*Serduszko*, look at me," he requests in a soft voice.

I turn and take in his down-turned mouth and worried eyes. "How are *you* doing?"

I lean my head back. How *am* I doing? That's a good question. "I don't know. I haven't really had a chance to think about it, ya know? I found out that he set me up at the same time we found Gregory. And since finding Gregory, everything has been focused on him and that's been at the forefront of my mind."

"And now?" he prods.

I let my mind drift to Tony. There's anger there, and so much sadness. "My heart hurts," I tell him. "It hurts from the anger I can't seem to let go of. It hurts because my friend is so lost. It hurts because I'm afraid of what the guilt will do to him."

"That's to be expected," he tells me.

"I know, and I get that. But my mind is constantly on edge, afraid he's going to do something dumb. I know he's changed. I've changed. But nothing brings any light to his eyes. And I don't know how to help change that."

"You can't."

Two words. It's all he says, but they fall like a sledgehammer. I stop rocking and finally look over at him. "What?" I ask, sitting up.

"You can't change him," he says, leaning forward. "You can be there, offer support, be a friend, but ultimately, it's him that needs to reach that place. For him to get to being happy again is completely dependent on himself. It's probably going to be a long road, and he'll need you cheering him on. But don't try and take on the responsibility of someone else's happiness. You'll fail every time."

I slump in the recliner. "Well, that sucks."

His rough laughter tumbles past his lips. "Wait till you have kids."

"I've got a long time before I need to worry about that, old man."

He looks me square in the eye. "Yes, you do, and don't you forget."

I smirk at the sternness in his voice.

We both continue rocking in our recliners until the back door swings open. "Have a good visit?" Walter calls out.

Gregory comes into view. He walks to my side and puts a hand on my shoulder. His thumb lightly rubs the back of my neck and I close my eyes. That feels good. "Yeah," he tells Walter. "She just ran off with some of the other kids."

Walter nods once. "Good."

"How's she been doing?" Gregory asks.

Walter rubs at the scruff on his chin. "A lot better since we got here. It helps having other kids around with powers. After Ania died I had to pull her out of school. It was just too dangerous. And then with everything else going on..."

Gregory and I nod, totally getting it. "I bet they were super happy when a doctor showed up here in Fordlandia," Gregory says.

"That they were," Walter says.

Gregory looks down at me. "Ready to go?" he asks.

"Yeah." I get out of the recliner and walk over to Walter. "Probably be seeing you real soon."

He stands from his chair and wraps his arms around me. "Anytime you want, you're welcome here. Plus, I know Bronia loves when you visit."

I quickly hug him tighter and then step back. He and Gregory shake hands, and then we're off.

"SO, *how* was your talk with Bronia?" I ask Gregory once we're clear from Walter's yard.

He runs a hand through his hair that the setting sun has turned golden. "Hard," he says. "She misses her mom, and so do I."

"I miss her too," I tell him, voice quiet. Even though I didn't know her as long as he did, she became like the big sister I always wanted.

"I wish she was here," I say.

"Me too. Her power was a lot for her to handle, and it's even more so for a ten-year-old to handle. But Bronia seems to be coming along really well." Gregory scans the houses. "Do you like living here?"

"Now I do. When I first came here after my grandparents were killed, it was hard. Everyone here has been pretty welcoming. They knew what had happened and kept trying to bring me food. But I didn't want condolences, I just wanted to get out there and track down the people responsible."

"What changed?" he asks.

I study the village, picturing all the people we've saved. "The first place we raided was in Germany. We rescued six people. Six. They were so scared. A couple didn't speak English. But luckily one of the guys spoke German and English. We brought them here and offered them a home. None of these people have ever had a home. Or they've been homeless for so long that they forgot what it was like to have a place of their own.

"We had them all come with us, because the powers that were forced on them can be out of control, and they can't be in normal society. One of the people we found was a little girl who controls lightning. We knew that she couldn't be in the real world, not until she was older and had a handle on things."

"Wow," he says, sounding genuinely surprised.

"Getting to know these people, helping them...it's changed how I see it here. I've needed this place as much as they do."

He grabs my hand. "I'm happy then."

We walk up Tiberius's front walk and head inside. We walk through the house, following the sound of voices coming from the living room. Lucy and Tiberius are sitting on the couch, bodies turned towards each other, heads close. "Hey guys," I say, probably interrupting a personal moment.

Both of them look up and Lucy offers us a warm smile. "What do you think of Fordlandia?" she asks Gregory.

He looks towards the open window. "It's amazing that this place is here. Becca told me about your safeguards, and the history of this place, but it's still surreal walking down the street."

"It's what a lot of us have needed," she tells him. "It's definitely been a place where a lot of us have been able to heal."

"How do you guys sustain yourself here?" he asks.

"Some, who can, work in town. Others work with me for my cyber security firm," Lucy tells him. "We have a few boats that make it easy to get into town and grab things. Plus, we have a huge communal garden."

"That's amazing," he says, looking awed.

I look at the clock on the mantel. "We need to get back. You ready to go?" I ask Tiberius.

Lucy jumps up from the couch. "Oh, before you go, I want to give you something," she says and rushes out of the room.

I raise a brow at Tiberius and he just shrugs. Lucy comes rushing back in the room, a small phone in her hand. "Here, take this. It is literally untraceable. I've programmed it so no one can trace where this phone is or who it's calling. Pretty proud of myself, actually. And the only numbers on there are me, Tiberius, and Luca."

I grab it and look it over. I've never seen anything like it before. "It's an old-school flip phone," she tells me and opens it to show me.

"This is awesome. Thanks," I say and put it in my pocket.

We all stand to leave. Tiberius walks to Lucy and cups her face. Gregory and I turn away, trying to give them a little privacy. He gives me a bright smile and I grab his hand.

"Let's head on back," Tiberius calls from over my shoulder.

Lucy grabs me and gives me a quick hug. "Be safe, and don't do anything stupid," she warns.

I laugh and grab the guys' hands. "No promises," I tell her, and in a blink, we're back in Tiberius's room at Project Lightning.

Tiberius lets out a huge yawn. "I need to get to bed. I'll see you two in the morning for breakfast."

He gives me a hug and shakes Gregory's hand. "See you in the morning," I say, grabbing Gregory's hand, and before he can say anything, I transport us to my room, right near my door.

"How are you feeling?" I ask, giving his hand a squeeze. "Your ribs have to be killing you."

"Dex gave me something that's basically a miracle," he says, leaning against the door.

We stare at one another. We really haven't been alone much, at least away from prying eyes. There's still so much we've got to figure out, but it can wait.

"You haven't said anything about me kissing you in the cafeteria." I pull on his hand, leading him to sit down on my bed.

"Haven't really had the chance," he says. He lies down and gathers me close. I nestle into the spot underneath his arm. "I feel like we're always going somewhere or something big is happening. This is the first time we've had together without people lurking or waiting for us."

He presses his lips into the top of my head. I wrap an arm around him, snuggling in close. "Stay with me tonight?" I ask.

His thumb strokes my arm. "Anytime," he promises.

I close my eyes and let the steady beat of his heart lull me to sleep.

THIRTY-FOUR

Tall pine trees surround us on all sides, standing guard...or trapping us in. The air feels crisp, but I love it because it's fresh, untainted. The moss under my feet feels like a cushion, and the trail ahead is something I'd love to explore. I have no clue where we are in the dream world this time, but that's okay, because it's amazing. I close my eyes, filling my lungs.

"This place is beautiful," I tell my mom.

"I lived near here, years ago," she tells me, and that little bit of revelation makes the euphoric feeling fade a bit.

"Yeah? When was that?" I ask, finally looking at her.

She looks around, her face looking younger somehow; this place must hold a lot of good memories that I know nothing about. "When your dad and I were first married, we lived here for a short time." Her voice is heavy, filled with longing. "This is where I learned that I was pregnant with you," she says, her voice breaking. "I always planned to move back here someday, but that never happened. But being here right now is a gift I'll treasure."

"How did you die, Mom?" I finally ask her the question that's constantly lurking in the back of my mind. "When we got the call, they

said you overdosed, but Ania told me that you were clean when you died. You told me you were hunted down. I think it's time."

She stares up into the green canopy, lost in thought, maybe memories. But maybe being in a place she loves will make it easier.

She takes a deep breath. "I know Ania told you that she and I kept in touch after I left Project Lightning. There were years when we didn't, and that's on me. When I was using, there were many times I was living on the streets. I did things, saw things, that I wish I could forget, but I can't. Drugs took everything from me, and I let them. About two years ago I did overdose, but they were able to rescue me in time. It was a badly needed wake-up call.

"I called Ania, we got me into rehab, and I started to slowly piece my life back together. I had such big plans." She shakes her head at that. "I was going to start talking to your grandpa so I could be in your life. I didn't want to take you from them; I just wanted you to know me, and I wanted to know you."

I stay quiet. Fearing that anything uttered from my mouth will shatter this dream.

"I was leaving my AA meeting. I had just gotten my two-year sobriety coin. It was great. I felt so happy and light, and I was ready to start trying to see you again. I was almost to my car when two men came up behind me. They bashed me in the head, tied me up, and threw me in the trunk of a car. They took me somewhere; I don't even know where. Things were so fuzzy, but I heard a man say that my body was too damaged from the years of drug use. I was no good to them. They were going to need my daughter."

"It had to be Rivers," I tell her, anger flaring in my chest. "He's been experimenting on our people for years."

She nods. "I know that now. Even if I knew that then, there wasn't anything I could have done about that. But we're here now," she tells me.

Yeah, we're here now, where I finally have a relationship with one of my parents, but she's dead. All because one man is on a stupid mission, and for what?

"I'm going to stop him," I vow to her. "I won't let him keep doing what's he's been doing."

She walks closer to me and grabs my hand. "They have a warning for you. A choice is coming, and depending on the decision you make, you'll either have incredible aid, or you'll be alone in this fight."

I stare at her, waiting for more, but she doesn't say anything else. "Really?" I ask. "That's all you've got. More cryptic advice."

"You know the rules," she says, lecturing me.

I drop her hand and step back. My hands clench at my sides. "Yeah, but come on now. I thought we'd moved past that."

She gives me a "don't-push-it" look.

"Will I at least know this choice when it comes to me?" I ask, not caring how sarcastic I sound.

"I hope so," she says, and it's not very convincing. I wonder if she knows the answer to that question.

Mom starts walking down the path and I fall in step with her. If it weren't for the lack of animal sounds, I'd forget we were in a dream. She doesn't say anything, just worries her lower lip. "What's going on?" I ask her, noticing the worry lining her face.

Her eyes dart to me and then away. "I don't know how many more times they're going to let me come to you."

My steps falter. "Why? What makes you think that?"

She slows her stride, waiting for me. "It's just a feeling I have," she says, rubbing the spot over her heart.

I've gone back and forth about these dreams with my mom. At first, they scared me, and then I didn't believe they were real. There's still the anger at times when I think about all the times they could have warned me. Like with my grandparents. Two lives could have been spared. And a part of my brain knows that my mom isn't to blame for that, but another part still feels that anger. And now I might not see her anymore? I finally have somewhat of a relationship with her, but it sounds like that's going to be gone too.

"You know, eventually, when we won't see each other in your dreams, just remember I'm always there. I'm always listening.

You've got so many people cheering you on, whether you know it or not."

"Are you going to be in any more of my dreams?" I ask again, because this feels a lot like goodbye.

She stops on the dirt path and reaches out for my hand. I let her hold it, and she gives it a squeeze. "I think you'll see me again soon," she tells me.

She drops my hand and steps off the path into the tree line, her form fading.

"Bye, Mom." I whisper once she disappears.

"Bye, baby," I hear her whisper back.

<hr>

THE TRANQUIL FOREST disappears and is replaced by the scratchy sheets on my bed in my room at headquarters. I reach over, finding warm, empty sheets. I sit up on an elbow. The bathroom light seeps underneath the door.

I flop back down and stare up at the ceiling, and my thoughts filter through all the information from another dream with my mom. I rub away the grit in my eyes.

What choice am I going to have to make? And why do they have to keep up with this cryptic B.S.? Can't they just be like, *"If you do this we won't help, but if you do the opposite, we'll back you up?"*

The sound of the bathroom door opening cuts off my inner monologue. I turn my head and lock eyes with Gregory as he leans against the doorframe.

"Heavy thoughts," he says to me.

I don't have earrings in.

"When were you going to tell me about your mom?" he asks.

I open my mouth but he stops me. "I heard your dream."

I run a hand over my face and let out a sigh. I swallow thickly. "They aren't really dreams."

He pushes off the door and sits on the bed next to me. "How long?"

"Since she died."

He curses and looks away for a moment. "Any other secrets you're keeping?"

I reach out and grab his hand. "It wasn't on purpose. For the longest time I thought it was my mind conjuring things. I didn't intentionally hide it from you."

"I know," he says, bringing our linked hands to his lips. He gives them a soft kiss before he puts them back on the bed. "I'm sorry about how on-edge I am."

He shifts, and I can see the pain flash across his face. I launch up to a sitting position. "Hey," I say cupping his face. "Are you okay?"

"Yeah," he says, gritting his teeth. "Think I need another dose of medicine from Dex."

"Well then, let's go get you some," I tell him, getting ready to stand. I probably shouldn't have slept on him last night. Damn it, why didn't I think of that?

"I would take any pain if it meant having you in my arms," he says, and I melt. "But we're not done talking about these dreams," he says in all seriousness.

"I know, but that can wait. You being in pain can't," I tell him, walking over to my dresser and grabbing clean clothes.

He stands slowly from the bed, hissing out a breath. "Get dressed, I'll meet you at the cafeteria."

I drop my clothes on the bed, and reach out a hand to him. "I can transport you to the infirmary," I tell him.

He waves away the comment. "It's okay, I want to walk."

He grabs my hand and tenderly pulls me into his body. He grips my hip with his other hand and leans forward to rest his forehead against mine. My hands leisurely travel up his arms until I reach his shoulders. His breath hitches as I caress the back of his neck. I lift up on my toes and he bends down, meeting my lips halfway. He places slow, intoxicating kisses on my lips. An electric feeling courses through my veins, making my heart race and feel light all at the same time.

He caresses my lips once more with his before he pulls away. I drop down on my heels. Both of us try to control our breathing.

He lifts my chin. "I love you," he says with such conviction. "Whatever comes, whatever your mom hinted at, I will not leave you."

I bury my face into his chest, wanting to hug him so tightly, but I know I can't. Tears stream down my face. "I love you." I manage to push the words out.

He holds me in his arms, and I lock this memory away, knowing in the coming days, weeks, maybe months, I'm going to have to pull it out and hold it close to my heart.

He moves a little, and I feel him wince. I push out of his arms. "You need to get to the infirmary and get more medicine."

"You're right. I'll see you in a few minutes," he says, and gives me one last kiss.

He walks out the door, and I hurry to get ready for the day.

THIRTY-FIVE

"**B**ecca!" Tiberius screams as he runs into the cafeteria, causing me to jump in my seat next to Tony. "We need to get back to Lucy, now!"

I've never heard him yell before, not even once. And we've been in some crazy situations before. The entire room stops talking. We really need to stop having all these events happen in the cafeteria. "What's going on?" I ask, scrambling up from the table.

Tiberius rushes across the room, laser-focused on us. "Lucy said they found them. Luca captured a man who somehow got into the village."

"Slow down," Xavier says from my other side.

"Whoa. Wait. How is that even possible? How would they find out about it?" I ask.

"What the hell is going on, man?" Mike whispers to Tony, but he ignores him.

"Tony?" Tiberius somehow asks and accuses in the same breath.

Tony shakes his head violently back and forth and holds his hands up in the air. "I've never told them about it, or where you guys were hiding people. I swear."

I believe him. I step in front of Tony, blocking Tiberius. "All right, let's go."

Xavier grabs my arm. "Whoa, wait a minute. You can't just go rushing off. What if it's a trap?"

"I can be there and back in a moment," I tell him.

"And what if Chelsea's there? You'll be a sitting duck."

"I'm not unarmed this time," I say, showing off the gun holstered in the waist of my jeans.

"When did you get that?" Tony asks, but I wave him off.

"Hurry back, because I do not want to be the one to tell Gregory what's going on," Xavier says, not even fazed that I have a gun on me.

I give him a nod and grab Tiberius's hand. And right before we leave, I turn and look at Tony. "Don't worry. It'll be okay," I whisper to him, giving him a wink.

I TRANSPORT us straight to his living room. "Oh, thank goodness." The relief in Lucy's voice is thick.

"Where is he?" Tiberius asks, looking around like the guy should be duct-taped to a chair next to the couch.

Lucy rubs his arm, trying to calm him. "Luca's got him at his house. Right now, it's just this guy. And I scanned him. He's got no tracking equipment on him. He says he came here to warn us, but I've got to doubt it."

I start pacing in front of the coffee table.

Tiberius plants his hands on his hips and looks off into the distance, hopefully coming up with a plan. "Okay. This is what we're going to do." He starts laying out his plan and I could hug him for it. "Lucy, double-check the border. Make sure everything is working. I'm going to call Walter and have him gather everyone to meet at the building next to the water tower. Becca, I'll meet you at Luca's and we'll see what we can find out."

I nod, and in a blink, I'm standing at Luca's front door. I knock and hear Luca yell for me to come in. I walk in the house and I immediately see who supposedly came to warn us.

"The last time I saw you, you were throwing a fireball at the car I was riding in," I say to Daemon. "Never thought I'd see you here."

He's sitting on a chair in the middle of the living room. But he doesn't look nervous or uneasy being around Luca. His legs are spread wide and the way he's slouched screams arrogance. Maybe being able to shoot fire out of your hands makes you cocky.

"He says he's here to help," Luca tells me, and apparently being angry makes his Italian accent super thick.

I drag a chair over from the kitchen and sit across from Daemon. "And what are you here to help us with?"

He leans forward, staring me straight in the eye. "Rivers is coming. And soon. You need to get all these people out."

My insides clench in fear. "And what's their plan when he gets here?" I ask him. My voice may seem calm, but I'm freaking out right now. Because this is a village with a lot of women and children. And even if we could get them out of here, I don't know where we'd take them.

Daemon leans forward in his seat. "Those who have actual powers will be taken, and those who were deemed experiments will be eradicated." He says it in such a detached way.

Luca's body goes scarily still next to me, and he starts talking heatedly to him in Italian.

"Cool it, lizard boy," Daemon says.

I throw my arm out to stop Luca from charging him.

"Don't be a jerk," I warn Daemon, but he just shrugs.

I keep my arm out, just in case. "And you're okay with Rivers coming and kidnapping these people? Do you know how many kids we've rescued from his labs?"

He sits up straighter. "That's why I'm here."

I search Daemon's face, trying to find deceit, but I'm leaning towards believing him. Because with his power, he could have blown

Luca away. But I'm not a hundred percent. "And how do you guys even know about this place?"

They shouldn't. With all that Lucy has done, we should be hidden from the world.

"Tony."

It feels like the world stops at him saying that name. I lean forward. He couldn't have said the name I think he said. *No. No way.* "Excuse me?"

He waves away my question like he didn't just drop a huge bombshell. "He didn't tell us, so don't worry about that. But the video game he was always playing? What he didn't know was that one of the guys he was playing with was Thompson. They were able to track him through the game. Back door IP address."

I hang my head. This is going to destroy him. I take a deep breath and look back at Daemon. "And why are *you* warning us? Because I've got to be honest, I'm having a hard time not believing this is just a trap. I don't even know what you could gain by being here."

He shifts and suddenly looks super uncomfortable. "I don't know if there's anything I can say that'll make you believe, but get Mr. Smith and Gregory here. They'll tell you what you need to know."

Okay, he obviously doesn't want to tell me, but I've got to wonder... "I'll get them. And probably Xavier and Raven too."

His eyes flare just a little at her name, but he quickly schools his features back to the arrogant mask he's been wearing. I bet she's the real reason why he's here.

The front door opens and Tiberius stalks into the room. "He says he's here to warn us that Rivers is coming," I tell him without taking my eyes off Daemon.

Tiberius stares him down, and I've never seen him look so scary. But this is his home, this is a place he built, and now he's got people coming to invade and destroy it. The room fills with his anger like a palpable living thing. I get up, drawing his attention, and carefully walk over to him.

"I kinda believe him," I say. "But I'm going to go grab Mr. Smith and Gregory so they can tell us even more. It was actually his suggestion."

I see him hesitate for a fraction of a second. Mr. Smith doesn't know about Fordlandia. He knows we've taken these people somewhere, but we haven't told him anything about it where it is.

"Go," he orders me. "Who knows how much time we have before they get here."

I close my eyes and picture the door of Mr. Smith's office, and in a blink I'm there.

I pound on his door.

No one answers, so I raise my fist to beat against it again when it opens. "Becca? What's going on?" Mr. Smith asks, eyeing my fist poised in the air.

I push past him into his office. "I'm taking you somewhere. You and Gregory. Probably Xavier and Raven too."

He leans against the doorframe, arms crossed, eyes stern. "Where?" he asks.

"I don't want to say here," I tell him. I still don't trust it here. And even if there's a small chance that Rivers doesn't know, I don't want that information to get back to him. "Where's Gregory?" I ask.

He gives me a long stare, but then he pulls out his phone and starts typing away. "They should be here soon. I told them to hurry," he tells me once he's done typing. "What's going on?" He may ask, but it sounds more like a demand.

"We've got big problems." And that's an understatement.

The office door swings all the way open and Gregory stands there breathless. I rush across the room to him, but he stops me before I get there. "Just give me a minute," he says in between shaky breaths.

Xavier and Raven come up behind him. "What's going on?" Xavier asks, looking between Mr. Smith and me.

"I need to take you guys to Tiberius, right now," I tell all of them.

Both Xavier's and Gregory's faces harden. I hold out my hands, and everyone grabs on. I look at Raven. "Brace yourself," I warn her, and she scrunches up her face.

THIRTY-SIX

The moment we appear in the room and the group sees who's in the chair, everyone starts yelling at the same time. Except for Raven. She lets out a surprised gasp.

"You've got some nerve—" Xavier starts.

"What the hell is he doing—" Gregory's voice rises.

"Enough!" Mr. Smith yells, cutting everyone off.

Daemon smirks from his chair, until Luca smacks him on the back of the head, effectively wiping away that smug grin. It also causes Raven and Mr. Smith to get their first look at Luca.

The room falls silent until Raven blurts out, "Do you have scales?"

Mr. Smith shoots her a *will you shut up look*. He nods at Luca, like it's every day you meet a lizard man. "Before we go any further, someone fill me in on where the hell we are and what's going on," Mr. Smith says.

I step forward and give him a brief explanation on where we are and what Daemon told us. Mr. Smith sits down heavily on the couch. He steeples his fingers in front of his face. After a few moments he says, "Gregory, pull up a chair."

Daemon squirms in his seat. I grab Gregory's hand before he can sit down. He looks down at me. *Let me see if I can help. I don't know what enhancing you and Mr. Smith will do, but we need to know everything.*

He gives me a small nod and I walk over with him, still hand in hand. Daemon's gaze stays fixed on our clasped palms. His eyes dart to Raven and then back to us. "Golden child gets to break the rules, huh?"

"Really?" I ask Daemon, rolling my eyes

He rubs a hand over his face, and after a deep breath he looks straight at Mr. Smith. "Ask away," he tells him.

I put a hand on Mr. Smith's arm. "Can we try something a little different?" I ask. "What if Gregory reads his mind, and you decide if it's truthful?"

"Do you think that'll work?" Mr. Smith asks.

I shrug. "Worth a try," I tell him.

He nods and looks at Daemon. "Show us what you know," he tells him.

I grab both Gregory and Mr. Smith's hands and close my eyes. Gregory delves into Daemon's mind, and it's a little chaotic at first until Daemon focuses in on a memory with Thompson.

"Do you have the location?" Rivers asks Daemon and Thompson.

"It was hard," Thompson says. "Whoever is their IT person is amazing. I never thought we'd be able to figure this out. But I planted a pretty small virus in the game that helps get in through the back door. It finally worked."

Rivers moves closer to the computer screen, leaning heavily on his cane. "Good. Pull up their location on the satellite."

Thompson starts working away on his computer. Daemon stands a little taller so he can see the screen. "What does that say on the map?" he asks, squinting at it.

"Fordlandia?" Thompson asks. "What is that?"

Rivers chuckles. "Ford built a compound in the middle of the Amazon so they could harvest the rubber for tires. They tried to put

American suburbia in the middle of the jungle. It failed." Rivers shakes his head, looking impressed. "Genius place to hide."

"It's not showing anything on the infrared," Thompson says, typing some more.

"What do you mean?" Rivers asks, practically growling.

"There's no one there," he says, pointing at the screen.

Rivers shuffles closer. "Could they be cloaking themselves?" he asks, hovering closer to Thompson's shoulder.

Thompson shudders slightly, and I wonder if anyone else caught that. "If they are, there's no way to tell. We'd have to actually go there."

Rivers steps back up. "Let me think on this," he says and slowly walks out of the room.

"What do you think?" Daemon asks once Rivers leaves the room.

Thompson turns in his chair. "I don't know. I've never met anyone that can cloak an entire town. But this is where Tony was playing the game, so I've got to assume they're still there."

"And you're sure it's Tony?" Daemon asks.

Thompson leans back in his chair. "Yeah. When he was brought in, they went through every piece of his life. If he signed onto anything Henderson immediately knew and alerted Rivers."

Daemon looks back at the door Rivers just left through. "What do you think he's going to do?"

"Probably capture all he can and then take out those he can't." He says it like it's not a big deal. Like there aren't kids here, little innocent babies.

I drop Gregory's and Mr. Smith's hands and slouch back against the couch. I rub a hand across my forehead. Gregory opens his mouth, but I stop him. "Just give me a moment." That took so much energy out of me, and yet I still want to get up and punch Daemon in the face.

I turn my head to Mr. Smith. "Was that memory true?"

"Yes," he says, and in that one word I can hear, and feel, his fury.

Daemon's cocky demeanor has fled. His eyes stay on the floor. I shake my head, anger surging to the forefront. I push myself off the couch, and on unsteady legs I walk over to Daemon. He looks up at the sound of my steps.

"Do you know how many kids I've found in cages? Treated like lab rats?" His eyes dart away.

No one stops me. No one tries to intervene.

"No, look at me." The words snap out of me like a whip. "You don't get to avoid this. You helped that man. You helped him ruin the lives of so many. Were you there when Eloise had to watch them murder her parents? Were you there when they left Luca to die, trapped in a cage? How many lives have you ruined?" With every question I get closer and closer to him, until I'm right in his face, forcing him to hear my words.

"I know, all right?" he says, agitated. "But do you remember who we're talking about? Rivers has the power of persuasion. And he wields that so well. At first you think you're doing something good. He makes it seem like a noble cause. But then when we realize what's going on, it's like we're in too deep."

My mind flashes to Sariah and when I tracked her down in England after she kidnapped Poppy. Her anger about kidnapping Poppy was so vivid, but those men quickly pointed out that she was a part of this now. She went down that road, and instead of getting off of it, she kept going.

Daemon leans in to me. And I stand my ground, not backing up. "I'm here because I've got to do something, and I can't do it alone."

"He's being honest," Mr. Smith says, and for a moment I had forgotten everyone was here.

I turn back to the room. "What do we do?" I ask, lost. "These people here are only somewhat trained. And those with any control of their powers are no match for the people with Rivers."

"How long do we have?" Tiberius asks, looking at Daemon.

Daemon rubs at his face. "I don't know," he says, frustrated.

"Where do they think you are?" Mr. Smith asks him.

Daemon runs a hand roughly through his hair. "I'm supposed to be back in the states. Meeting with a contact at Project Lightning."

That causes everyone in the room to come to attention. "Who?" Mr. Smith asks.

"Arianna."

Xavier curses and Mr. Smith looks livid. "How did I not see that?" Mr. Smith says to himself.

I lean closer to Gregory. "Who the heck is that?" I ask him.

"She did orientation with you. Redhead from South Carolina?" He says it like a question, probably trying to jog my memory.

I tilt my head back and forth. "Yeah, not really ringing a bell. I remember a Southern accent. But that's about it."

He shakes his head at me. "Her dad was a close friend of Mr. Smith."

"I wonder if Rivers got to her like he got to Sariah," I say.

Gregory makes a humming noise. "You might be right."

Tiberius's phone rings and he steps out of the room to answer it.

"We can worry about that later," Mr. Smith butts in. "With how long it took you to get here, and how long you've been out of contact, they've got to know something is up."

Tiberius walks back into the room. "Walter has everyone assembled. We need to go and give them a heads-up. Daemon, you better stay here in the house. The last thing I want is to incite panic, and I know there are people here who will recognize you."

Daemon nods.

"I'll stay here with him," Luca offers.

"Sounds good. Don't drop your guard," Tiberius says, pointing at Daemon.

We all walk out of the house and Mr. Smith and Raven pause. "Welcome to Fordlandia," Tiberius says to them, and takes off for the warehouse next to the water tower.

We follow him down the road. "This place is insane," Raven says to Xavier.

They walk ahead of us and I turn to Mr. Smith. "Thoughts?" I ask him.

Mr. Smith's eyes drift from house to house, taking it all in. "Part of me doesn't believe it. I haven't seen what you two have seen. But watching the memory of Daemon, how was I so wrong about Rivers?" His vulnerability is shocking. Who is this man?

"I don't know, but we can't let him keep going," I say.

Gregory grabs my hand and gives it a squeeze. "There's something else you need to know," Gregory tells Mr. Smith. "My mind reading is spotty here. There's a lot of this stone called carnelian here, and that helps block mind reading."

Mr. Smith lets out a huff of air. "That's going to be a problem, especially if we can't figure out a plan and get everyone out of here."

"I'm starting to think that no matter where we go, he's going to find us and keep kidnapping more people," I tell them. "I'm afraid if we don't take a stand now, we never will."

We're closer to the warehouse, and the sound of multiple voices reaches us. "One step at a time," Mr. Smith says. "Let's first figure out how to keep the children safe."

We walk into the warehouse and I search the crowd until I find Tiberius. Lucy's close to his side, along with Walter and Bronia. I head that way, Gregory and Mr. Smith following behind.

As I get closer, the noise starts to die down, and everyone's stare is on us. I do my best to smile at some of the kids, but I'm pretty sure it's just a grimace. Lucy takes a step closer to Tiberius as soon as Mr. Smith comes into view.

"Walter," Mr. Smith says, stepping closer and holding out his hand. "It's so good to see you."

Xavier and Raven walk up to our side.

"Jeremy," Walter says, shaking Mr. Smith's hand.

Jeremy? That's his name? "Does it freak anyone else out to know his first name?" I whisper to the group.

"I feel like when he was born, he was wearing a suit and even his mom called him Mr. Smith," Xavier answers back quietly.

We all laugh a little.

"Did you know that was his name?" I side-whisper to Gregory.

"Maybe? No one *ever* calls him that, so if I had heard it, it would have been years ago," Gregory says, looking as surprised as the rest of us.

I don't think I can ever think of him by his first name. It's too weird.

Walter ignores all of us. "When Ania died, I was afraid for Bronia. I won't apologize for leaving."

"After what I've learned, I don't blame you one bit," Mr. Smith says. They share a look that I can't quite discern, but they obviously do. And by the nods they exchange, I assume they've come to some agreement.

"Everyone's here now, so let's get this going," Tiberius says, cutting through the tension.

"Can I get everyone's attention?" he calls out to the crowd. Everyone settles down and focuses on him. "I hate to have to tell you this, especially because I promised you a safe haven here. But we just found out that there's a strong possibility that we've been discovered."

Cries of anguish and fear sound throughout the room. I watch a mother clutch her daughter close to her. Tiberius holds his hands up, trying to calm everyone down. "You need to know what's happening, but what I need right now is for you all to try and stay calm. We have to work together. This is our home. We're coming up with a plan now, but I need everyone who thinks they have a handle on their powers to come see me."

I turn to Gregory and Mr. Smith. "We're going to fight back and defend Fordlandia. What are the odds of Project Lightning aiding us?"

"We're already invested in this. And these are my people too, no matter how they became that way. I won't turn my back on them," Mr. Smith says firmly.

Over his shoulder I see a look of pride on Walter's face. Gregory squeezes my hand. "Together," he says.

THIRTY-SEVEN

For the next two hours the majority of the village comes to Tiberius's house, wanting to fight in any way they can. Even some of the kids. But we've agreed unanimously that the kids need to be put somewhere safe.

"You can't make me go with them," Bronia says, stomping her foot and unfortunately putting a hole in the wood floor of Tiberius's living room, aka our war room. At least she looks a little bit sheepish about it.

"It's not safe—" Walter starts to say, but I interrupt him.

"We need you to protect them," I tell her. "I know Luca's been working with you. We need your strength. We need to guard these kids. All their parents are going to be here, but with you keeping them safe, it'll make them feel a lot better and be able to concentrate."

I'm stretching the truth a bit here. But I know Bronia can keep them safe. Plus, some of these kids have a good handle on their powers. I have no doubt these guys are a formidable force, but none of us want them to watch what will probably unfold. They've already endured too much. They've already seen more than any child should have to see. People are going to die, and they shouldn't be a witness of that.

"Can you do that for us?" I ask Bronia.

"Yes." Her voice is firm and filled with conviction. And I'm pretty sure I hear Walter let out a sigh of relief.

"Good. Now, where should we move the kids?" Mr. Smith asks.

"I don't think it's a good idea to keep them here. Even hidden, it's too dangerous," Lucy says.

Thankfully, she seems okay with Mr. Smith. I wasn't sure how she'd feel about him since Rivers was his mentor. But once he offered the help of all the agents at his disposal, she seemed comfortable with him.

"What about my home back in the states?" Walter offers. "No one would even think to check there. And it would take a while for them to get back to the states."

"That could definitely work," Gregory says. "We need to move them soon, though. Because with the amount Becca is going to be transporting, it's going to tire her out quickly."

"There's a lot of globe hopping you're going to have to do," Mr. Smith warns me.

I stand tall, steel infusing my spine. "Don't have much of a choice, do we?" I ask him.

"I suggest we move the children first," Tiberius says, wiping at his eyes. "We need everyone else focusing on strategy. We've got to somehow turn these people into soldiers in a day."

Lucy puts a hand on his arm, and he grabs it with his other hand. I know he's feeling horrible right now. Sadly, the guilt is threatening to swallow me. I'm the one who put everyone in the spotlight.

"If you hadn't been pushing to dismantle more of these labs, then more people would be taken and experimented on. Do *not* feel guilt for saving lives." I look down and Gregory's hand is on my knee, letting him read my thoughts.

"The only person to blame is Rivers," Lucy says, hatred flooding her voice when she says his name. "He's the one who is doing this.

Don't look at yourself as an enemy. Because you aren't. And you need to remember that; otherwise it'll cripple you. *We* are the victims. Not that man. *That* man is the reason your grandparents aren't here right now working alongside us. *That* man is the reason Gregory was tortured for months. *That* horrid man is the reason I'll never be able to carry my own children."

Tears stream down Lucy's face. And I feel my throat work to hold the ugly emotions that want to come spilling out. "So don't you dare feel anything bad about this. Don't you even feel an ounce of guilt." She throws her arm out, pointing towards the window. "Those little girls are out playing because you gave them a chance at childhood. They are able to smile because you pushed yourself to be able use your enhancing power to help track them faster and sooner than we could ever imagine. Without you, it could have taken years to uncover all these places. And by then...who knows what the world would look like now."

The room falls silent, her words causing it to fill with an emotion I can't even name. Because it's more than sadness, more than determination. We're at a precipice here. And I think we all can feel it.

"I'VE BEEN HAVING Luca train the people," I blurt out to the room.

Tiberius's brows rise at that bit of news, and Lucy smiles wide.

"Whether they were born with powers or had them forced upon them, they have them now. They should know how to use them so they can protect themselves. And I think we all knew deep down that this day would come. It was only a matter of time," I tell them, my voice rising with conviction.

"I'm glad you asked Luca to do that. I should have done that from the beginning," Tiberius says.

Lucy puts a hand on his arm. "They needed normalcy at first. And you gave them that."

"You've created a community in which people trust one another. That alone is a hard thing to accomplish. Don't diminish that," Mr. Smith says.

I clear my throat, drawing the attention of the room. "There's something else I need to tell you guys," I say.

Everyone in the room exchanges looks. "Since I got my powers, I started having dreams. But they aren't normal. I'm not even sure if they count as dreams." I take a deep breath and brace. "My mom is in them."

Mr. Smith sits up in his seat, and I watch Walter's eyes widen.

"And before you guys say anything about it's just my mind conjuring her, it's not. There's someone, somewhere out there, whose power is to dream walk."

Gregory stiffens at my side, but I grab his hand, letting him into my mind while I tell the rest of the group.

Xavier swears, and Raven turns white.

"In the beginning she would give me warnings, and the dreams were always so cryptic, but lately it's been more specific. And during the last dream, they told me that a choice was coming that would either render us more aid or leave us to our own devices."

"What does that even mean?" Xavier asks, hands fisted by his side.

"I have no clue," I tell him, sounding as confused as I feel. "It's like being in every cliché mystery movie you can think of." Sadly, I'm being completely honest.

"Why haven't you told us sooner?" Tiberius asks.

I look over at Walter, and his face scrunches in confusion. "Because Ania told me not to. She knew my mom didn't really overdose. She knew my mom was killed and told me to have my guard up."

"What?" Walter whispers, and the room goes still.

"Mr. Rivers had her killed because she was no use to him. Her body was so ruined from all the drug use that she was worthless for his experiments, but he knew I existed."

Lucy drops Tiberius's hand and rushes over to me. She throws her arms around me, hugging me tightly. "I'm so sorry," she says into my hair.

"He's taken so much," I tell her.

"I know," she whispers back.

"I can't let him take anymore," I tell her, trying to make her hear my resolve. Because I'll die before I let him hurt anyone else I love.

"He won't," Mr. Smith says, fury making his voice shake. "This ends now."

I look around the room, and everyone nods their heads in agreement. Raven's basically baring her teeth, which makes me have to swallow down the urge to laugh.

Lucy squeezes me once more and I step back into Gregory's embrace.

"What do you think the choice we have to make is?" Raven asks, bringing us all back.

I've thought about this, but it wasn't until I saw Daemon that something struck me. "I think we need Daemon—"

"No," Gregory says harshly, his face set like stone.

I turn into him, my hands coming up and gently grabbing onto his shoulders. "Yes."

His face softens at my touch.

"He came here to warn us. And I don't think he's the only one who would leave Mr. Rivers given the chance."

I send an image of Sariah's face after she broke my rib.

"You can't be serious," he says, taking a step back.

"What?" Mr. Smith asks looking between us, but Gregory ignores him.

"Look at everything she's done," he says, shaking his head.

"She could have been me," I say, jabbing a hand at my chest.

"Never," he says vehemently.

"Who the hell are you two talking about?" Tiberius asks, making me jolt in surprise at the anger in his voice.

"She thinks Sariah could help us," Gregory says.

Walter's brows shoot up to his hairline and Xavier lets out a low whistle.

I turn to the group gathered in Tiberius's living room. "That could have been me. The most important person in her world up and disappeared and no one would tell her anything. If that had been my grandpa, I would have done anything."

"No, you wouldn't have," Lucy tries to tell me, but I whip a hand out, stopping her.

"Yes. What do you think I've been doing these last few months? I burn buildings down. How many times has Tiberius told me I'm being reckless? And what—"

"You didn't kill anyone," Mr. Smith says in a deadly calm voice. "You didn't take a little girl from her dad. And you sure as hell didn't torture a defenseless person hanging from cuffs."

"She's gone too far," Raven says softly.

I shake my head. Because a part of me still feels this unchecked rage toward her, but there's this voice that keeps asking, *What if she's been controlled all along?*

Tiberius walks over to me and puts a hand on my shoulder. "Let's work on getting the kids out of here first," he says, looking around the room before turning to me. "And I agree, I think Daemon is here to help us."

"Let me talk to him," Raven says. She takes a deep breath and some resolve passes over her. "He'll help us."

"How do you know that?" Mr. Smith asks.

She looks him dead in the eyes. "Because I know he still loves me."

Mr. Smith looks shocked, but me? "Not really surprised," I tell her, and she just smiles.

THIRTY-EIGHT

"I think I should be in there," Mr. Smith says in a huff.

"Later," I say. "He doesn't really know me enough to hate me yet, and I get the feeling you're not his favorite person."

Mr. Smith looks down the dirt road to Tiberius's house. We left everyone else there so they could start talking with parents about our plans for the kids. We also need a volunteer to stay with them. So many moving parts, with such a small amount of time.

"He left," Mr. Smith says, still looking into the distance. "After I told him and Raven to end their relationship."

Ahh. That makes a lot of sense. I can also see how that made it so easy for Rivers to swoop in and recruit Daemon.

"Don't really blame him for being mad," I tell him.

He shakes his head and scoffs, finally turning back to face me. I shrug, because I was pissed at him for a while too.

"I'll let you know when you can come in," I tell him and walk into the house.

Raven, Luca, and Daemon all sit in the living room in complete silence. I take a seat next to Raven on the lone couch. "Uh, I know this is awkward and all right now, but we don't have a lot of time," I tell them. "Raven, you're up."

Daemon looks between the two of us. He leans forward in the same chair he's been sitting in. Luca probably wouldn't let him up.

"We need your help," Raven says to him. She keeps clasping and unclasping her hands in her lap. "You came to warn them, so does that mean you'll stand against Rivers?"

"Are you asking me to fight with you?" he asks her, completely focused on Raven like Luca and I aren't here.

"Yes," she says.

"I'd do anything for you, Ray," he whispers, but even I can feel the impact those words have on her.

She searches his eyes. "Are there others that would leave him and help?" she asks.

I lean forward, my body tensing just waiting for his answer. He tilts his head back and stares at the ceiling. Luca locks eyes with me. Raven grabs one of my hands. The three of us hold our breath, waiting, praying.

"Possibly," Daemon says, and a whoosh of air passes past my lips. He turns towards me. "I'm doing this for her," he tells me.

"I don't care what your reasons are," I tell him in all seriousness. "I've got a bunch of innocent people who've already suffered enough. If the only thing that's going to motivate you is Raven, then so be it."

I stand from the couch. "You're going to have to talk strategy with Tiberius and Mr. Smith." He opens his mouth, but I wave him off. "I know how you feel about him, but it doesn't matter. I've got to go get children to safety. Luca, can you come with me?" I ask.

He nods, still watching Daemon, but follows me out of the house nonetheless.

Mr. Smith startles at our appearance. "He's agreed. Better go in there and smooth things over," I tell him.

He gives a short nod and walks past us. "I'd love to know how that conversation goes," I tell Luca.

"*Si.* Me too," he tells me.

"I'm going to be transporting the kids to safety. I really need you to go talk with Gregory and Lucy. Tell them who's gotten a little bit better with their powers. I'm going to head to Walter's. He should have all the kids there with their parents."

"How long do you think we have?" Luca asks, nerves showing in his voice.

There's a strange stillness in the jungle, and it makes all the hair on my arm stand up. "I don't know, but my gut is saying not long."

"*Mannaggia la miseria,*" he says, kicking at the ground.

"Exactly," I tell him, not understanding the word but agreeing with the frustration in his tone.

"I'll see you in a little bit," I say, and with a wave I transport to Walter's.

"SO THE POWER and water are still on?" I ask Walter, grabbing a bag to put on my back.

Most of the kids are still saying their goodbyes to their parents while Walter loads me up with some groceries. Hopefully they won't need to be gone for too long, but at this point I've got no idea.

"Yes. I've kept everything going. The neighbors think we're on vacation," he says, loading another bag.

"Aren't you worried about the neighbors hearing fifteen kids at the house?"

He zips up the bag and hands it off to Bronia. She adds it to her collection of the other three bags she's holding. Man, it must be amazing to have that kind of strength. "No," he says. "They'll have to be quiet, but these aren't normal children. I think they can already feel something bad is going to happen."

"Here's hoping they'll be quiet," I tell him. I turn to Bronia. "Ready to head home?" I ask her.

She turns to Walter, her mouth opening and closing but no words coming out. He opens up his arms and she rushes into them. He rocks back on his heels from the impact, but he quickly wraps her up in his embrace. "Do not worry. I will see you soon," he tells her as he strokes her head.

"What if...what if something...bad happens to you?" she asks through ragged breaths.

He steps back a little and cups her face. "I will be just fine. I promise you," he tells her.

"Mama said that too," she says in such a soft voice I barely catch it.

Walter's face contorts in pain, and I have to turn around to compose myself. "She would do anything to be here. But I will not leave you alone. You have my word, *robaczku*."

I take a deep breath and turn back to see her give him a shaky nod. Walter kisses her on the forehead. He clears his throat. "Go with Becca and do whatever you need to protect yourself and the little ones."

Bronia stands a little taller. "I will, JaJa," she says.

I walk over and grab her hand. "I'll be back in a minute to start transporting the rest," I tell him.

"Be safe," he tells us, and in a blink we're gone.

"IS THAT ALL OF THEM?" Lucy asks as she turns in her computer chair.

I fall back onto the couch, desperately trying to keep my eyes open. "Walter's on the phone, doing one more count with Maria, but I'm pretty sure my last trip with Eloise was the last of them. And it only took an hour."

I shift a little on the couch and can't suppress the groan that spills out. Five transports across the world in an hour about killed me. I could probably sleep for a year.

"I think I saw Luca shed a tear," Lucy says.

I smile. "He does care a lot for Eloise."

I roll my head on the back of the couch so I can see her better. "Where is everyone?" I ask.

I hear the clicking of her keyboard. "Looks like they're on the boat here. Tiberius and Gregory went to gather the other Project Lightning agents from Itaituba. They all flew in."

"Good. How's the perimeter?" I ask, the heaviness of my eyes causing them to close again.

"All my scans show it's fine, but I don't know what powers Rivers's people have."

I feel my head start to bob and try to shake myself awake.

Lucy's soft footsteps approach from my side and my eyes flutter open for a moment. "Sleep, Becca. I'll wake you when everyone gets here."

THIRTY-NINE

They wouldn't be so cruel, would they? I walk closer to the tree swing I sat on more times than I could count in my grandparents' backyard. I can feel the house looming behind me, but I can't bring myself to turn around. What if it's a burned-out husk? What if it's whole?

I sit on the swing, my back to the only home I've known, and wait. Lately, Mom has been here right away, but it's quiet now. Not even the sound of birds or the rush of wind. I sway back and forth on the swing until the snap of a twig has my head whipping to the left.

I can just make out someone moving closer through the tree line, but they're still shrouded in darkness. "Mom," I call out as I stand.

They don't answer, just move closer to the light. I walk closer, and it's then I see it isn't only one person.

Five people walk over the tree line, and I drop to my knees.

Mom. Dad. Ania. Grandma. Grandpa.

It's not possible. Unless...

"Am I dead?" I ask, because they shouldn't be here.

"No, sweets," I hear Grandpa say as they walk closer.

At the sound of his voice I explode from my kneeling position and run to him. He opens his arms and I barrel into him, almost knocking us both over.

The tears pour out and I let them. He rubs a hand up and down my back, soothing me. I keep trying to say something, anything, but the words are trapped in my throat.

Another hand lands on my shoulder and I look up into a pair of eyes identical to my own.

"Dad," I croak out his name.

His smile is blinding. "I've waited so long to meet you, Becca." His voice startles me more than his looks. I've seen him so many times when I look at Tiberius, but instead of a Russian accent, he has a New England one.

I step out of Grandpa's arms so I can face my dad. He takes a step towards me, and I go the rest of the way, hugging him tight. "It feels so good to hold you, baby girl," he says.

I back up, giving him a big smile. Grandma clears her throat and she's next for a huge dose of affection. From the comfort of Grandma's arms, I look at everyone I love that I don't have anymore.

"I miss you guys. I miss you so much it hurts," I tell them.

Ania grabs my hand, making me move away from Grandma. Her eyes glisten with unshed tears. "Thank you for everything you've done for Bronia."

"I'll be there for her as long as I can," I tell her.

"We don't have a lot of time," my mom interrupts.

"What are you guys all doing here?" I ask. "I'm so excited to see you, but this isn't the norm."

"We're here to help," Mom says, and points behind her.

Hundreds of souls fill the spaces between the trees. I lift a hand, covering my mouth. "Is that Cleopatra?" I ask Ania quietly.

"Yes," she answers in an excited whisper.

The group parts and a woman marches towards me with a determined look. My mom leans into me. "That's Sariah's mom."

"No way," I say, bracing myself.

She stops in front of me. Her face blank.

"*Thank you,*" she says.

Uh, what?

"*You were the only one to stand and say Sariah deserved another shot. I know she's strayed so far. But you believe that anyone can come back. And for that I'm grateful. I'll help any way I can.*"

I look at the group and then back at my mom. "*I don't understand. How are you going to help?*"

"*Shemnon, the dream walker, is coming to you and you're going to enhance him,*" she tells me.

"*Wait. Are you guys going to be alive?*" I ask, looking at the faces of my family and friends.

"*No, sweets,*" Grandpa says. "*But we'll be able to interact with the world for a time to help you.*"

Mom's eyes shoot to the sky. "*We're out of time,*" she warns.

"*No,*" I say, grabbing onto Grandpa's and Dad's hands.

"*It's okay, baby,*" my dad says, giving my hand a squeeze. "*We're never really far.*"

No.

The ground shakes, but I'm the only one knocked off balance.

"*Becca,*" someone calls.

The earth rolls, throwing me to the ground. My side slams into the dirt. "*No!*"

"*The time has come,*" my mom says urgently.

"*How will I know him?*" I ask her.

"*You'll know. You'll feel us with him,*" she tells me, and I guess she's not done being cryptic.

"*Becca!*"

Who's shouting?

"Wake up," Ania commands.

A deafening clap of thunder booms around me.

I shoot up, gasping for breath.

"Becca." Walter shakes my shoulder, causing me to jump.

"What is it?" I ask, still panting.

Lucy walks up behind Walter, looking as confused as I am.

"We can't find Melanie," he says, and I finally take a good look at him. His hair is standing up straight like he was pulling it and his shirt is half untucked.

Lucy rushes over to her computer, fingers frantically moving over her keyboard.

"Are you sure? I thought I transported her," I say, picturing the little girl who can throw lightning bolts.

"I just got off the phone with Maria. She's not there."

"We need to call Tiberius," I say, standing up.

"He won't be able to hear you from the boat. Too much noise," Lucy says, fingers flying over the keys. I watch the screen constantly changing from all the different cameras.

"How soon till he gets here?" Walter asks from beside me.

"Ten minutes," she says, still focusing.

I bite my thumb nail. That'll take too long. "I'm transporting to him," I tell them. "Pull up his GPS coordinates and get the remaining adults here in Fordlandia at the house."

Her fingers pause and she finally looks at me. "Don't even try to talk me out this," I say before she can object. "Pull it up. Please."

She stares at me for a beat longer, but switches screens, bringing up a map. I study it. I picture Tiberius. He's driving the boat; he wouldn't let anyone else. I picture myself standing next to him at the wheel.

I squeeze my eyes tight, saying a little prayer.

My heart beats once, Lucy calls my name. But in the next beat I'm knocking Mr. Smith to the floor of the boat.

People start shouting. Someone tries to grab my arms, but Gregory's voice cuts through it all. "Stop! It's Becca."

"What the hell is going on?" Mr. Smith asks, half of his body pinned under mine and sprawled across the deck.

I scramble off of him and turn to face a boat full of gawking faces, including Tiberius. "We can't find Melanie," I tell Tiberius, ignoring everyone else.

"Xavier, take the wheel," he orders, stepping away.

He closes his eyes.

He's taking too long. I grab his hand and pump him with as much enhancing as I can, my fear escalating with each passing second. He staggers to the side and I grab his other hand to anchor him.

"She's still here. She's in the abandoned building behind the range."

I drop his hands, stepping back to give myself some room, but before I can transport, he roughly grabs my arm.

"She's not alone," he says hurriedly. "There're others with powers with her, but I don't know them."

I look around the boat. There are too many. "You can't take us all," he says, reading my thoughts.

My eyes search the group. "Gregory, Tony, and Mike, you're with me," I say, not caring one bit that I'm taking charge.

Mike hesitates, eyes shooting towards Mr. Smith. "Go. Becca and Tiberius are in charge here," Mr. Smith tells him and the rest of the group.

Mike gives him a firm nod. "Hold on tight," I tell them.

They each latch on to me and I transport us to Daemon. Because I need the firestarter. Gregory sucks in a harsh breath at that thought. But in a blink we're gone.

FORTY

"I need you," I blurt out, interrupting the kiss he's having with Raven.

He raises a brow. "Not like that, you perv. One of the little girls has been taken. I need you to encircle Fordlandia in a ring of fire."

Voices start shouting over each other.

"You'll burn down the jungle."

"Someone might die."

"Are you insane?"

I don't bother answering. "I don't think I can do that," he says, his cocky attitude erasing and turning into dread.

"With me you can," I tell him. "You just need to grab my hand and focus on the fire not burning anything you don't want it to."

He lets out a heavy sigh. "A lot easier said than done."

"We don't have time for this, so suck it up," I say, making Raven's eyes widen and Daemon's jaw hit the floor, while the guys behind me start to shift in place.

"Don't pull any punches," he says.

I turn away from him and look at Raven. "Can you ask the animals to scout?"

"Yes," she says and heads out the door.

"Tony, head out to the water tower. But run by Lucy and grab a walkie-talkie first," I say, and before he can move away, I grab his arm. "You've got this."

"I won't let you down," he tells me.

"I know you won't."

I watch his throat work, but he gives me a nod and heads out.

"Mike, I need you with me. The jungle is dense and dark. We might need to hide."

"Got it," he says, and I have to blink a few times because I didn't expect him to agree so quickly.

"And me," Gregory whispers into my ear.

"With me, always," I tell him.

I open the maps on my phone and pull up a satellite picture of the main living area. I turn back to Daemon and hold out my hand. "This is where we are, and this is the boundary I want you to put up," I say, showing him on the phone.

He hesitates with his hand hovering in the air, but then he clasps it with mine.

"Picture the fire acting like a wall, not burning or destroying, but waiting for your command."

He looks at the map once more and then closes his eyes. I squeeze his hand, hoping that I'm enhancing him enough to pull this off. Because I'm terrified that Rivers is already here or he's having his people hide in the jungle.

Daemon eyes pop open. "Okay, I think I did it. But I've got no clue how long it's going to last."

"Let's go see," I tell them and grab everyone's hands.

I transport us to just outside of the range, somewhat hidden by the shed that holds the targets. I grip Gregory's hand.

Do you think you could cripple someone's mind if I enhance you? I ask.

He blows out a breath. *Probably, but I've never even attempted something like that.*

If someone has Melanie, can you try?

He nods once.

"Is your fire still burning?" I ask Daemon quietly.

He lifts up his hands, as if he's feeling something in the air. "Yeah. I can sense it's holding."

"Good. I don't know if we'll be able to use Mike's shadows until we're closer. The flames might make it too bright. But we'll find out in a minute. Tiberius said Melanie was in the abandoned building on the north side of the range."

"Are we transporting in?" Gregory asks.

I peek around the shed at the building. Nothing looks amiss, but I'm too afraid I'm missing something.

"No. I've got no clue if she's alone."

"Shouldn't we wait for everyone else?" Mike asks, looking over his shoulder like he can see them.

"Can't Gregory see if he can read anyone's minds from here?" Daemon asks, arching a brow.

"There's too much of a certain stone here that's blocking me. I can't hear anything. Let's go," Gregory says.

"We've got a little girl who's probably terrified, and we need to get her to safety. Time is something we don't have," I tell him, still looking at the building.

"Stay close and within touching distance so we can transport in a moment's notice."

I take the lead with Gregory right behind me, grumbling about me being the one in the line of fire. His hand rests on my lower back. The closer we get, the more I can just make out the top of Daemon's flame wall.

"Awesome," I hear Mike say in awe. He's not wrong.

Flames lick at the sky, but they don't touch the canopy of trees. We move closer and I can finally see the wall more clearly running behind the abandoned building in both directions. Gregory's tightens his grip on the back of my shirt. He slides his hand under it and lays his palm on the skin of my back.

I turn my head and quirk my brow. *With his free hand he holds up three fingers.*

Who? I ask him.

Thompson, Sariah, and Melanie.

I drop to the ground and motion everyone to come closer. Gregory keeps his hand on my back, and I grab the hands of the other two guys.

We've got two people in there besides Melanie. Mike jolts at the sound of my voice in his head, but quickly shakes it off.

Thompson and Sariah are in there.

Daemon curses.

Mike, can you handle this? I ask him, widening my eyes.

His eyes dart from the building to mine. I give his hand a squeeze. *If we can get Sariah to turn against Rivers and help us then we will. But we can't let her hurt another kid.* With Gregory's help I send him the images from when she kidnapped Poppy in England.

Mike's face drops.

Maybe away from Rivers she'll want to be different, but we've got to be careful.

He nods.

Good. Bring your shadows to you and I'll see if I can cover all of us.

Daemon mouths the word *shadow* like a question. And I tilt my head towards Mike. Daemon's eyes widen as the shadows pool around Mike's feet and slither up his body. I grip everyone's hand and pump some enhancing into Mike.

Gregory curses as we're plunged into Mike's smoky shadow world. "Let's go save a little girl," I whisper and make a move for the building.

We run hunched over until we get to a small opening in one of the crumbling walls. I really hope we're blending in and not looking like a floating black blob. I lean forward to look into the opening. Melanie sits in the corner, her knees up to her chest. Sariah is planted against the wall and Thompson stalks back and forth. They're too far apart. We're going to have to split up.

Thompson will be able to freeze one of us, and Sariah is probably carrying a gun. Do whatever you have to do to get Melanie out, I tell the guys.

Why don't you just transport in and grab her? Daemon asks.

If she does that, Thompson is going to freeze her before she has a chance to get away, Gregory tells him.

Mike, what if you try knocking out Sariah? That way we can get her out of here.

He nods once, but then his eyes shoot to my forehead and I feel the sweat gathering there.

You've got to slow down or you're going to burn out, Gregory warns.

I wave away his comment. *I'm fine,* I assure him and hold up my hand. *On my signal.*

I watch Thompson and Sariah for a beat more and then lower my hand, dropping our shadow shield.

We sprint into the building.

"Now!" Gregory screams, startling everyone.

I lock onto Melanie. Her wide, scared eyes find me. I try to let her know with my eyes that I'm coming for her. She gets on to her knees, hands frantically waving in the air. Thompson shouts and he freezes me in place. Daemon throws a fireball at Thompson's feet. He jumps out the way of Daemon's fire, and my body stumbles forward.

Sariah raises a shaky hand and points a gun at Melanie.

Everyone stops. Eyes trained on her.

"I'll shoot," she says.

"No. You won't," I tell her.

Someone crawls in the window behind Melanie. My stomach revolts at the sight of Henderson. "Melanie! Use your power!" I scream at her, and everyone bolts into action.

Mike races towards Sariah, while Gregory and Daemon work to attack Thompson.

Melanie bites her lip, eyes darting all around the room.

"Now!" I command her.

My heart is racing as more Hendersons climb into the room.

Melanie turns, letting loose a blood-curdling scream, and throws her hands up. Lightning bolts shoot out of her palms, hitting Henderson directly in the chest. It must be the original one, because he staggers to the side and the other ones disappear.

I close the distance between us and open my arms for her. She hesitates but jumps to her feet and runs to me. I scoop her up and turn to get the guys.

Mike has the gun out of Sariah's hand. He raises his hand like he's going to strike her, and she closes her eyes like she welcomes it. His fist connects with her temple and her body starts to drop until he picks her up, throwing her over his shoulder. She wanted him to knock her out. I only hope he saw that too.

"Gregory. Daemon. Let's go," I yell. We need to get to Lucy because I don't know what else is happening.

Daemon throws another fireball, but Thompson freezes him and his fire. "Gregory, his mind!" I call out as I come up behind him with Melanie in tow. I plant my hand on his back, pushing my power into him.

Gregory focuses on Thompson and in a moment he's on the ground, clutching his head. Daemon unfreezes, and he and Mike each snatch up one of my hands. Gregory turns and grabs my waist. I close my eyes and picture Lucy's living room.

FORTY-ONE

We stumble into Tiberius's living room. I sway to the side and Gregory scoops me up his arms, taking me over to the couch. Lucy's computer chair crashes against the wall and she runs to Melanie.

"Are you okay?" she asks me as she holds Melanie close.

"I'm fine," I say, waving her off. "Take care of Melanie."

Lucy keeps her close and leads her out of the room.

"You're almost spent," Gregory says as he stands over me.

"I'm fine," I say through gritted teeth.

"You won't be able to help anyone if you pass out," Daemon says.

Walter hurries into the room from the kitchen, doctor bag in hand. "Who is that?" he says, heading for Sariah's prone form.

"That would be Sariah."

He does a double take but doesn't pause as he squats down at her side where Mike laid her on the floor.

"I knocked her out," Mike says, shifting from foot to foot.

"Better out than dead," Daemon says bluntly.

Walter rolls his eyes but takes his stethoscope and checks over

Sariah. "She seems fine. Probably will come to in around twenty minutes or so."

"We need to tie her up before she wakes up," I tell them.

The front door swings open and Tiberius charges in the house with Mr. Smith and Xavier following close behind. He looks at Sariah on the floor, but quickly dismisses her.

"Rivers's group is surrounding the village," Tiberius says, out of breath. "A large group is making their way to the water tower."

I push to standing and sway a little on my feet. Gregory reaches out and grabs my waist to steady me. "Get Tony on the walkie talkie," I tell him.

Tiberius grabs it off Lucy's desk. "Tony, it's Tiberius. What do you see?"

The line crackles and we all lean forward, waiting for him to respond.

"I count at least twenty people coming in from the west side of the tower. They're picking their way through the jungle. There are about ten more coming in from the south and the east. Did he hire mercenaries or something? How did he get so many people?"

"We're outnumbered," Xavier says quietly, his face pale.

I open my mouth to tell them about my dream with my mom when Luca crashes through the front door. His shirt is torn, like bullets ripped through it.

"What happened?" I ask, meeting him as he leans against the wall.

He takes huge, gulping breaths. "We need to get out there right now. Dante's been hit. And I might be bulletproof, but it hurts getting shot at."

We fly out the front door, spilling onto the front walk. Dante hobbles around the fence, clutching his side, blood seeping through his fingers. Xavier curses and runs over to grab him, ushering him towards the house where Walter stands in the doorway. "My house is now the infirmary," Tiberius yells to us.

The walkie talkie crackles. "Incoming!" Tony's voice booms out of the speaker.

Together we run onto the dirt street. A huge group has all of us pulling up short. Daemon's hands become completely engulfed. Raven comes from across the street, and I blink rapidly to make sure I'm seeing the three jaguars walking on either side of her.

The group across from us parts and Chelsea walks forward, Henderson on her left. Where's Mr. Rivers? I scan the faces, but I'm not seeing him.

"Surrender now and save yourselves. Or don't. Your DNA is still good to us whether you're alive or not," Chelsea yells.

A maniacal grin spreads across Henderson's face. Guess Melanie's lightning bolt didn't knock him out for long.

"You've got another group coming in behind you," Tony frantically yells at us.

Gregory curses, and I turn. They aren't past Tiberius's house. With Project Lightning agents and the people from Fordlandia, we number about sixty, but it's not enough.

I reach out and slap a hand to Daemon's back. "Encircle us and the house in fire."

The flames covering his hands grow and brighten. I turn my face away because it's so bright. Screams break out from our group.

"It's okay," I yell over the roar from the inferno. "Stay together."

Everyone huddles close. "This isn't going to last long," Daemon shouts, sweat falling in steady streams down his face.

The flames start to lessen, and I try pumping more enhancing into Daemon, but they hardly budge. "What's wrong?" I ask him.

"I don't know," he says through gritted teeth.

I kick at the dirt. I can't see through the flames.

"It's Chelsea," Gregory yells.

"Can you cripple her mind?" I ask.

He shakes his head. "There's too much carnelian. I can't get a good enough lock on her."

"Daemon can make an opening in the flames and Raven, can you send you jaguars to attack her?" Mr. Smith asks.

Raven nods, and Daemon grits his teeth. "I can try," he says, and he slowly lowers his arms.

The flames part like curtains and the three jaguars rush through. The flames crash back together, blocking our view, but not the sound. Screams from the other side of the flames reach my ears, but then I hear the distinct sound of three gun shots. Raven clutches her head, screaming. The flames completely extinguish.

"Daemon!" I scream at him, fisting his shirt.

"I can't," he yells back, panicking.

A sound starts, shrill and harsh. "What the hell is that?" Mike yells, his hands covering his ears.

A man walks on the other side of Chelsea. His mouth is wide open. Chelsea jabs a syringe into his arm and almost instantly the sound becomes earsplitting. One by one my group starts dropping to their knees, hands covering their ears. Mr. Smith howls in agony, blood trickling through his fingers covering his ears.

He's got a supersonic voice, he tells me, and even his inner voice sounds pained.

What was in that syringe? I ask.

Probably your—

"No!" I try to catch Gregory as he lists to the side. His eyes roll in the back of his head, and he starts seizing.

The sound increases and I cry out. It's like someone is pushing a hot needle through my eardrum.

The group in front of us starts moving in closer. I think Tony's yelling through the walkie talkie, but I can't hear him.

Things can't end this way.

I try to stand but my body won't obey me.

Something flickers to my right. A man comes strolling towards me. His hair is long and dark. Skin a deep bronze. He holds out a hand and I grab onto it.

"Enhance," he commands.

Shemnon?

He nods once, and I pump every last drop of power left into him. His long hair flies around his face from an unearthly wind. The hairs on my arms stand and the feeling of electricity crackles through the air.

Shemnon drops my hand and walks slowly forward. I fall to my knees and sway until my body topples to the side. But my eyes track him. He lifts his arms to the sky. The clouds darken, and thunder booms. Lightning strikes a nearby tree, causing sparks to rain down on us. He brings his arms down in a swift strike. Ghostly apparitions surround him, numbering in the thousands. As one, they walk forward and the ground shakes, cutting off the supersonic voice.

"You have angered your ancestors." Shemnon's voice booms across the space like a cannon. "You have defied the laws of nature."

With each step forward lightning strikes, felling trees.

"Face your judgment."

Screams rise up from Mr. Rivers's people. "What's happening?" Tiberius yells.

"I think our ancestors are attacking them," I tell him.

One by one the group surrounding us drops to their knees, hands fisting over their hearts. "You do not deserve the powers given to you," Shemnon roars.

The souls of ancestors raise their hands, arms outstretched. Small lights stream out of the chests of Chelsea and Henderson.

Henderson splits into five. His clones try to run at Shemnon, but they freeze and then burst into bright lights. A ghostly man steps forward, and the light from Henderson rushes into him.

Two women walk over to Chelsea. She screams and grabs at her chest. It looks like her power is being ripped from her, the light streaming into her ancestors' bodies. Chelsea and Henderson flop to the ground, screaming and moaning in pain.

"Becca."

I turn my head and come face to face with my mom.

"Mom," I say, crying out her name.

"There isn't time. You need to make them all forget," she says, her voice urgent.

My brow furrows. "What? How?"

She points to Gregory. He's starting to come to. I look back at my mom and bite my lip. "I don't think I have enough left in me," I tell her.

"You need to try. You'll never be safe. These people will never be safe. Gregory needs to make them forget about Mr. Rivers. Forget their hatred for their own kind and work toward making this world better. Just like our ancestors intended."

"Rivers isn't even here," I tell her.

"He's close by," my mom says. "I can feel him. Do this and we'll help deal with him."

My grandparents, my dad, and Ania walk up behind Mom. "You've got this, sweets," Grandpa says, smiling brightly at me.

I drag myself over the rough, charred dirt towards Gregory. His head is moving back and forth. I place my head on his chest, too tired to sit up.

Gregory. I need you. I need your help, I tell him.

A quiet moan slips out.

Please, I beg.

His eyes start to flutter open. "Becca?" he asks, his voice sounding like sandpaper.

I tell him what my mom said. "I need you to try. If we have a shot at the future, this is the time. This all needs to stop," I say.

He grabs my hand. I start to give him everything I have. Even as black spots start to fill my vision and the world starts to sway, I give it all.

"It's working," he says. I think he's shouting, but I can't really hear him. It's like he's at the opposite end of a tunnel.

"Almost done," my mom whispers to me.

I let myself go, opening my heart and mind.

Surprise shouts reach my ears, but it's muffled. The black spots fill my vision until everything fades.

FORTY-TWO

The scraping of rocks and dirt against my cheek is what finally wakes me from the nothing I was submerged in. My eyes blink open. I'm outside still, but who's dragging me, and why?

I pull my leg to try to dislodge it, but nothing happens. Nothing moves. I'm frozen.

"Oh, looks like she's waking up," Mr. Rivers says, and my eyes shoot to the left.

He's hobbling along beside me, and since I'm frozen, that must mean Thompson is dragging me.

"You really messed up my plans."

I strain to say something, anything. He raises a brow. "Thompson, release her mouth."

"How?" I ask through heavy breaths when my mouth can move again.

"That was easy. I just injected Thompson with your blood. It's amazing stuff, by the way. Imagine everyone's surprise when they all froze."

The dragging suddenly stops and Thompson drops me like a sack of potatoes. The sound of a door opening makes my heart pound in my chest.

Thompson picks me up again and brings me into one of the abandoned houses in the village.

"Drop her over there," Rivers commands.

Thompson drops me on my side against a wall. I still can't move anything but my eyes and mouth.

Rivers grabs a syringe from his pocket. It's filled with blood, probably mine, and he injects it into his arm like a heroin addict. After the plunger completely pushes my blood into his veins, he lets out a soft sigh.

"Good," Rivers says to Thompson. "Now release her and go outside to keep watch."

Thompson walks robotically out the door, and Rivers turns to me.

"On. Your. Knees." The command in his voice washes over me, forcing me.

My stomach clenches in dread and I feel my body get to my knees without me telling it to.

His hand reaches for the gun on his hip and he slaps it into my hand. "Put that to your temple," he instructs.

He fixes his shirtsleeves like what he's having me do is nothing. I feel the cool barrel of the gun touch my temple. My heart starts beating out of control, but there's nothing I can do. I keep trying to transport, but nothing works. I can't break his compulsion.

He pulls out a chair and gets comfortable in his seat. Like I'm not kneeling here with my hands shaking, sweat dripping down my face, gun to my head. "Did you know I was in the Korean War?" he asks.

I don't say anything.

"Answer," he says, his voice ugly, vicious.

"No," the word feels unnatural as it pushes out of my mouth, and his lips curl in cruel satisfaction.

"You know I bled for my country. And then later I watched my best friends being tortured in Vietnam. I was forced to be a POW so I could learn the enemy's secrets. My body is filled with scars for this country, and yet I'm not allowed to exist out in the open with my powers. I'm not allowed to use my power for personal gain, or they'll find a way to put me down. I'm not allowed to have more than one child. So yes, I started trying to create more of us. I found all these *undesirables*. I rid the streets of homeless people, whores, addicts. I wanted change. I want to take back what's ours. We used to be treated like gods."

"You went too far," I say through clenched teeth.

"Excuse me?" he asks, like he can't believe I have the nerve to contradict him.

"Do you even realize the horrible things you've done? What you've destroyed? And for what? To stroke your ego?"

He *tsks* at me like I'm a child. "Brave words for a girl with a gun to her head. Press it harder to your temple," he says with a flick of the wrist.

The barrel digs into my skin, and I can't stop myself from wincing in pain.

"Weak. Just like your mother," he says.

I grit my teeth, trying to move my hand away, but I can't.

"You could have been a part of all of this," he says waving his hands in the air. "No matter; your DNA will still be around whether you're breathing or not."

My stomach drops at his words. No. No, this is not how this is supposed to be. This is not how I die. I can't. He leans towards me, a manic look in his eyes. "Pull the—"

The door beside him bursts open. He spins in his chair, but before he has a chance to open his mouth, Lucy puts a bullet in each of his legs.

He crumples to the floor, screaming in agony.

My arm falls to my side, and a sob breaks free. Gregory rushes into the room. He rips the gun out of my hand and gives it to someone behind him. His arms surge around me, and I can't stop shaking.

"I got you," he says in my ear.

"Not so scary now, are you?" Lucy spits out the words, standing above him, her gun trained on him.

A strange gurgling sound comes from Rivers. "What's happening?" I ask.

We all stare at him as he clutches his chest. "You hit a major artery," Mr. Smith says from the door, Walter right on his heels.

Mr. Smith walks into the room and stands over Rivers. "Before you die—because that's what's happening—I want you to know that your plan has failed. Our people are united. Project Lightning has just gained a large amount of help. I hope you rot in Hell for the things you've done."

"Jeremy," Rivers says, blood trickling past his lips.

Rivers takes one more gasping breath and then goes completely still. Walter leans down and puts two fingers to Rivers's neck. After a moment he looks up at us. "He's gone."

Mr. Smith steps over his body, completely ignoring the man who was his mentor and friend for years. He squats down next to me. "Are you okay?" he asks, looking me over.

"Yeah," I say. "Just banged up like everyone else."

My eyes stray to Rivers's body. "Let's get out of here," Gregory says and picks me up.

We all leave out of the house, except for Mr. Smith.

"Is he going to be okay?" I ask Gregory.

He keeps walking down the road and towards Tiberius's house. Lucy, Walter, and Xavier follow behind. "I don't know."

I nod once. I don't know what I would do if it had turned out Mr. Smith was a psycho who tortured and murdered people.

"Where is everyone?" I ask.

"Tiberius is at the house helping the injured and talking with...I guess our allies now?" Lucy looks as confused as me.

"It'll take time to figure it all out," Walter says, patting her arm. "We won't know the true extent of their willingness to change until Mr. Smith and Gregory can interview them all."

"Where's Tony?" I ask, scanning the roads.

"I don't know," Gregory says. "We all watched your unconscious body be dragged away, and as soon as we were unfrozen Tiberius tracked you down."

After another right turn, we approach my house. "There're too many people at Tiberius's right now," Gregory explains, answering my unspoken question.

Xavier walks ahead and opens the front door and we walk inside.

Tony jumps up from the couch and rushes over to me. "Are you hurt?" he asks.

"I'll be fine."

He takes a deep breath and his whole body relaxes. "Becca, I saw him. I saw my dad," Tony tells me.

"I know," I say. "I didn't get a chance to tell you that my mom gave me a heads-up in a dream. They were all there to help."

Gregory drops us down on the couch. "Ania was here?" Walter asks.

I nod and start to choke up at the tears he lets fall. "She loves you so much and she wishes she was here," I tell him.

"How?" Lucy asks.

"Shemnon. Where is he?" I ask, looking around.

"Who?" Gregory asks, face scrunched.

"The guy with the long hair that summoned all of the spirits. He's the dream-walker."

"He disappeared with all the spirits when we were unfrozen," Xavier says.

The front door opens, and Tiberius, Mr. Smith, Raven, Daemon, and Luca walk into the house. We all look horrible. And tired.

"What now?" I ask Mr. Smith.

The most amazing thing happens. Mr. Smith smiles. "We get to save the world every day."

Gregory lets out a tired laugh and I lean against him and close my eyes.

"How about a vacation first?" I ask.

"We'll see," Mr. Smith says, and I can hear the smirk in his voice.

"It's done," Lucy whispers and my eyes open to find her.

She grabs Tiberius's hand. "Yes," he says.

I rise from the couch and walk over to my aunt and uncle. They wrap me up, and it's at that moment I feel the arms of my family around me, living and dead. Everyone I love is in this room.

"Do you have room for a lizard man?" Luca asks, causing Xavier to burst out laughing.

"We'll make room," Mr. Smith says.

"Does this feel weird? It feels weird to me. Are you sure we should be gone like this?" I ask Gregory as he pulls out a chair for me.

"Becca," he says, leaning down to kiss my temple. "For the hundredth time, it's just a date. We're probably going to go on thousands of these."

He takes a seat across from me. "I know, but Luca was almost completely transformed. And Lucy and Tiberius haven't been out without Eloise, and *you* just hashed everything out with Mr. Smith—"

He grabs my hand and gives it a tug. "It's just dinner. We'll be back later. Besides, how often do you get to eat at Vito and Lucille's Restaurant?"

He's right. I haven't been here since I went with my grandparents years ago. And this is the first time we've really been alone since the showdown in Fordlandia.

But we've been busy. Everyone has. Tony has been in counseling, and he and Mike went on a backpacking trip around Alaska. Dex thinks he finally found the cure for breast cancer. Raven and Daemon got married last month. Life has been crazy, but amazing.

"How was your talk with your dad?" I ask.

He winces a little at the "dad."

"Sorry," I say.

"It's okay," he says, waving away my concern. "It was a good talk today with the therapist. He finally opened up about my mom. She cut the relationship when she found out she was pregnant with me. They never told anyone about their relationship. Rivers never had any clue about me."

Our waiter comes over and takes our order.

"Enough with the heavy," I tell him once we're alone again. "I'm pretty sure I saw Mike kissing Sariah."

"Becca."

"What?" I ask, confused.

His face softens and he shakes his head. "I love you," he says.

I smile at him. "I love you too."

He starts to tell me about Raven's work with finding trafficked women, when both our phones start to buzz.

I pull mine out. "Damn it. Looks like our date is getting cut short."

He looks at his phone. "Xavier said it's urgent," he says, placing his napkin on the table. "We'd better hurry back to headquarters."

He reaches for my hand.

"Let's go then," I say.

Gregory leaves a twenty on the table to cover our drinks and we head out of the restaurant. Once we're around the side of the building, Gregory pulls me close to his body. "One last kiss before we go," he says, and dips his head down.

Our lips connect, and that same all-consuming heat fills my veins, shooting from my toes up to my fingertips.

"Never gets old," I tell him, and transport us to the cafeteria at headquarters.

"Happy birthday!" A chorus of voices slams into us the moment we appear.

"What?" I say, looking around at everyone I love.

Everyone is here, from Bronia and Walter to Lucy and Tiberius. Even Daemon made an appearance. "My birthday was a month ago," I tell them.

"We were hunting down Thompson then and didn't have the chance," Gregory tells me, hugging me close.

"At least he's now rotting away in a jail cell with Henderson. And since Dex found that stone to block powers, there's no way they're getting out."

Only Chelsea and Henderson had their powers stripped from them forever. Everyone else that worked with Rivers is blocked until Mr. Smith decides otherwise.

Gregory squeezes me once more and I walk around, talking to all my family and friends.

The night flies by. And it's filled with laughter and joy, things that seemed unachievable six months ago. And after several hours, I can barely keep my eyes open. Gregory walks me to my room and helps me inside.

"Did you have fun tonight?" he asks.

I throw my arms around his neck and play with his hair at the nape of his neck. "It was amazing. Thank you, because I know you were probably behind it."

He gives me a shy smile, so I reach up on my tiptoes and kiss him.

"I'm glad," he says. "Get some sleep. I'll see you in the morning."

He leans down and kisses me once more. "Love you," he whispers.

"Love you too," I say and watch him walk out the door.

I stagger over to the bed and plop down. In no time at all, sleep pulls me under.

THE TREE SWING IN MY GRANDPARENTS' backyard is a welcome sight. I sit down and push off, feeling the wind blow my hair.

"Hey, baby," my mom says, and I drop my feet to stop the swing.

"Mom," I say, my voice breaking. I haven't seen her since Fordlandia. I never thought I'd get the chance again.

She opens her arms and I run into them. "I never got to say goodbye," I say into her hair.

"Shemnon let me come back one more time," she says.

"If I ever see that guy again, I'm going to hug him."

She laughs. "He'll be around."

She steps back and holds me at arm's length. "I'm so proud of you. I'm so proud to be able to be your mom. And I can't wait to watch all the amazing things you're going to do."

I look down at our feet. "I wish you were here still."

She lifts my chin with a finger. "I am here," she says, tapping my chest. "I am always here. I will always be here for you, rooting for you, and loving you. Don't ever forget that."

I give her a small smile. "I won't."

"Good. Give me one last hug," she says.

I squeeze her tight. "I love you," she whispers to me. "Keep conquering the world, my extraordinary girl."

The End

ACKNOWLEDGMENTS

I can't believe I just wrote "The End" on book three in The Extraordinary Series. I started writing the first book over eight years ago. Took me a while to get that one done. It's been an amazing ride seeing so many people read it. It fills me with so much joy when people tell me that they enjoy my words. But it's not just me behind all of this. There are so many to thank.

First, I'd like to thank my editor, Jana Miller. She's been with me since she read book one over three years ago. Her comments and edits have truly helped me become a better writer. Next I need to thank my dear friend and fellow author, Kathy Cowley. Thank you for always being willing to proofread my work, even when I only give you a few days' notice. Also, Susan Allred, thank you for proofreading, giving advice, and being an amazing cheerleader.

To my lady authors from the Red Mountain Chapter, thank you for your support, critiques, and friendship. I truly cherish our time together. And to the rest of the American Night Writers Association, I am a better person from knowing and working with all of you.

To my amazing book cover designer, Molly Phipps, you did an

amazing job yet again. I can't wait to see what other covers you'll create for my books to come.

To my parents: thank you, Mom, for being as excited about these books as I am. And thank you for giving me your honest opinion. Thank you, Dad, for always believing in me and letting me know that you're proud of me.

I know there are so many more people I need to name, but I want to thank my husband and my children. My kids have been the best cheerleaders for me during this series. I love you more than you'll ever know. No dream is too big or too far away; you just have to try and work for it. And know that I am always proud of you. Nick, your unwavering support means the world to me. I love you and I'm glad I have you by my side.

Finally, to the readers. Thank you for taking on me and reading my second book.

If you liked this book, please consider leaving a review. Thank you!

ABOUT THE AUTHOR

Pam Eaton lives in the deserts of Arizona, but she'll always consider herself a New Englander at heart. She graduated from Arizona State University with degrees involving education and history. While she loves history, it'll always take a backseat to the fictional world she stumbled into as a young girl.

She lives with her husband, three kids, and two crazy but lovable labs. It's a chaotic life, but she wouldn't have it any other way. Especially since they let her read an insane amount of books, and watch way too many Food Network shows.

You can find out more at Pam's website
www.pameaton.com
Or email her peaton.ya@gmail.com

facebook.com/authorpameaton

instagram.com/author_pam_eaton